Green Longmans

Stories of the saints for children

The black letter saints

Green Longmans

Stories of the saints for children
The black letter saints

ISBN/EAN: 9783337202279

Printed in Europe, USA, Canada, Australia, Japan

Cover: Foto ©Andreas Hilbeck / pixelio.de

More available books at **www.hansebooks.com**

STORIES OF THE SAINTS
FOR CHILDREN.

𝕭𝖆𝖑𝖑𝖆𝖓𝖙𝖞𝖓𝖊 𝕻𝖗𝖊𝖘𝖘

BALLANTYNE, HANSON AND CO.
EDINBURGH AND LONDON

S. Boniface embarks at Southampton.

STORIES OF THE SAINTS

FOR CHILDREN

The Black Letter Saints

BY

MRS. MOLESWORTH

AUTHOR OF "THE PALACE IN THE GARDEN," ETC.

"Roses and Lilies among the Church's flowers—white for faithful labour—red for the Martyr's sufferings—both fair in God's sight."—*From the Writings of S. Cyprian.*

LONDON

LONGMANS, GREEN, AND CO.

AND NEW YORK: 15 EAST 16th STREET

1892

CONTENTS.

——◆——

CHAPTER I.

PAGE

S. Nicomede.—S. John ante Portam Latinam.—S. Clement.—
S. Perpetua 1

CHAPTER II.

S. Fabian.—S. Agatha.—S. Laurence.—S. Cyprian . . 17

CHAPTER III.

S. Prisca.—S. Valentine.—S. Denys.—S. Cicely.—S. Crispin
and S. Crispinian.—S. Lucian.—S. Alban.—S. Faith . . 35

CHAPTER IV.

S. George.—S. Lucy.—S. Agnes.—S. Vincent.—S. Margaret.—
S. Katharine.—S. Blaise 53

CHAPTER V.

Invention of the Holy Cross.—Exaltation of the Holy Cross.—
S. Sylvester.—S. Enurchus.—S. Nicholas.—S. Hilary.—
S. Ambrose.—S. Martin 71

CHAPTER VI.

S. Jerome.—S. Augustin of Hippo . . . 95

CHAPTER VII.

PAGE

S. Britius.—Lammas Day.—S. Remigius.—S. Benedict.—S. David.—S. Leonard.—S. Machutus 115

CHAPTER VIII.

S. Gregory the Great.—S. Augustin of Canterbury . . . 135

CHAPTER IX.

S. Chad.—S. Etheldreda.—S. Lambert.—S. Giles . . . 153

CHAPTER X.

The Venerable Bede.—S. Boniface.—S. Swithin . . . 173

CHAPTER XI.

S. Edmund the Martyr.—S. Edward the Martyr.—S. Dunstan . 191

CHAPTER XII.

S. Alphege.—S. Edward the Confessor.—S. Hugh.—S. Richard. —O Sapientia.—Holy Name of Jesus 211

ALPHABETICAL INDEX 232

CHRONOLOGICAL TABLE.

SAINTS OF FIRST CENTURY.

Name.	Day of Commemoration.	Home or Country.	Martyrdom or Death.
S. Nicomede, *m.*	June 1 . . .	Rome	September 15, A.D. 81, at Rome.
,, Clement, *m.*	November 23	Rome	November 23, A.D. 100, at Rome.

SAINTS OF THIRD CENTURY.

Name.	Day of Commemoration.	Home or Country.	Martyrdom or Death.
S. Perpetua, *m.*	March 7 . .	Carthage . . .	March 7, A.D. 203, at Carthage.
,, Fabian, *m.*	January 20	Rome	January 20, A.D. 250, at Rome.
,, Agatha, *m.*	February 5 .	Catania, Sicily . .	February 5, A.D. 251, at Catania.
,, Laurence, *m.*	August 10 .	Aragon	August 10, A.D. 258, at Rome.
,, Cyprian, *m.*	September 13	Carthage	September 13, A.D. 258, at Carthage.
,, Prisca, *m.*	January 18 .	Rome	January 18, A.D. 270, at Rome.
,, Valentine, *m.*	February 14 .	Rome	February 14, A.D. 270, at Rome.
,, Denys, *m.*	October 9 . .	Rome and France .	October 9, A.D. 272 (or 289), at Paris.
,, Cicely, *m.*	November 22	Rome	November 22, *about* A.D. 280, at Rome.
,, Crispin and Crispinian, *m.*	October 25 .	Rome and France .	October 25, A.D. 283, at Soissons.
,, Lucian, *m.*	January 8. .	Rome and France .	January 8, A.D. 287, at Beauvais.
,, Faith, *m.*	October 6 . .	Aquitaine	October 6, *about* A.D. 300, at Agen.

SAINTS OF FOURTH CENTURY.

Name.	Day of Commemoration.	Home or Country.	Martyrdom or Death.
S. Alban, *m.*	June 17 . .	Verulam (S. Albans)	June 17, A.D. 303, at Verulam.
,, George, *m.*	April 23 . .	Cappadocia . . .	April 23, A.D. 303, at Nicomedia.
,, Lucy, *m.*	December 13 .	Sicily	December 13, A.D. 303, at Syracuse.
,, Agnes, *m.*	January 21 .	Rome	January 21, A.D. 304, at Rome.
,, Vincent, *m.*	January 22 .	Saragossa	January 22, A.D. 304, at Saragossa.
,, Margaret, *m.*	July 20 . .	Antioch	July 20, A.D. 306, at Antioch.
,, Katharine, *m.*	November 25	Alexandria . . .	November 25, A.D. 307, at Alexandria.
,, Blaise, *m.*	February 3 .	Cappadocia . . .	February 3, A.D. 316, at Cappadocia.
,, Sylvester	December 31	Rome	December 31, A.D. 335, *d.* at Rome.
,, Enurchus	September 7 .	Rome and France .	September 7, A.D. 340, *d.* at Orleans.
,, Nicholas	December 6 .	Lycia—Asia Minor	December 6, A.D. 342, *d.* at Myra.
,, Hilary	January 13 .	France	January 13, A.D. 368, *d.* at Poitiers.
,, Ambrose	April 4 . .	Rome and Milan	April 4, A.D. 397, *d.* at Milan.
,, Martin . .	November 11	Hungary and France	November 11, A.D. 397, *d.* at Tours.

SAINTS OF FIFTH CENTURY.

Name.	Day of Commemoration.	Home or Country.	Martyrdom or Death.
S. Jerome . .	September 30	Hungary—Rome, Palestine	September 30, A.D. 420, *d.* at Bethlehem.
,, Augustin .	August 28 .	Africa and Rome .	August 28, A.D. 430, *d.* at Hippo.
,, Britius . .	November 13	France	November 13, A.D. 444, *d.* at Tours.

SAINTS OF SIXTH CENTURY.

S. Remigius .	October 1 . .	France	January 13, A.D. 533, *d.* at Rheims.
,, Benedict .	March 21 . .	Italy	March 21, A.D. 543, *d.* at Monte Cassino.
,, David . .	March 1 . .	Wales	March 1, A.D. 544 (or 601), *d.* at S. David's.
,, Leonard. .	November 6 .	France	November 6, A.D. 559, *d.* at Limoges.
,, Machutus or Malo	November 15	Wales and Brittany	November 15, A.D. 566, *d.* near Saintes.

SAINTS OF SEVENTH CENTURY.

S. Gregory. .	March 12 . .	Rome	March 12, A.D. 604, *d.* at Rome.
,, Augustin of Canterbury	May 26 . .	Rome and England	May 26, A.D. 604, *d.* at Canterbury.
,, Chad. . .	March 2 . .	England	March 2, A.D. 672, *d.* at Lichfield.
,, Etheldreda.	October 17 .	England	June 23, A.D. 679, *d.* at Ely.

SAINTS OF EIGHTH CENTURY.

S. Lambert, *m.*	September 17	Flanders	September 17, A.D. 709, *m.* near Liège.
,, Giles . . .	September 1 .	France	September 1, *about* A.D. 724, *d.* in Provence.
,, Bede . . .	May 27 . .	England	May 27, A.D. 735, *d.* at Jarrow.
,, Boniface, *m.*	June 5 . . .	England and Germany.	June 5, A.D. 755, *m.* near Dockum.

SAINTS OF NINTH CENTURY.

S. Swithin . .	July 15 . .	England	July 2, A.D. 862, *d.* at Winchester.
,, Edmund, *m.*	November 20	England	November 20, A.D. 870, *m.* at Framlingham.

SAINTS OF TENTH CENTURY.

S. Edward, *m.*	June 20 . .	England	March 18, A.D. 978, *m.* at Corfe Castle.
,, Dunstan .	May 19 . .	England	May 19, A.D. 988, *d.* at Canterbury.

SAINTS OF ELEVENTH CENTURY.

S. Alphege, *m.*	April 19 . .	England	April 13, 1012, *m.* at Canterbury.
,, Edward the Confessor	October 13 .	France and England	January 5, 1066, *d.* in London.

SAINTS OF TWELFTH CENTURY.

S. Hugh . .	November 17	France and England	November 17, 1200, *d.* in London.
,, Richard . .	April 3. . .	England	April 3, 1253, *d.* at Dover.

CHAPTER I.

Introductory.

S. Nicomede, June 1, A.D. 81.—S. John ante Portam Latinam, May 6, A.D. 95.—S. Clement, November 23, A.D. 100.—S. Perpetua, March 7, A.D. 203.

THE first three centuries of the Church's history stand out in a striking manner from all the later ones. Of the fifty or more Saints, of whose lives, dear children, I am going to try in simple words to tell you something, the names of twenty-six are marked, in what is called the "Black Letter Calendar" of our own Prayer-Book, by the letter "M." You know, most of you at least, that this stands for the wonderful word "Martyr"—a word which means, in the original Greek, "witness." And of these twenty-six, no less than twenty-two lived and died within three hundred years of our Blessed Lord's "Ascension," so shortly followed by the promised gift of the Holy Spirit on the Day of Pentecost. This day, once a great Jewish festival, we now commemorate as the birthday of the Christian Church, under the name of Whit-Sunday, which has probably come from "White Sunday," in allusion to the white robes worn by the newly baptized.

And these twenty-two martyrs are but a small, a very

A

small, number among the multitudes who, faithful unto death itself, treading in His very footsteps, suffered, in what at first sight seems so terrible a way, for their beloved Master. Of these multitudes the names of not a few, written in golden letters in the Book of Life, have yet not been handed down to us. In other calendars or lists there are also many, about some of whom I may afterwards be able to tell you a little.*

But just now, before entering upon the histories of the saints of our own list, I wish you well to understand what this great record of martyrdom really means, and why it concerns us Christians of these present peaceful times so closely. This is the answer: These blessed martyrs were not only true to their Lord and to themselves; they were martyrs for *us*, for the whole Church in the days to come. It was for us, for all human beings we may indeed say, that they, these holy ones—strong men, tender women, even sometimes little children—gave their bodies to be tortured and destroyed. For through and by these very sacrifices did the Church take root and gather strength; it was the actual sight of human beings suffering and dying rather than give up their faith which led others to understand,

---

* It is impossible not specially to regret the absence in our calendar of the names of the early saints—S. Ignatius, S. Polycarp, Bishop Pothinus, the aged martyr of ninety, and his fellow-sufferers of Lyons and Vienne—for of all of these there exist undoubtedly true and marvellously interesting historical accounts, unconfused by legend or exaggeration. Several of the very greatest of the Fathers of the Church, from Justin Martyr in the second century to S. Bernard in the twelfth, are also, strange to say, unmentioned.

to *feel*, that this same faith must have a living source in truths such as the world had never yet known; that this "Master," of whom each martyr spoke with his latest breath, was indeed One whose like had never before lived as a man among men and women. There have been martyrs in all ages; there are martyrs in the present day, some unknown and unmarked by human eye, some whose names have been on our lips but recently. But these *first* martyrs had a special mission, and deserve from all Christians a special gratitude which should never be forgotten. They were indeed, as has been well said, "the foundation stones on which the Church was built;" they were the soldiers who fought her first battles and gained her first victories. And this thought explains the meaning of the expression we know so well—that of "the noble *army* of martyrs," an expression which at the first glance seems hardly suited to the gentle and loving spirits of these all-enduring, saintly sufferers.

So, though it may be in one sense painful and even terrible to read of the martyrs' trials, it is, in another and a higher sense, both glorious and beautiful. And as one writer on this subject says: "The sufferings which the soldiers of Christ were content to endure, we who follow in the same Christian chivalry may not refuse to hear of." It is indeed only right that even as children we should know something about these sufferings, believing at the same time that, fearful as they were, the grace and strength specially granted enabled the holy martyrs to bear with more than human courage what, for us, it is *almost* too awful to think of. Nay, it is even in some cases recorded that they became actually unconscious of the agony, in the bliss and joy of knowing for whom they suffered, for whom they died.

We may leave out such of the festivals as you have doubtless learnt about already: that of the Transfiguration of our Lord, and those in honour of the Blessed Virgin, of her mother S. Anne, of S. Mary Magdalen, and of the Beheading of S. John the Baptist. After these, the earliest saint's day, *historically* speaking, in our Black Letter Calendar, is the 1st of June, dedicated to S. Nico-mede. Very little is known of this faithful-hearted man, but his story, slight as it is, makes him not unfitted to be the first on our list. For S. Nicomede was a martyr *for* martyrs.

Some histories tell us that he was a personal disciple of S. Peter, but this is uncertain, though, if it were true, S. Nicomede showed himself worthy of such a teacher. He was a holy and humble-minded Christian priest at Rome, too humble and insignificant probably to have attracted attention on his own account; but in the persecutions of the Emperor Domitian, near the end of the first century, he devoted himself to the service of the martyrs, tending and comforting them, doubtless, in their sufferings whenever it was possible for him to do so, and especially, we are told, showing loving and reverent care for their poor life-less bodies. We can picture to ourselves the gentle, yet courageous priest searching, alone and unaided, for the disfigured corpses, all that was left to earthly sight of his beloved friends, and burying them with Christian rites, unmindful of the danger to himself. And at last his own time came. He was seized when thus employed, ordered to sacrifice to the gods, and on his refusal to do so, condemned to die. His death was a fearful one: he was beaten with leaded whips till he expired. One is pleased to think that in its turn kind Nicomede's dead body was cared for as he had cared for others: a priest named Justus buried it in hallowed ground in the Via Nomentana, at Rome, where his tomb used to be shown. And the Christian Church has never allowed his faithful and courageous devotion to be forgotten. The martyrdom of S. Nicomede took place on the 15th of September, but the 1st of June is more generally observed in his honour, as on that day a church at Rome was dedicated to him. He died in the year of our Lord 81.

Fourteen years later, on the 6th of May, our record brings before us another and much more familiar figure in the person of S. John the Evangelist. On this day our Black Letter Calendar describes him as "S. John ante Portam Latinam," or "S. John before the Latin Gate." This is the same S. John written of as "the disciple whom Jesus loved," the author of the fourth version of the Gospel, as well as of the three epistles bearing his name, and the Book of the Revelation; the same S. John to whose honour is dedicated the 27th of December, one of the greater saints' days of the Church. But this 6th of May is also consecrated to his memory because on that day, according to a tradition handed down to us, S. John, already a very aged man, underwent a cruel trial. By the order of the inhuman tyrant Domitian he was thrown into a caldron of boiling oil, just outside what was called at Rome the

S. John (*Hans Hemling*).

"Latin Gate," or the gate on the road to Latium. The holy disciple suffered, we are told, no injury from this intended torture, but seemed, on the contrary, to be strengthened and refreshed by it; so that the Emperor, seeing this miracle, was terrified, and dared not attempt anything more, contenting himself with banishing S. John to the mines at Patmos.

The Evangelist was at this time about eighty-nine years of age, but he lived five years longer, and died peacefully at Ephesus, where he was allowed to go after the cruel Domitian's death. There is no certain historical account of this story of the 6th of May, but still there is no reason why it may not be true. Indeed, S. Jerome and others think that by this trial was fulfilled to S. John our Lord's prediction that both the beloved disciple and his brother S. James should indeed "drink of His cup," or, in other words, suffer with Him. S. James was beheaded by Herod, and "in will," says S. Jerome, "John was a martyr, and did indeed drink the chalice of confession."

On the 23rd of November, in the year 100 A.D., died S. Clement, whose name is the third on our list. As is the case with many of the early saints, especially the martyrs, we know the day of his death, but not that of his birth. We do not even know the year in which he was born, nor is it certain to what nation he belonged, though most writers think it probable that he was a Jew by descent, though born and brought up at Rome. Some believe him to be the same Clement as he whom S. Paul, in his Epistle to the Philippians, speaks of as "a fellow-labourer." Late in life he was made Bishop of Rome. He may have been a Christian from his birth, or he may have been con-

verted by S. Peter or S. Paul. This we cannot tell. But
that he was, indeed, a Christian of the best and noblest is
proved by the interesting and beautiful writings which have
come down to us in his name. In the early days these
writings were read in the churches, and looked upon almost
as belonging to the New Testament. But for many centuries they were lost, and only restored again in the year
1633, when a very ancient manuscript Bible containing
them was sent as a present to our King James I., whose
librarian translated and published them as the " Epistle
of S. Clement to the Corinthians." This epistle or letter of
Bishop Clement was called forth by unhappy quarrels at
that time in the church at Corinth. It is very beautiful
and touching, full of good and wise advice, breathing all
through a spirit of holy love and charity and Christian
courage. For at the very time he was writing it, Clement's
own life and the lives of all his flock were in daily and
hourly danger. That he died the death of a martyr is not
certain, though probable. For it was in this very year,
100 A.D., that a short, though fierce, persecution of the
Christians broke out again at Rome under the Emperor
Trajan. There is a legend, beautiful enough to make us
wish to think it quite true, about Clement's last days. It
tells that he was banished to the country now called the
Crimea, to work there in the mines with many other Christian prisoners. He found these poor exiles suffering fearfully from want of pure water, and in answer to his fervent
prayers for their relief, he saw in a vision a lovely white
lamb, pointing with its foot to a certain spot on the ground,

S. Clement immediately sought for the spot, and on digging but a little way, a spring of delicious water burst forth. According to this same legend, the Roman prefect, enraged at the saint's success in converting many of the heathen miners to Christianity, put him to death by drowning. A heavy anchor was tied to the good bishop's neck, so that his body should never be seen again. But according to one version of the story, some of his living disciples succeeded in recovering it, and in later days his bones were reverently cared for in the Church of San Clemente at Rome, dedicated to his memory. One would love to know more of the facts of the life of this great and good man, but yet of himself and his own heart and mind we are able to learn much by his earnest and holy writings.

A long time passes, more than a hundred years, between the date of Bishop Clement's death and that of the next saint's day in our Prayer-Book. This is the 7th of March, dedicated to S. Perpetua, who, with several others on that day, in the year of our Lord 203, suffered martyrdom under the Roman Emperor Severus. This century, though passed over in silence in our smaller record, was yet marked in the great annals of the Church's history by many persecutions. No details have come down to us of the sufferers in the fearful persecutions of the insanely wicked Nero, in the first century, many though they were, and in the same way it is certain that multitudes, of various nations and at widely separated places, were martyred in the second century whose names have been lost to history. We know of but a few: Ignatius, the noble Bishop of Antioch, A.D. 107; Polycarp, also a bishop, at Smyrna, A.D. 140; the slave-girl Blandina, with the boy of fifteen, Saturus, two among the many martyred in France, then called Gaul, A.D. 177; Symphorius, a youth of noble birth, also martyred in France. For these second-century persecutions were sharp and short, bursting out suddenly and unexpectedly here and there, as do smouldering fires; not like the great *planned* onslaught against Christianity which I must tell you of in the next chapter. But first I must relate the beautiful and wonderful story of S. Perpetua. Among all the martyr stories of ancient or later days, it is one of the most interesting, for we have all the details of it, up to the very night before her death, related in the saint's own simple, yet dignified, words. Is it not marvellous to think of, that across this long stretch of nearly seventeen hundred years sweet Perpetua's account of her own sufferings and noble courage, written by herself in her prison, should have been preserved? Not that she praises herself or seems to think there was anything wonderful in her holy heroism. She ascribes all her strength to her dear Lord's goodness, and through all the horrors of her dreadful imprisonment is never weary of thanking and praising her Master. Some day, when you, dear children, are men and women, I trust you will read this story for yourselves; those of you who are learning Latin may do so in the saint's *very own original words*. It would spoil it for me to attempt to quote much from it, but I will tell you all that I have space for.

Vivia Perpetua, to give her full name, was a young married lady, living with her family at Carthage, in Africa. Her mother and brothers were Christians, but not her father. Nor do we know if her husband was a Christian; it is only said that he was a wealthy and respected man. She had one dear little baby, whom she tenderly loved. Her youngest brother of seven had died just before the persecution broke out. This child had suffered from a very painful disease, and his death was evidently a great grief to his sister, for she relates how, in the prison, she had a wonderful dream about this little boy, which shows how much he was in her thoughts. But except for this sorrow it seems as if Vivia Perpetua's life had been a very happy one. She was young, rich, and beautiful, surrounded by friends who loved her dearly—it is said that her father cared for her most of all his children—no doubt courted and admired. There does not seem much in such a life to prepare one for a martyr's death. But the true martyr spirit was in this fair young lady, as firm and fervent as in the strong soldier S. George, or the tried and experienced Clement—as humbly faithful and self-forgetting as in the poor slave Felicitas, who suffered with her.

We know no particulars of the beginning of this persecution, or what directed it to Carthage, and especially to this rich and important family. Perpetua's account begins when already in prison. She tells how for some days she and her companions—two young slaves, Revocatus and Felicitas (probably his sister), two young men, most likely of high rank, Saturninus and Secundulus—were arrested on suspicion of being Christians, shut up for some days in a house, under a strong guard, and then taken to one of the dreadful Roman prisons, where, she says, "I was shocked at the horror and darkness of the place, never having known what such places were." No wonder, for these prisons were "dismal holes," with no windows, only a very small aperture high up in the wall for the light to come in by. The heat also, she says, was fearful, and the rudeness of the soldiers very hard to bear. In the house, their first quarters, they had been joined by Saturus, whom Perpetua speaks of as her brother. He gave himself up in order to comfort and instruct the others, for he was a learned as well as a holy man, and he arranged that they should all be baptized, as they had not yet received baptism. Perpetua's worst trouble at first was the thought of her poor baby, but two Christian deacons who were allowed to see the prisoners, managed to have the little fellow brought to her, which made her happier, though she was obliged to send him back to her mother to be taken care of. Another terrible trial to her was the visits of her old father, who came constantly entreating her to renounce her faith—"for the sake of his grey hairs to take pity on him." He kissed her hands and her feet with many tears, and she, "full of pain and grieved at heart," yet had strength to repeat that she *could* not give up her Master.

"I *cannot* call myself other than a Christian," she had already said to him at the first, and she touched a pitcher which happened to stand beside her. "Can I call this aught but a pitcher, which it is?"

And he answered, "No."

"Nor can I say of myself that I am not what I am—a Christian," she repeated.

She had some wonderful and mysteriously beautiful dreams in the prison, which comforted her and the others greatly. Her brother, too, had a vision, which made them feel sure that they were soon to die, while it opened heaven and its blessedness to their faithful eyes. These visions are too long for me to relate here, but some day I hope you will read about them.

At last came the day so terrible to these poor people as human beings, so glorious as the followers of their Lord. The slave Felicitas had a little baby, too, even younger and more tender than the Lady Perpetua's infant son. It must have been a bitter sorrow to both these young mothers to have to say good-bye to their children. One would like to know what became of them; one could hope that they grew up Christians worthy of the name and of their noble mothers.

I do not want to say too much about the actual sufferings of these martyrs: it is very terrible and heartrending. They were first forced to fight with wild beasts, but none of them were killed in this combat. Perpetua and Felicitas were exposed to a wild cow, who tossed them both. Perpetua, as soon as she came to her senses, raised herself and tried to bind up her long hair, not wishing "to seem forlorn in what was her hour of victory." Then, looking round and seeing her poor slave friend in worse case than herself, she tenderly tried to support her.   And even the hard hearts of the brutalised spectators were a little touched.   They called out that it was enough; the victims might now be despatched by the sword.   So they were led away to the gate of the arena.   And then, it is related, Perpetua seemed to awake out of sleep.   She had been stunned, doubtless, by the shock of her cruel fall, and we may also believe that in God's love for His noble child He had softened her sufferings.   For she looked round and asked dreamily how soon she and Felicitas were to be given to the wild cow, and when told that that part of their trial was over, she seemed to rejoice and gather new strength, though she could scarcely believe it.   For it was the fearful thought of the wild beasts that had been the worst to her gentle spirit: death itself she did not fear.

And it came soon, though to the last all Perpetua's courage was called for.   The gladiator who was to kill her trembled and shook; it is said he was unskilful—rather would one think he was conscience-stricken and filled with remorse.   It was her own hand which guided the sword-thrust to her tender throat.   Her dear brother Saturus was already dead, though to the last, with holy unselfishness, he had encouraged and supported the others.   That he would be the first to die had been foretold in one of her visions to Perpetua, in which she had seen a golden stair, up which Saturus ascended before her, ready to welcome her when she came.   And so it was.

In the vision Saturus heard his sister say, "Whatever happiness I have had in life is as nothing compared with what I have now."

And the blessedness of heaven is no short-lived joy. "Eye hath not seen, nor ear heard, neither have entered into the heart of man, the things which God hath prepared for them that love Him."

CHAPTER II.

S. Fabian, January 20, A.D. 250.—**S. Agatha**, February 5, A.D. 251.—**S. Laurence**, August 10, A.D. 258.—**S. Cyprian**, September 16, A.D. 258.

THERE is again a lapse of many years in the record of our saints. From the death of S. Perpetua, in 203 A.D., we come upon no name till that of S. Fabian, whose martyrdom in the year 250 is commemorated on the 20th of January.

We do not know much of Fabian's life. He was a Roman, belonging to a great and powerful family; a Christian when we first hear of him, and probably a Christian from his birth. He was living in the country at the time of the death of Anteros, the Bishop of Rome; and he came to Rome to take part in the gathering of the Christians for the purpose of choosing a new bishop. At that time the only place where the followers of our Lord could safely assemble for religious purposes was the catacombs, or great underground cemeteries, which the Christians had themselves constructed from the earliest days of the Church's existence. The Roman authorities allowed them to make these burial-places, but it is probable that no one but the Christians themselves had any idea how very large they became, as from one generation to another they were added to.   And in times of persecution—which times, however, it must be remembered, were not constant; now and then, for many years together, the Christians were left at peace—this great extent of underground chambers and passages, none of them very large, but as puzzling as an enormous labyrinth, offered excellent places of conceal-ment.   Not that any one could have lived long in these strange cellars—the want of pure air would have made this impossible; but for some hours, or even days at a time, it was easy to hide in them, especially as there were secret ways of getting in and out, often by the sand quarries near that side of the city, unknown to any but the Christians themselves.

It was in one of these underground chambers, conse-crated as a church, that the "brethren" were met together on the important question of the choice of a bishop from among them, when they were joined by Fabian, "an un-known stranger," we are told, to most of them.   We do not know how old he was at the time, but his life till then had probably been quiet and uneventful; he had come to Rome with no thought of putting himself forward in any way.   He was not even a priest.   Suddenly, in the midst of the discussion, a dove, fluttering down through one of the small openings overhead, alighted on the stranger, recalling the scene of old, when the Holy Spirit descended in the same form upon our Blessed Lord.   And the eyes of all present turned upon Fabian, while all voices exclaimed together, as if they were but one, "He is worthy."

And thus he was chosen.

The Bishop's future life showed that the choice had indeed been divinely guided. He governed the Church wisely and well for fourteen years, not caring only for his own flock at Rome, but choosing and sending missionaries to foreign lands. Among these was Dionysius, or Denys, whose work in France I shall have to tell you about soon.

Fabian's name is marked by " M," as well as by the " B " which stands for " Bishop." For in 249 Decius became Emperor of Rome, and during the two years of his short reign the persecutions he instituted against the Christians were very severe. The Emperor Decius and some of his successors were not so inhumanly cruel as several of the earlier Roman rulers. They believed that it was necessary to put down Christianity in order to revive the ancient pagan religion. For they saw that the nation was becoming more and more corrupt, and in their ignorance they tried to stamp out the one cure, to silence the teaching inspired by God's Holy Spirit Himself. But even where love of cruelty is not the motive at first, all injustice and tyranny are sure before long to awaken it. And in many cases where the emperors themselves would not have wished it to be so, their orders were entrusted to brutal governors or prefects, who heaped insult and torture and horrors of all kinds on to their defenceless victims.

There is no record of the particulars of S. Fabian's death. A letter written to S. Cyprian, then Bishop of Carthage, telling about it, once existed, but has been lost. We only know that the good Bishop was beheaded at Rome on this

20th of January, and in Cyprian's own writings he is spoken of as " Fabian, of most noble memory."

At the time we have been speaking of, while Fabian was

S. Agatha (*Malta, 15th century*).

Bishop of Rome, there was growing up in Catania, in the island of Sicily, a sweet and beautiful young girl, named

Agatha. She was the daughter of a noble and wealthy family, and from her earliest childhood she was loved and admired, not only for her beauty, but for her peculiarly gentle and charming manners. Her life, as far as we can judge, must have been a very bright and happy one. And this was the case with several of the early saints—saints in the days when the word was almost sure to mean "martyrs" also. It was not only the poor and sorrowful, the aged and the oppressed, that accepted the tidings of the Gospel of hope and joy, of rest for the weary and comfort for the miserable. The young and prosperous, the rich and beautiful, were to be found among the most earnest of the followers of the lowly Jesus, eager to give Him their all, their love and devotion, their very life itself.

Such an one was Agatha.

We are not told distinctly that she was born a Christian, but it seems certain that she was, for from her earliest youth, the ancient writers tell us, "she was consecrated to God." These words no doubt mean that her parents, and she herself when she was old enough to decide, resolved that she should never marry, but devote her life to serving God in the ways that an unmarried woman has more leisure for. Not that the Christian religion has ever taught that marriage is wrong, but in those days for a Christian maiden to marry worthily was very difficult. The pagan idea of marriage was a low one; women were not considered in any way fit to be the "helpmates" of men. They were treated more like dolls or slaves. Few of the best and noblest Christian men felt free to marry in those troubled times; there was work for all to do—far more, indeed, than all *could* do, in continuing the mission of the Apostles. And if a Christian girl married an unbeliever, though in some cases the wife's influence refined and ennobled the husband, even when she did not succeed in converting him, yet the risks were very great, and to a maiden brought up in a Christian home it would have seemed almost certain degradation to marry a pagan, however rich and great and powerful. We cannot, therefore, wonder at Agatha's choice.

But her beauty and her many charms—perhaps, too, her wealth—made some of the rich Romans, living in Sicily, very angry when they heard what she had decided. And Christians, even when of noble and important birth, were fair game for tyranny. No risk was run by any one who oppressed them. Quintian, the Roman governor at Catania, admired the beautiful girl, and when he found that there was no use in his doing so—Agatha wished for neither admirers nor suitors—he grew furious. Under pretext of zeal to carry out the Emperor's orders against Christians, he seized and imprisoned her, hoping to terrify her into sacrificing to the pagan gods. Then he gave her into the keeping of a cruel and heartless woman, who, with flattery and coaxing, in turn with frightful threats, tried to make the girl yield. But Agatha stood firm.

"My soul," she said, "is founded and built on Christ."

And when brought before the governor she spoke out bravely, telling him, when he boasted of his noble birth, that his nobility was poor indeed, as he was a slave to sin and to the worship of gods who did not exist. Much more she said, till he ordered her to be silent, and gave her over to most dreadful tortures. She was beaten and scourged, and her tender flesh torn with pincers, and then, wounded and fainting, she was thrown into a dungeon.

But into the dreary darkness and suffering there came to Agatha a wonderful vision. Angels, and one whom she believed to be the Blessed S. Peter, came and ministered to her, so that her pain ceased and her heart was filled with joy. Four days after, her trials began again. More furious than ever at the sight of her calmness and renewed strength, the governor caused her to be thrown on to a great fire, where she was fearfully burnt, but yet not left there till she expired. As they carried her back again to prison she prayed to God earnestly, though submissively still, that she might die; and her gentle prayer was granted. "Sweetly," we are told, "she rendered up her spirit."

Her friends buried her in a beautiful tomb of porphyry, and though Agatha, humble in her holiness, would little have thought of such honour, it was well that even her dead body should not be forgotten. For our bodies, we are told, are "the temples of the Holy Ghost," and it is right and true to think of the bodies of the holy martyrs as indeed temples glorious and undefiled—"channels for the grace of God." And even the very tombs of the martyrs have their uses. To God alone is it known how many of the heathen may have been influenced by the sight of that of Agatha to ask about her story and the wonderful faith which had given strength to a young and tender girl to dare and endure all for her dear Lord's sake.

Within two years of this martyrdom the Emperor Decius died. During the first part of the reign of his successor, Valerian, the Christians were left in peace. But these quiet years increased their numbers and even their riches, as many great people joined them. Then again broke forth the hatred and jealousy of their power, and the year 258 saw the eighth great persecution at its worst. In this year, on the 10th of August, was put to death the next saint we commemorate, the young Archdeacon Laurence, of whom it is said that "there are few martyrs whose names are so famous."

He was by birth a Spaniard, the son of Christian parents, and (like S. Agatha) it is probable that his childhood and boyhood, passed in a country home in Aragon, were very happy and peaceful. While still very young he became the friend, perhaps at the college where he was educated, of a priest named Sixtus or Xystus, who afterwards was made Bishop of Rome. The Bishop never forgot his young friend, whose holy and beautiful character was shown even in his boyhood, and when he was himself the head of the Church he sent for Laurence, then a deacon, and made him *arch*deacon. The friends had but a few months together, for Sixtus was one of the first to be seized and condemned to death. As the good Bishop was led away to prison, Laurence followed him, weeping, entreating to be allowed to suffer with him.

"Whither art thou going, O my father," he said, "without thy son? Whither, O holy priest, dost thou hasten without thy deacon? Wast thou ever wont to offer the Sacrifice without thy minister? Dost thou refuse me a bloody death,

when thou hast admitted me to be with thee at the consecration of the Blood of the Lord? Abraham offered his

S. Laurence (*Vivarini*).

son; Peter sent Stephen before him. O father, let thy

strength be shown in thy son; offer him whom thou hast trained up!"

And the Bishop answered him with affection, foretelling that Laurence, "his son in the faith," would not have long to wait, and that he should be strengthened to endure a yet more terrible and glorious death for their Master. Then, perhaps partly to comfort the young man for the time, he commissioned him to sell the Church treasures at once, and distribute the money among their poor, who, as he foresaw, would be left desolate indeed without their beloved pastor. Laurence obeyed him, and spent the rest of the day in going round to all the Christians in need of help, and distributing to them the value of the golden chalices and candlesticks which he had sold. And the next day he contrived to have one more last glance of his well-loved friend, by standing in the way by which Sixtus must go to the place of execution. There Laurence called out to the Bishop as he passed, that his wishes about the treasure had been carried out. The word "treasure" caught the greedy ears of the Roman soldiers, and Laurence was sent for and commanded to give it up. He allowed that the Church still possessed much treasure, and promised to return with it. And they let him go for this purpose, in the charge of a Roman officer named Hippolytus.*

What do you think were S. Laurence's "treasures"?

---

* There is a story that, while imprisoned in the house of Hippolytus, S. Laurence restored sight to a poor captive named Lucillus, at the same time that he instructed and baptized him. It is told also that the sight of this miracle and the holy words of the young deacon led to the conversion of Hippolytus and his household. .

Two days later he reappeared before the Emperor—some accounts say that he begged Valerian to come to the church to see the treasures—leading a strange and motley crowd. There were the poor and suffering; "the halt, the maimed, and the blind ;" widows and orphans, some of them doubtless widows and orphans of imprisoned or martyred Christians ; the aged, too old to work for themselves ; little children with none to care for them—all who needed love and sympathy and help.

"These," said the young Archdeacon, "are the Church's treasures ; treasures confided to her by Christ himself, in whom He himself is to be seen. For does He not say, 'Forasmuch as ye did it unto one of the least of these, ye did it unto Me'?"

The Emperor was infuriated, and ordered that Laurence should be given over to be tortured.

I could not tell you all that the holy young deacon had to bear. Bishop Sixtus had foretold that "a more glorious trial" than his own awaited Laurence, and his words proved indeed true. Not hours only, but *days* of agony were the youthful martyr's portion. At the end of the first tortures he thought himself dying, and prayed to God to receive his soul, while thanking Him for the courage which had been given him to endure. And new strength was sent, so that, through the long hours of the bright August day, Laurence lay on his awful couch—for, children, he was gradually burnt, or rather roasted, to death on an iron frame, like a gridiron, over a slow fire—gazing up at the deep blue sky, his face illumined by the summer sunshine which fell upon it, and by the still more glorious sunshine of the spirit within, serene and even smiling, not a groan or murmur passing his lips, till at last his pure and faithful spirit was permitted to escape to the happy home awaiting it.

There is something very touching as well as grand in what we know of the character of this saint. He seems so young, and almost boyishly sensitive and affectionate. He was not ashamed of his tears in the public streets, as he followed his dear friend and teacher; sweet stories are told of his tender pity for his suffering poor; and yet with courage, equalling that of the most experienced and tried of Christ's soldiers, he bore unflinchingly such horrors of bodily agony as one would fain hope the world has not often seen. So certain is it that the truly strong are the truly gentle; above all, those who, like S. Laurence, are strong with the strength of God.

S. Laurence was buried outside Rome, on the road to Tivoli. A church was afterwards built over his tomb, and thither came numberless visitors from far and near to pray, many believing and attesting that their prayers were miraculously answered. There are now a great many churches—hundreds—dedicated to S. Laurence, in various countries all over the world. But he is commemorated also in Spain by the palace of the Escurial, a magnificent building, or buildings, in the form of a gridiron. This was the work of Philip II. of Spain, and the motive of it was gratitude for a great victory he won on the Feast of S. Laurence.

Another saint is commemorated in our Black Letter Calendar, whose martyrdom took place the same year as that of S. Laurence, and indeed but a very few weeks later. This was the great and good Cyprian, Bishop of Carthage. There are strong contrasts in the history of the saints. S. Laurence, a Christian from his birth, was probably little more than a youth when he died; S. Cyprian, born and bred a pagan, only learnt the true faith when past middle age, a man of forty-six, nor was it without great struggles of mind and spirit, much questioning and distress, that through the grace of God he was at last enabled to feel himself, in his own words, "a changed man in heart and mind." Then, he goes on to say, "in a wonderful manner doubtful things were made certain; what had been closed was opened, dark became light, power was given where had been difficulty."

Cyprian was a very clever and learned man; he was rich too, belonging to an important family of Cyprus who had settled in Carthage, and before his conversion he was famed as a teacher of rhetoric and philosophy in the colleges. His own teacher, in the truest learning, was an aged Christian priest, named Cecilius, whom Cyprian loved so much and with such gratitude that, when baptized into the Church, he added his friend's name to his own. Cyprian threw his whole heart and mind into Christianity. He was not a man to do things by halves, and his life became a model of holy beauty for all to follow. He gave of all he possessed to his poorer brethren, selling indeed a great part of his property in order to do more for others.

His house and lovely gardens, we are told, were open to all comers, and none in sorrow or trouble returned from him unconsoled. He soon became so well known and respected among the Christians of that part of Africa, that, on the death of Donatus, the Bishop of Carthage, he was chosen to succeed him. Cyprian had been but a short time in the priesthood, and he thought himself quite unworthy of such honour, but the people insisted on his election, and he had to yield. This was in the year A.D. 247. Less than eleven years later he was put to death, but in those eleven years he did more work for Christianity than many even good and zealous men achieve in a long lifetime. Almost immediately after he became Bishop, the short though terrible persecution under the Emperor Decius, which I have told you of, broke out, and Cyprian, who took no step save with the most earnest prayer for God's guidance, concealed himself for some time, till he could with safety appear again. In this he showed even greater courage than if he had sought martyrdom, for he braved the reproach of cowardice for the Church's sake, knowing how sorely his life and influence were needed, and in this his example was of great value. For the true Christian martyr should above all desire to fulfil his Master's will, and be in no haste to seek death while work clearly remains for him to do.*

---

* "It is one thing for the spirit to be ready for martyrdom, and another for martyrdom to be ready for the spirit. . . . For God does not ask for our blood, but our faith " (Translation of S. Cyprian's writings).

From his concealment the Bishop wrote a great number
of treatises and letters, and directed the affairs of his own
charge with wonderful wisdom and skill. There was much
to do in this way, for during the long period of peace
many evils had crept into the Church. The zeal and
earnestness of many had failed; there were disputes and
jealousies even among the sincere and devoted. And
Cyprian's rare character, the union of great firmness with
Christlike charity which he possessed, fitted him peculiarly
for his most difficult post. We seem to know him well
through his writings, a great number of which are still
preserved. Many painful questions arose at this time:
one of the most perplexing was about the treatment of
those unhappy Christians—" the lapsed," as they are called
—whose courage and faith failed them in the hour of
danger or loss, and whom some of the heads of the Church
wished to consider as outcasts for ever. In Cyprian these
poor people, when truly penitent, found a gentle judge
and pitying friend, though at the same time he was careful
to be assured of their thorough sincerity and real repentance
before receiving them again.

The few years of his life as a Christian were full of
troubles. Even when, for a time, persecution ceased
again, for this devoted man there was no breathing space.
Quarrels and strife within the Church herself, sad to say,
must have been harder for him to bear than attacks from
without; jealousy of himself, generously though he met it,
must yet have sorely wounded his loving spirit. But in the
end he seems to have won nearly all hearts; he was ever

calm and self-forgetting, cheerful and gracious. In one of his letters he describes his garden and speaks of his love of it; and his deacon, Pontius, who wrote his Life, relates how the Bishop was walking among his flowers, with a gay and cheerful countenance, the very day he was expecting the Roman soldiers to carry him away to prison and to death.

Perhaps no part of his life shows his noble and beautiful character more perfectly than the account of his behaviour during a most awful pestilence that broke out at Carthage and in the neighbouring country, five or six years before his martyrdom. He was unceasing in his tender care of all the sufferers, carrying the Blessed Sacrament to the dying Christians at one moment, at the next soothing the last anguish of some poor pagan ; tending the deathbeds of many of the very men who but a short time before had been loud in the cry of "Cyprian to the lions !" and by his eager words and untiring labour encouraging his fellow-believers to join in his noble task. So that this fearful time was indeed a triumph for the Christians, who, led by their Bishop, spared neither labour nor wealth in the work of succour. "Men," we are told, "with the scars or mutilations of recent tortures on their bodies, were seen exposing their lives for others"—and these others their cruel foes—"to a yet more honourable martyrdom ;" encouraged by Cyprian's reminder that death in whatever guise—in that of a loathsome disease as well as in the more heroic form—if it finds us doing God's will, is indeed blessed.

"Not our own will, but God's," are the words which seem most frequent on his lips. Whatever He sends is best. "There are both roses and lilies among the Church's flowers—white for faithful labour, red for the martyr's suffering—both fair in God's sight."

And *both* were to be S. Cyprian's. The years of faithfullest labour were crowned by the martyr's death. On the 13th of September, A.D. 258, a few months after the beginning of the eighth general persecution, that under Valerian, the great and good Bishop knew that his own hour had come. "With a glad countenance and a lofty bearing" he came forward to meet the messengers sent to fetch him, though the news of his arrest filled the streets near his dwelling with weeping and bitterly sorrowing crowds; "even the pagans coming forth to do honour to him" whose heroic goodness had won their hearts. And the next day, a bright and cloudless September day, after the mockery of a trial, in which Cyprian's dignity made him seem more like a victor than a victim, came the quiet end.

"Deo Gratias" (thanks be unto God), he said when he heard his sentence; and in prayer to Him he knelt to receive the sword-stroke which opened to his pure and faithful spirit the gates of Paradise.

CHAPTER III.

S. **Prisca**, January 18, A.D. 270.—S. **Valentine**, February 14, A.D. 270.—S. **Denys**, October 9, A.D. 272.—S. **Cicely**, November 22, A.D. 280.—S. **Crispin** and S. **Crispinian**, October 25, A.D. 287.—S. **Lucian**, January 8, A.D. 287.—S. **Alban**, June 17, A.D. 303.—S. **Faith**, October 6, about A.D. 303.

THE great persecution under the Emperor Valerian, which began, as I told you in the last chapter, A.D 257, lasted about three years. S. Laurence and S. Cyprian are the only martyrs in our calendar who suffered under Valerian. And in the year 261, Gallienus, who was then emperor, formally granted to the Christians liberty to follow their religion in peace. This state of things continued till nearly the end of the century, when under Diocletian the slumbering hatred and jealousy of the Christians began again to awaken, and in 303 A.D. the edict of this emperor appeared, by which all privileges were taken from them, and cruelty and insult of every kind to the followers of Christ throughout the Roman empire were made law. This edict of Diocletian ushered in the last general persecution.

For through all these forty and more years of seeming grace and liberty the spirit of persecution was, as I have said, only sleeping, ready to break out again at any moment, in another wild effort to crush the Church, now more and more firmly taking root, and with every year of comparative peace extending still further among all classes of men and women.   And there were many martyrs during those forty years, for the underlying hatred of the imperial government was often counted upon as certain to excuse and condone any cruelty against a Christian.   The question of religion could at any time be safely taken up as a pretext under cover of which to give way to personal spite; and the pure lives and holy example of those who really walked in the footsteps of our Lord often irritated and infuriated the most wicked and degraded of the pagans among whom they dwelt; and, as must be the case where a government is based on unsound principles, those in high places and in authority were very often the worst men of the nation.

The next date on our list is the 18th of January, 270 A.D., commemorated as that of the martyrdom of S. Prisca. But little is known of this child-saint, for she was only thirteen at the time of her death—and the reason of her cruel suffering seems almost a mystery, happening as it did at a time when persecution had for the moment nearly ceased.   It is possible that her family may in some way have incurred the ill-will of the Emperor, and that the fact of their being Christians was taken advantage of.   Be this as it may, the story remains the same; and even though it has been a good deal confused with legends, there is no reason to doubt the chief points of it.   The very fact of her name being found in so many of the calendars shows

how widely S. Prisca was revered, and through how many
centuries.

She was the little daughter of a great Roman family.
For some reason she was accused as a Christian of refusing to offer incense to the gods, and brought before the
Emperor, who laid his commands upon her thus to do
honour to his deities. But Prisca bravely refused. She
was punished by scourging and blows, and other tortures
yet more dreadful, but all in vain. Then for a time she
was sent back to prison, and only brought out again to be
exposed to a lion; who, it is said, would not harm her,
but crouched at her feet like a gentle dog. In the end
the sweet child—for every account describes her as both
sweet and lovely—was beheaded, and all through the long
roll of more than fifteen centuries her name has been
remembered in the Church's records.

Barely a month later, in this same year, 270, another
Roman martyr gave his life for his faith. This was S.
Valentine; a holy Christian priest, who was imprisoned by
the Emperor in consequence of his having tended and
comforted other Christian martyrs. The child Prisca may
have been one of these; it would seem probable that her
family was among the good priest's friends, and in several
of the ancient records he is spoken of as especially kind
to young girls. Perhaps his friendship for Prisca was the
origin of this idea, though so few details of either have
come down to us. S. Valentine was imprisoned in the
house of a Roman judge, and it is said that, during the
two or three days he spent there, the sight of his holy

bearing and his earnest words converted to Christianity his gaoler, with all his household. Some accounts say that Valentine was beaten to death, others that he was first beaten and afterwards beheaded.

It is strange to think that the 14th of February, the day on which this saint's martyrdom is remembered, has for so many years been associated with pleasure and merriment. For this same day was once a pagan festival, and when Christianity became the religion of the civilised world, this festival was changed into one in honour of the good and kind priest; and thus the name "Valentine" came to be given to the fancy letters we all know, though of late years the fashion of Christmas cards has almost caused them to be forgotten.

The name of S. Denys, the patron saint of France, which follows next, for he was martyred on the 4th of October, in the year 272, carries us back to the good Bishop Fabian of Rome; for Denys was one of seven missionaries sent by him to France, where at that time but a small number of Christians was left, though it is believed that many converts had been made there in the first century by the preaching of S. Luke and S. Paul, or if not by either of these great teachers themselves, certainly by some of their disciples.

S. Denys first landed at Arles, where he remained a short time preaching to the few Christians he found there, and then with some of his companions went on to Paris, where he stayed, and in process of time consecrated a church and appointed clergy. No personal records exist of him, but he is spoken of as a most zealous missionary. He must have laboured fully thirty years in his adopted country, possibly more than forty, as it is not certain if he was put to death in this year, 272, or not till seventeen years later. Persecutions of the Christian churches in the Roman provinces often took place even when there was peace at Rome itself. The government was jealous of the growing and extending power of the Church, and any prefect or consul, if he happened to be of a tyrannical nature, could indulge his love of cruelty and win favour at the same time with his rulers, by ill-treating the Christian subjects under his power.

The French nation has always, and rightly, for their Denys must have been a devoted and noble evangelist, greatly reverenced this saint. But unfortunately, in the desire to do him honour impossible facts have been mingled with his true history. Some writers have stated that he was the same Dionysius as the convert and friend of S. Paul, the member of the court of the Areopagus, before whom the great Christian teacher spoke, and to whom were falsely attributed some very valuable and beautiful writings, *really* the work of an unknown author about the end of the fifth century. It is certain that they were not written by S. Denys, and it is also certain that he lived and died two centuries later than S. Paul. The bodies of S. Denys and two companions who died with him were thrown into the Seine, but a Christian lady recovered them and buried them near the place of their martyrdom. There now stands the great abbey, dedicated to the missionary saint, where for many ages the kings of France were interred. The ancient war-cry of France, "Montjoie S. Denys," recalls his memory, though *his* message was one of peace and good-will, and his death one of holy self-sacrifice.

On the 22nd of November we commemorate the martyr-dom of another Roman lady of high birth. This was Cecilia, or, as we love to call her in our English tongue, S. Cicely. Not very much is known of her as certain fact, but through all the legends that have gathered round her sweet name, many of them very charming, some almost as fanciful as fairy tales, enough can be gathered to give us a just idea of her true history. For that she really lived and died there is no doubt, even though the actual dates vary according to the different accounts. It seems most probable that she suffered in the year 280 A.D. Her name is to be found in most of the calendars, and has "always," we are told on good authority, "been most illustrious in the Church."

She was young and beautiful, of a noble and wealthy family. But her parents were pagans, and though like S. Agatha, and for the same reasons as I explained to you in relating her history, S. Cicely wished never to marry, she was obliged to yield to her parents' authority in the matter. Her husband, Valerian by name, was young and lovable, good and kind, though a heathen. But her sin-cere and earnest religious faith, her sweetness and gentle-ness, succeeded in converting not only him, but a brother of his, called Tiburtius, and the three young people lived

together most happily, trying to teach others and to succour
and console such of their Christian neighbours as suffered
for their devotion. The usual fate overtook them—being

S. Cecilia (*Raphael*).

rich and important was often in those days but a greater
danger to Christians. The two brothers and Cicely herself
were arrested, and ordered to sacrifice to the heathen gods.
They refused without the slightest hesitation, and then

first Valerian and Tiburtius, and a few days later S. Cicely herself, were put to death. It is said that though fearfully wounded, she lingered for three days, and that her brave and loving spirit so rose above the sore bodily sufferings that through those long hours she never wearied of speaking to and instructing those about her, and of singing psalms and hymns. For all accounts agree in saying that she had a most lovely voice, and could sing with marvellous sweetness, for which reason she has always been looked upon as the patroness of sacred music. In one of the service books of S. Gregory, of the sixth century, there is a beautiful prayer to be used on S. Cicely's day. There is a story which relates that her body, and those of her husband and brother, were found in the ninth century in a Roman cemetery, and buried afresh, or "translated" to a tomb in a church already dedicated to her in Rome. This is the more probably true because at a much later date—in 1599—on the restoration of this church, three bodies were found in a tomb near the altar, exactly corresponding to the description in the old account of their re-burial.

We must return to France again to hear about the next three saints—all of them martyrs—whose dates follow that of S. Cicely. You remember that I told you that with S. Denys there came to France, then called Gaul, several other missionary priests. Among these were three, whose names are in our English calendar to be commemorated. These are S. Crispin and his brother Crispinian on the 25th of October, and S. Lucian on the 8th of January. S. Crispin's name is sometimes given alone, but in every account of him, he and his brother are mentioned together. They were of noble Roman birth, what we nowadays would call thorough "gentlemen," yet they were shoe-makers! This was of their own choice. They were de-votedly attached to each other, had together become Christians, and when they heard of S. Denys setting out as a missionary to the distant (for such it must have seemed) heathen land of Gaul, they volunteered to accompany him. Arrived there, the little band soon separated, S. Denys himself, as we have seen, journeying to the north. But the brothers kept together. They made their home in the small town of Soissons, and there they set up as shoe-makers, and menders too doubtless. In this they were influenced by the example of S. Paul, who was himself, you remember, a tent-maker, and very probably too they found that by living as working men among the rough natives they were able better to win their confidence. The brothers are described in the ancient writings of S. Jerome, our own Bede, and others, as models of "charity, disin-terestedness, and heavenly piety," and the effect of their example as well as of their teaching was the conversion of numbers to the Christian faith. They lived many years in their adopted home peacefully and happily, for their missionary work prospered greatly. But, humble as they made themselves, they were not to escape the glory of the martyr's death. In the year 287 they were summoned before the Roman governor of that part of Gaul, and questioned as to their religious belief.

"We worship the one God," they replied. They were

then threatened and bribed in turns, but nothing moved them, and in the end—probably after undergoing tortures—they were beheaded. A church was afterwards built over their tomb, and up to a few years ago at least, one of the yearly religious processions at Soissons used to stop in front of the house now standing where the church formerly was, to do honour to the memory of the Christian shoemakers.

S. Lucian, who must have been a friend of these brothers, was another of the missionary band sent to Gaul. He was of a noble Roman family, and still very young when he left his own country. Like most of the priests who came with S. Denys, he lived to be an old man, and to see much good result of his labours, both among the native Gauls and Romans who had settled in France. S. Lucian made his home at Beauvais, and now and then he and S. Denys were able to see each other, which must have greatly cheered them both. Lucian trained young priests to help him in his work, and it is probable that this aroused the jealousy of the Roman government. For two of his pupils were seized and put to death, and then the aged priest himself was imprisoned in his turn, first cruelly beaten, and then beheaded.

Now, for the first time in the history of the saints of our English calendar, we come to our own country—Britain, as it was then called. It is believed by all the most learned writers on the subject that the Christian faith was taught and preached in England during the time of the Apostles themselves—that is to say, during the latter part of the first century. There is even some reason for thinking it probable

that S. Paul or S. Peter may have visited this country in
person. But the earliest actual detail that has come down
to us dates from the year 180 A.D., when, it is stated, a
native British king, Lucius, was converted and sent to Rome
for further instruction. It is historically certain that within
thirty years of that date Christianity had made its way
among the Britons. Tertullian, writing about the close
of the second century, speaks of it as having spread to
"Britons beyond the Roman pale." But it was not till the
outbreak of the tenth and last general persecution—that
under Diocletian—that the terrors usually so closely following the acceptance of the true faith came to test the courage
and devotion of the British Church. These islands were a
long way from Rome and its tyranny; it could not have
been difficult for a small body of Christians to conceal
themselves from any specially prejudiced Roman governor
in the wild hill fastnesses of Wales or the North, and many
of the governors were mild and temperate in their rule.
Very likely too they cared little whether the native Britons
kept to their own Druid worship or adopted the new faith,
which it was the Roman fashion to speak of as beneath
contempt, "fit but for the dregs of the population," so long
as they were submissive and docile subjects. So that, from
all these causes, the early British Christians seem for a time
to have been left in peace. But with the terrible persecution of Diocletian this state of things changed. "The
storm," we are told, "fell with great fury," and the first
martyr on British soil was S. Alban; "Alban the proto (or
first) martyr of Britain," as he is always called.

He was a Briton by birth, but an educated and cultivated man. He had, indeed, been sent to Rome as a boy "to improve himself in learning," though he seems to have returned to his own home without having learned anything about the most valuable of all knowledge. He lived at Verulam, an important Roman city in those days, and he was one of the most respected of the native citizens there. He is described as "hospitable, compassionate, and charitable." To this pleasant and kindly home, in a lovely part of the country, came one day a travel-spent, all but worn-out man. He was a Christian priest flying before his enemies, for already the spirit of persecution was abroad. Alban received and succoured him, as with his character he would have received and succoured any one in distress, and for some time the fugitive was safely concealed in the wealthy citizen's house. These days were a crisis in Alban's life. He was at first struck and interested by the earnest devotion and prayers of his guest, and thus led to inquire what it meant, with what invisible friend the gentle priest seemed so constantly in communion? The stranger gladly answered; he told all the wonderful story to the eager and intelligent Briton, told it faithfully as a message from heaven, and without concealing that the acceptance of it would all but certainly lead to suffering and death. And it was not told in vain. There are times when days do the work of years, when minutes even, perfect what we might despair of completing in a lifetime. Thus it was with the good Alban. Before it was discovered where the Christian priest had taken refuge, the work which he had been sent to do was done; his kind pagan host was an avowed believer in the faith of the Cross. And almost at once came to the new Christian the trial and the triumph for which often all the threescore years and ten would seem scarcely enough preparation. The hiding-place of the priest was found out, and soldiers sent to seize him. And Alban, in the delight of his enthusiasm, and in gratitude to his teacher, was not content to face danger when it came, he must meet it half-way, so he wrapped himself in the priest's cloak, and thus disguised by the long "caracalla," as it was called, he gave himself up in the father's stead; and the change was not discovered till the prisoner was led to the Roman judge, who was at that moment standing before the images of his gods, sacrificing to them. The rich Briton was probably known to the magistrate by sight, and he was at once ordered to join in the Roman worship. Alban refused, and in answer to the questions which were put to him, replied simply that he was a Christian, a worshipper of "the true and living God who created all things." Then he was cruelly scourged, and afterwards led away to be beheaded. The spot is still known, near the town called by his name, where the martyr met his death, and several legends have gathered round the story, as is, indeed, scarcely to be wondered at when one considers its unusual and striking facts. The priest was stoned to death about three miles from the town. The beautiful cathedral of S. Albans was built in the Saxon times by a king of Mercia named Offa. He founded a monastery beside it, which was destroyed in Henry VIII.'s reign, but the church was saved by the townsfolk joining together to buy it.

We must cross back again to France to hear the story of the next saint of our roll. It is, indeed, a little uncertain if her martyrdom did not occur before the year 303, which we have been considering as the date of S. Alban's death. All that is sure is that it took place early in the fearful Diocletian persecution, which seems to have spread into the outlying Roman provinces far more quickly than any other. It was in the old town of Agen, in Aquitaine, a name so familiar to us all in history, that lived the little maiden Faith—Fides, as she is called in Latin. A true martyr's name it sounds, and well borne by the child confessor. Like Prisca, Agatha, and Cicely, she was the daughter of wealthy Roman parents, though her home was in France; and she was a Christian from her birth. The actual edict of Diocletian against the Church was not issued till 303, but for some years before, there had been the beginnings of fresh persecution, and the Roman governor in Spain, Datian, was a fearfully cruel man. He came to Agen, hearing of the spread of Christianity there, on purpose to torture and kill. But the news of his visit reached the town in time for most of the members of the Church, led by their Bishop—Caprasius—to take refuge in the hills in the neighbourhood. How it was that the family to which the child-martyr belonged had not also escaped, we do not know. Perhaps her relations may have thought that their important position would place them above danger; possibly some accidental circumstance may have

left some of them behind, and among them the young girl
Faith. When the governor of Spain arrived, bent on persecution, there were no victims to be found in Agen. Infuriated at this, he caused close inquiry to be made, and
his officers succeeded in finding this one innocent lamb.
She was brought before Datian, and the usual mockery of a
choice was offered to her.

"Sacrifice to our gods, or submit to torture and death."

And her answer came, clear and unfaltering—

" I will not sacrifice to your gods. From a child I have
served the Lord Jesus Christ with all my heart, and have
confessed His name."

Thereupon followed tortures unspeakable, endured by
the young girl with a strength and courage such as we
can scarcely picture to ourselves, however firmly we may
believe in them. They beheaded her at last, and to the
end her gentle voice could be heard witnessing to her
Master, and rejoicing in being permitted to suffer for Him.

Some accounts relate that the sight of this martyrdom
drew many of the spectators to Christianity, so marvellous
was the patience and courage of the holy maiden, so
fiendish the cruelty of her tormentors. The Bishop Caprasius returned to Agen shortly after S. Faith's death—
the legend tells that in his concealment in the hills he
had a vision of her sufferings—and was himself put to
death but a few days later. The child-saint has had many
churches dedicated to her honour; among them two in
our own country existed in the eleventh and twelfth centuries. And what is more interesting, at the present time

D

a small chapel in S. Paul's Cathedral is still known by her name. Before it was destroyed by the Great Fire of London, the crypt underneath the choir was dedicated to her.

My chapter began with S. Prisca, and closes with S. Faith. We cannot but think of these two children martyrs together, though thirty years divide the dates of their deaths, and S. Prisca, if living at the time of S. Faith's martyrdom, would have been a middle-aged woman. But they will always seem children to us—children of the Church, faithful lambs of the Good Shepherd. And though they never met on earth, their pure spirits, we may assuredly believe, are friends and sisters in the paradise of God's best beloved.

S. George (*Carlo Crivelli.*)

CHAPTER IV.

✠. George, April 23, A.D. 303.—✠. Lucy, December 13, A.D. 303.—
✠. Agnes, January 21, A.D. 304.—✠. Vincent, January 22, A.D.
304.—✠. Margaret, July 20, A.D. 306.—✠. Katharine, November
25, A.D. 307.—✠. Blaise, February 3, A.D. 316.

THE year 303, that of the next date on our list, bursts
upon us in the full blaze of the last and most
terrific persecution. It had actually begun some years
before, but 303 saw it made law; nay, more, encouraged
and stirred up to fury by every means, and by the united
efforts of all in authority or with influence in the Roman
government. Yet fearful as it was during the seven or
eight years through which it raged, it was really but a last
and dying effort on the part of her enemies to make an
end of the Christian Church. It was a well-planned and
well-considered effort. It did not take its rise in any
personal hatred of the Christians on the part of the
Emperor Diocletian; indeed, for some time he hung back
from publishing any actual order for it. But he was
worked upon by all about him: the clever and learned
men of his court saw that it was "now or never;" the
new religion was gaining ground and depth, and promised
before long to rule the spirits of all classes of society, so
it was determined this time to strike at the very roots of

it by especially attacking the clergy, and by the destruction of the churches and of all the sacred books and writings.

"All who should refuse to sacrifice," we read in one history, "should lose their offices, their property, and their rank; slaves should lose the hope of liberty; Christians of all ranks should bè liable to torture; all churches should be razed to the ground; the Scriptures and service-books be committed to the flames."

These orders were to some extent carried out. Many of the older and greater members of the Church were martyred, among them Peter, Bishop of Alexandria, Lucian of Antioch, Methodius of Tyre, and a learned Christian writer named Pamphilus. None of those saints are in our calendar, however. On the contrary, of the seven martyrs distinctly of the Diocletian persecution whose names we have, five are young girls; one, S. Vincent, a youthful deacon of only twenty, and the seventh a soldier, our own patron saint of England, S. George.

His name comes next in our history to that of S. Faith, for he was martryed at Nicomedia, in Asia Minor, on the 23rd of April, A.D. 303. Very few saints have received more honour, and the devotion which his memory inspired began to be shown but a few years after his death, for in the reign and by command of the Emperor Constantine a beautiful church was built over his tomb and dedicated to him about the date 330 A.D. From that time to the present day the number of places in which his name is venerated is almost impossible to count. During the Crusades his aid was invoked by our King Richard, Cœur-de-Lion, in

favour of his armies, and it is related that, in response
to this, the saint appeared in a vision to the king. Since
then S. George has always been considered our national
saint. His true history has been so extraordinarily confused and mixed up with legends, and what we may almost
call fairy tales, that it is very difficult to come upon any
facts. But the widespread fame of his name, and the
honour accorded to it even in this exaggerated way
throughout all Christian countries, prove how great and
lasting an impression was made on the world by the
young soldier's brave life and holy death.

It seems historically certain that he was the son of
wealthy Christian parents in Cappadocia, that he was
brought up to be a soldier, and early in life held a high
appointment in the Roman army under Diocletian. At
the time of the edict against the Christians the young
tribune (a rank something like that of "colonel" in our
days) was passing through Nicomedia on his way to his
military post. Some say that he tore down and trampled
under foot the proclamation, and for this offence was at
once seized and brought before the Emperor. It is at
least certain that he boldly expressed his horror and
indignation, and upbraided Diocletian himself with his
cruelty. He was threatened and then bribed, both alike
in vain; the Emperor's rage seemed the greater on account
of the young man having been a favourite with him—for
George is described as gracious and handsome in person
and bearing, as well as courageous and trustworthy in his
profession—and tortures of unusual severity were employed

to shake his constancy. It was based on too firm a foundation.

"Sooner shalt thou be wearied of inflicting suffering than I of bearing it," he said, according to one account, addressing Diocletian.

The words were true. Cruelty loses its zest in such a case, and at last the order was given for the undaunted soldier to be beheaded. This was on a day specially suited for a martyr's death—Good Friday, which fell that year on the 23rd of April.

S. George is often represented as trampling on a dragon, and several curious stories have gathered round this to explain it. But the real meaning of it is an allegory, showing how the Christian soldier fought and conquered evil. In this noblest of combats we may all follow our patron saint; and like him, if we look to our dear Lord for strength and courage, we shall not be worsted in the fight.

On the 13th of December of this same year 303, another young, rich, and beautiful Roman lady suffered as a martyr for Christ. This was S. Lucy, or Lucia. Her family was Christian, and, like that of S. Agatha, had settled in the island of Sicily, where at Syracuse Lucy was born and brought up. We cannot be certain that the particulars of her story are altogether true as they come down to us, but they do not vary much in the different accounts, and there is nothing improbable or exaggerated in them. Lucy, as I have said, was a Christian by birth; she was also a most earnest Christian in soul and spirit. From her earliest years she had been much impressed by the story of

S. Agatha, who, half a century before, had lived her holy
life and died her holy death in this same island of Sicily,

S. Lucia (*Angelico de Fiesole*).

and Lucy put the girl-martyr before herself as a model

to follow. Losing her father while she was still very young, she was left to the care of her mother, Eutychia. Eutychia, though a Christian and a loving parent, seems to have been more worldly in spirit than her child, for she promised Lucy in marriage to a rich pagan, altogether against her daughter's desire. But just at this time Eutychia fell ill of a troublesome and painful disease, for which all the doctors she consulted were able to do nothing. Lucy persuaded her mother to visit with her the shrine of S. Agatha at Catania, on the other side of the island, and there to pray for cure. Their prayers were heard, and in gratitude to her sweet child the mother gave up all thought of urging her to marry ; she also made over to Lucy the whole of the young girl's fortune, a great part of which Lucy at once devoted to helping the poor and suffering about her. The young nobleman who had wished to marry her must have been very different from Valerian, the betrothed of S. Cecilia, who, though a pagan, treated her faith with respect from the first, for Lucy's suitor was furiously angry, especially when he found out the use she was making of her wealth. There was always in those days a means of revenge at hand for any one who had a grudge against a Christian. And the vindictive and wicked man took advantage of it. He reported the maiden to the Roman governor, Paschasius, as a Christian, and threw blame upon her also for misusing the wealth which by this time he expected would have been his. It was at a moment when any rumour of Christianity brought danger and death. Lucy was at once arrested, and the remainder of her story follows almost exactly the terrible yet beautiful path we have already trod so often.

She was tortured, fearfully but uselessly, and at length put to death by the sword. It is said that her last words spoke of the speedy coming of peaceful times for Christianity—words which were certainly fulfilled some years later, when the Emperor Constantine not only put an end to persecution, but himself embraced the true faith.

Closely following each other, in the next year, 304, we find recorded the trial and triumph of two other youthful witnesses for Christ, S. Agnes and S. Vincent. Their martyrdoms took place on succeeding days, the 21st and 22nd of January, though at a distance from each other, for S. Agnes suffered at Rome, S. Vincent at Saragossa, in Spain, and in this world they never met. Both are especially interesting, and the memory of both has been widely and lastingly cherished in the Church.

Of what are called the "acts" of the martyrs, which means genuine and authentic accounts written at the time, or very shortly after each saint lived, we have none truly belonging to S. Agnes. Still we seem to know more about her, and that more certain than about many of the martyrs, through so much having been written concerning her by the early Fathers, who had the best opportunities of knowing what stories were fact and what were only legend. And many of the greatest of the Fathers have written about S. Agnes: S. Jerome, S. Ambrose, S. Augustin, and S. Gregory, all mention her, as well as S. Martin of Tours, and the Christian poet Prudentius;

and indeed, some of these great writers relate her history in detail. She was the daughter of Christian parents of high birth. They seem to have been truly religious, and

S. Agnes (*Martin Schoen*).

to have brought little Agnes up with the greatest wisdom and most careful teaching. And from her very earliest years her whole heart and soul were given to God. But she was both beautiful and rich—no safeguard, but rather an additional source of danger for a Christian maiden. And this proved the case for S. Agnes. She was but thirteen when the son of the Prefect of Rome fell in love with her, and asked for her in marriage. Agnes had no wish to marry; young as she was, she had made up her mind to this, and her parents, dreading for her no doubt the uncertainty and difficulties of a marriage with a pagan, agreed with her in refusing the young man, though it does not appear that the reason was fully explained. For the youth and his father, Sempronius, persisted for some time in their endeavour. At last it came to their ears that the real ground of the refusal lay in the question of religion, that Agnes and her parents were Christians. Thereupon their persistence turned to rage, for they must have known that their efforts would never succeed. The wretched young man who had loved her—though true and good love could not so change—became her bitterest enemy. He and his father denounced the young girl as a Christian, and she was brought before the judge—some say that it was Sempronius himself—and ordered either to promise to marry the Prefect's son, or to sacrifice to the goddess Vesta and become one of her attendants. The holy child refused to do either, and when dragged before the altar, instead of offering incense she calmly made the sign of the cross. The judge then tried to frighten her by a display of all the most dreadful instruments of torture, but Agnes only smiled. Then he determined to punish her in what to her innocent and delicately brought up nature must have been indeed more fearful than any bodily anguish. He caused her to be imprisoned in the house of some exceedingly wicked people, where she could not help hearing bad words, and seeing fighting and drinking and the rudest behaviour. It makes one shiver to think of the pure and holy child, fresh from the peaceful home where the love of God was the ruling spirit, in such a place; but even there she was safe, safe as "the three children" of old, in the fiery furnace, for she was held in the unseen arms of her Lord. It is related that a shining light like a mantle of glory seemed to be wrapped round her, so that even the most wicked of the degraded people about her were overawed. If this were so, it was but a foreshadowing of what was close at hand, for the next day S. Agnes was condemned to be beheaded. "Joyfully, as if in triumph, she went to the place of execution."

"She," says S. Ambrose, "in whose tiny body there was hardly place to receive the sword, had that in her which triumphed over it." "Hardly knowing what it was to die, yet unmoved; scarce able for the suffering, but ready for the victory; crowned, not with flowers, but with holiness."

And S. Augustin, in allusion to her name and its beautiful meanings, writes thus: "In Latin Agnes signifies a lamb, and in Greek it means pure. She was what she was called; and she was found worthy of her crown."

Of S. Vincent, who died the very day after the martyrdom of S. Agnes, whose fearful tortures must indeed have been going on at the very time the holy maiden was beheaded, we possess much fuller particulars than of most of the early saints. His "acts," written very soon after his death, are believed to be quite true. He was, like S. Laurence, born in Spain, of Christian parents, and many things in his history recall that of the young martyr who lived and died about half a century before him. Vincent too was a deacon ; he had been trained and prepared for the Church by Valerius, then Bishop of Saragossa, which was Vincent's home, and, like that of S. Laurence for the good Sixtus, the affection of the pupil for his teacher was very strong.

The Bishop and his deacon were arrested together in the early days of the Diocletian persecution, and carried before Datian, the cruel and bloodthirsty governor of Spain, at Valencia. Before examining them, Datian had caused his victims to be kept some days fasting in prison, with the intention of subduing their courage. But in spite of this, both the old and the young man seemed fresh and strong when led forth, so the governor scolded the gaolers for having, as he thought, secretly fed and nourished them —little knowing with what spiritual food they had indeed been sustained.

Then began the usual routine—the fair, false words of bribery and persuasion were first tried : and the aged Bishop, who had an impediment in his speech, finding the words could not come, turned, as he had often turned before—for the deacon, though so young, had already helped his learned but infirm master by preaching for him— to his brave and eloquent disciple. And Vincent was ready.

"Father," he said, "if you order me, I will speak."

And speak indeed he did. He was but twenty, but the words might have been those of a very father in the faith; and they brought their reward. The aged Bishop received a mild sentence of banishment only, but for Vincent there was the martyr's crown. And to win it he had to tread a fearful path; his tortures were, I think, the most awful we have to read of; and they were not only endured, they were triumphed over. When tried far beyond what the bravest hero-spirit, unsupported by Divine strength, could possibly have lived through, there came a lull. And the voice of the cruel fiend Datian was heard again in temptation, urging him to yield, "for the sake of the flower and beauty of thy youth," he said. But Vincent, undaunted, had strength to reply; till at last, in very weariedness of cruelty, the torturer owned that he was vanquished.

Then they bore the mangled but still conscious body to the prison, and laid it in a dungeon strewn with broken potsherds, as a chance the more of further anguish. But in the night angel visitants ministered to him. Vincent's voice was heard singing as he saw the gloomy, dreadful hole illumined with light, and felt the scent of flowers, surpassing the fragrance of earth's very sweetest, about him. And when at last his friends obtained leave to carry a soft bed to the dying saint, in which they laid him with tenderest care, perhaps it was no smoother to him than the rugged floor, on which angel hands had supported him through that last night, while they showed to him heavenly visions of peace, rest and joy unspeakable. It was too late for human succour; though surrounded once more by loving friends and care, Vincent gently died.

There are legends that the body of S. Vincent, thrown out in Datian's rage to lie unburied and dishonoured, was miraculously guarded by the birds and beasts, and afterwards even cared for by the sea, and safely washed into a harbour; and it is not to be wondered at that the story of his marvellous constancy should have given rise to these. But whether they are partly true or not matters little. We know that in God's own blessed keeping is the saintly spirit of Vincent, "the invincible" for Christ.

Dear children, I almost feel as if your gentle hearts could bear no more of these wonderful martyr stories, even though I trust that you try to think of "the far more exceeding weight of glory" that is their real meaning. But there are still two or three of these early hero-saints that we must not leave out. I will try to tell you of them shortly.

Two more sufferers in this fearful Diocletian persecution are enshrined in our prayer-book calendar—S. Margaret and S. Katharine.

We know little historically true of either, especially of S. Margaret. We may apply to them both the words of a writer in the seventeenth century, who, speaking of S. Katharine, says, "It would be hard to find a saint more generally reverenced, or one of whom so little is known on trustworthy authority." Yet we must believe that the Church has with reason deemed such worthy of great

E

reverence.   Often those saints of whom least is known are
most universally honoured.

It seems certain that Margaret was a holy Christian

S. Margaret.

maiden, martyred at Antioch about the year A.D. 306.   The
legend about her tells that she was the daughter of a priest
of the pagan gods, and that, her mother dying, she was

given as a little child to the care of a humble foster-mother,
a Christian. It goes on to tell that when the maiden grew
up and returned home, her father discovered that she had
become a believer in the Cross, and in his anger turned
her out, so that the poor girl again took refuge with her
peasant friend. There she lived in peace tending sheep,
till one day the Roman governor passing by, was struck by
her beauty, and carried her off to marry her. In her fear
and anxiety Margaret prayed aloud, thus telling her secret.
The governor was furious when he found she could not be
persuaded to renounce her faith and sacrifice to his gods;
she was threatened and tortured, and in the end beheaded.
Her memory is recalled to us on the 20th of July.

S. Katharine, or Catharine, was a Christian lady of Alexandria, famed for her wealth and beauty and learning.
She gained the ill-will of Maximin, the Roman Emperor;
some accounts relate that by her wisdom she put to silence
a company of heathen philosophers whom the Emperor had
sent to argue with her. She refused to give up her faith,
and after suffering a new and strange kind of torture, she
was beheaded. This was on the 25th November, A.D. 307.
There are several legends about this saint, or at least about
one of her name, but they are clearly stories of much later
date. It is, however, probably true that before she was
killed she was condemned to be tortured on a wheel with
sharp spikes, and one would like to believe what one account states—that the wheel flew to pieces before it could
be used. You all know the fireworks called "S. Catharine's
Wheel." Strange to say, this name is believed to have

S. Katharine (*Lucas and Leyden*).

come from the instrument of torture intended for this brave and holy maiden, unforgotten through all the roll of centuries down to our own days.

One other martyr's name connected with this last general persecution remains on our list. It is that of S. Blaise, or Blasius. The most probable date of his death is the year 316, and though this was after the Emperor Constantine had issued his edict in favour of the Christians, there were still, especially in the provinces at a distance from Rome, occasional outbreaks of the old rage and cruelty.

Blaise was Bishop of Sebaste, in Cappadocia, or Lesser Armenia. His life was more like that of a hermit than of a dignitary of the Church, but he was pastor of a simple flock, and from his retirement he was able to direct and counsel, and always ready to come forth when needed. He had escaped notice during the hottest times of persecution, but on the appointment as governor of Cappadocia of a cruel and bloodthirsty man—Agricola—the Bishop was hunted out and brought before the tyrant. He was subjected to terrible tortures, and then, on the 3rd of February, beheaded. There are some very sweet and touching stories of this good man, especially of his love for animals. It is told that even the wildest and fiercest were tame and gentle with him, and used to come to his cave for succour and help if they were hurt or wounded, and that if they found him at his prayers they waited patiently till he had finished ! We must, of course, look upon such stories almost as fairy tales, or rather *allegories;* still it is certain that they must have a foundation of truth. Doubtless the character of S. Blaise was one of extreme and loving gentleness, joined to the most heroic Christian courage.

With this last saint's death closes the roll of the martyrs of the early Church, whose names are in our own English calendar. Their stories are strangely similar in some ways ; it is indeed almost difficult to separate them in the memory. This resemblance is natural ; for however they may have altered as to age and sex, nationality or outward circumstances, as *martyrs* they stand together, inspired by one faith, disciples of one Master. And besides the likeness to each other, a more marvellous likeness strikes us as we read one by one the pathetic yet soul-stirring histories —the seizure, the imprisonment, the dragging before the judge—not seldom to more than one in turn—the cruel onlookers, across whose faces passes but rarely a softening gleam of pity, the heartbroken friends, who at best can only hope to be allowed to care for the lifeless body. Then the first tortures—in some instances the very scourging we read of in the one greatest martyr story of all. Ah ! children, I need not ask you what these saintly deaths remind you of ; and when we think of this, can we wonder that these holy ones trod unflinchingly the road already traversed by the Master Himself, glorying in their humiliation, rejoicing in their anguish, thanking God that they were thus honoured, trusting to our dear Lord's promise: "Whosoever, therefore, shall confess Me before men, him will I confess also before My Father which is in heaven."

CHAPTER V.

Invention of the Holy Cross, May 3, A.D. 326.—Exaltation of the Holy Cross, September 14, A.D. 335.—𝕾. 𝕾𝔶𝔩𝔳𝔢𝔰𝔱𝔢𝔯, December 31, A.D. 335.—𝕾. 𝕰𝔫𝔲𝔯𝔠𝔥𝔲𝔰, September 7, A.D. 340.—𝕾. 𝕹𝔦𝔠𝔥𝔬𝔩𝔞𝔰, December 6, A.D. 342.—𝕾. 𝕳𝔦𝔩𝔞𝔯𝔶, January 13, A.D. 368.—𝕾. 𝕬𝔪𝔟𝔯𝔬𝔰𝔢, April 4, A.D. 397.—𝕾. 𝕸𝔞𝔯𝔱𝔦𝔫, November 11, A.D. 397.

ON the 3rd of May is commemorated in our Black Letter Calendar what is called the "Invention of the Holy Cross," and on the 14th of September we find another minor festival in honour of the "Exaltation of the Holy Cross." These two days thus set apart differ from the other dates we have till now been hearing about, in that they recall events rather than persons. Still it would scarcely do to pass them over.

I will tell you the stories they refer to, shortly.

The word "invention," as here used, has not the meaning we commonly give to it—that of the finding out, or discovery, of something *new*. It does indeed mean a finding, but in the sense of finding again, or a *re*covery. For it was on this day, in the year 326 A.D., that, according to the tradition of the Church, the Empress Helena, the mother of Constantine, succeeded in finding the Cross, the actual frame of wood on which our Lord was crucified. At that time the Empress was already a very aged woman; she became a Christian only late in life, and fifteen years after her conversion she made a journey to the Holy Land to visit the sacred scenes she had learnt to reverence so deeply. Then the wish seized her to restore to honour the Holy Sepulchre and to find the Holy Cross. In both these endeavours it is said that she succeeded; a stately church was built by her son Constantine on the site, and the remains of the Cross were placed in different churches, to be preserved and reverenced. But it is now uncertain where they are, or if indeed any remain. The Church has gone through many troubles and disturbances since those days—the fragments of the sacred relic passed through many hands, sometimes seized by heathen foes, sometimes hidden for centuries at a time. On the 13th of September, eleven years after the "Invention of the Holy Cross," was consecrated the "Basilica," * erected on the site of the Holy Sepulchre. A portion of the recovered Cross is said to have been placed there, and on the day after the solemn service of consecration, this was lifted up to a high place in the building so that all the people should be able to see it. But this is only one of the explanations of this festival. Another is that nearly three hundred years later this same portion of the sacred wood, which had been carried away by the Persians in an onslaught on Jerusalem, was again recovered and restored to its place by the Emperor Heraclius,

---

* *Basilica.* A large hall having two ranges of pillars, and two aisles or wings with galleries over them. These buildings were first made for the palaces of princes, and afterwards for churches. A basilica is generally a magnificent church, as the basilica of S. Peter at Rome.

who entered the city barefoot to do honour to the Cross, which he bore high above his head. And in the Greek Church the "Exaltation of the Holy Cross" has still another meaning. It is taken to refer to the vision of the Emperor Constantine, before his conversion, of a gleaming cross in the sky, on which were inscribed Greek words signifying "In this conquer."

All these histories or legends—no doubt the truth is that they are a union of the two—are exceedingly interesting. But we are not required to decide precisely how much of them is fact. Nor is it well for Christians to attach too much importance to any actual material object, however precious its associations, or however we may venerate it as a symbol. This is taught us by the quaint words of S. Ambrose, when speaking of the Empress Helena, who, he says, "adored in this sacred wood, not the wood itself, which would have been the error of the heathen, but the King of Heaven, who had been placed upon the wood."

We now come to the first saint on our list who was not also a martyr. This is S. Sylvester, Bishop of Rome. He was a Roman by birth, and, at least on his mother's side, a Christian by descent. This mother, Justa, is described as a most excellent and virtuous woman, and she chose for the teacher of her son a priest named Charitius, who was both a very good and a very clever man. So that Sylvester had great privileges in his upbringing. He did not misuse them. From his earliest childhood he seems to have been intended for the priesthood, and he entered it as soon as he

was old enough.   A long life in the service of God and the
Church was before him, for he was ordained about the year
286, and lived till 335.   The last twenty-one years of his
life he was Bishop of Rome.   S. Sylvester passed, therefore, through eventful times.   He was an eye-witness of the
fearful Diocletian persecution, though he himself escaped.
It is stated in some accounts that he was for a time
imprisoned in Rome, but this is not certain.   The Bishop
in later days had great influence over the Emperor Constantine, and he seems to have been everywhere respected
and venerated.   During his last years he was frail, and
unable to take much active part in some very important
and distressing difficulties which arose in the Church,
though his name has been mixed up with these on evidence
not to be trusted.   There are also legends about him which
we cannot accept as true, though in one especially, which
relates how he made a fierce dragon harmless by tying a
thread round its mouth, there is plainly an allegorical
meaning, showing that the gentleness of truth may be
stronger than the fierceness of falsehood.

S. Enurchus or Evurtius was a priest sent from Rome
about 320 A.D. to the Church in France or Gaul ; you will
remember hearing about the band of missionaries under S.
Denys, who did such good work there nearly seventy years
before S. Enurchus followed in the same path, converting
and teaching many.   He was made Bishop of Orleans, and
died there on September 7, 340.   In a few dry lines we
seem to tell all that has to be told of some of these noble
lives ; but it is not difficult to fill up by the imagination

what is—what was—the real story of twenty years of devoted missionary work.

Now comes a name which every child has heard, though in another form. For in what family, of late years especially, since Christmas-trees have become so general in England, is the great winter festival celebrated without mention of "Santa Klaus," * the mysterious fairy godfather, so to speak, of all good children, who fills their stockings, who finds out what gift to hang for each on the magic fir-tree, who loves to hear Christmas carols, and to inspire all kind and generous Christmas bounties? And from the saint who is next on our list, the good Bishop Nicholas of Myra, in the far-away Eastern land—the kindly priest who lived and died more than fifteen centuries ago —the man of childlike virtues, "of meekness, simpleness, and without malice," as a very old writer describes him, have come these sweet and homely fancies about the unseen Christmas visitor.

Like the Master whom he served from his own earliest boyhood, He who bade the little ones come unto Him, Nicholas loved children, and was always ready to protect and care for them. So that it is only right and fitting that he should be thought of as their patron saint. He was born of Christian parents at Patara, in Lycia, a province of Asia Minor, and with the exception of a journey to visit all the sacred places in the Holy Land, he seems to have spent his life in his own native country, where he devoted all his wealth to the wise and careful succour of those in

* "Klaus" is, in German, the "short" for Nicholas.

S. Nicholas (*Botticelli*).

need. He wished at one time to give himself up entirely
to a life of seclusion, and for some years he was abbot of
a monastery; but then it was shown to him that more
active work was intended for him, and he was chosen to
be Bishop of Myra—Myra being the capital of the province,
and only three miles from the birthplace of the saint.
He died, greatly loved and greatly honoured, on the 6th of
December, 342 A.D. There are many legends about him;
one relates how by his prayers he stilled a storm at sea,
from which he is often called the patron of sailors;
another tells of his giving money to the three young
daughters of a poor gentleman in the city who were nearly
starving, and being so anxious not to be thanked that he
threw the coins in at the window while the family was
asleep; another, of his saving from death three unjustly
condemned prisoners; and, however the stories vary, they
all unite in showing how gratefully and affectionately he
was regarded by those he lived among. In the fourteenth
and fifteenth centuries there was a curious custom at some
places of celebrating S. Nicholas' Day by allowing the
boy choristers, one of whom was chosen "bishop" for the
time, to conduct part of the church services; but this was
given up, and wisely, for there are many more fitting ways
in which all, both boys and girls, can follow in the footsteps of the saint whom children of so many nations, and
in so many ages, have reverenced as their model in love
and kindness and all unselfishness.

A very different figure from the simple Nicholas is that
of another bishop, the learned S. Hilary of Poictiers. He

was by birth a pagan, but an earnest and thoughtful-minded man always. His conversion was greatly the result, under God's blessing, of his own sincere and eager desire to learn the truth. He studied the Holy Scriptures with the intelligence of a scholar, and yet the single-mindedness of a child. He tells in his own words how the writings of Moses impressed him and filled him with admiration, yet seemed to leave something wanting, and how when the Gospel burst upon him in the teachings of the New Testament, he felt that he had indeed fully found all he needed. It is believed that he was elected bishop even while still a layman, so great being already his distinction as a Christian. But to his talents he joined the virtue of extreme humility, and when the bishopric was pressed upon him he did his utmost to decline it. There is not very much to tell of this holy man's own history. As far as outside persecution was regarded, he lived in quieter times, but within the Church herself there were sad troubles; and doubtless to S. Hilary the worst pagan cruelty would have been easier to bear than the ill-will and enmity of fellow-Christians. It was a period of great strife about doctrines, and though it is never right to condemn harshly those who differ from us, still we cannot but sympathise with the orthodox Christians of those days in their thorough earnestness. And it is impossible to hold those who caused dissension as altogether honest in their opinions, when we see how much the love of power and jealousy of others were mingled with their refusal to accept the Church's teachings. The most serious trouble was that caused by a Christian priest named Arius. When you are older you may perhaps read more about this great " schism," as it is called. The Emperor of Rome was so much influenced by Arius, that he treated with great severity those priests and bishops who would not adopt the new doctrines, and among these S. Hilary was sent away from his own home for several years in banishment. While in exile he wrote a great number of learned and valuable works on religion. A letter of his is still preserved to his young daughter Abra, advising her not to marry, as she was thinking of doing. We do not know the reasons Bishop Hilary may have had for this, but the letter is most fatherly and kind, urging her to put the love of God and His service before all else. Perhaps he knew that the marriage she was considering would not have been for her good. Abra followed her father's wishes in this: she died young, and in another of his writings he alludes to her again, saying that he was happy to think of her as safe from trouble. For though not a martyr, he had much to bear in this world. He died on January 13, A.D. 368, only about seven years after his child. It is on this day, that of his death, that we commemorate his name.

About the year 335 A.D. there was living at Trèves, in France, a Roman family of all but princely birth and importance. The father, Ambrosius, held under the Emperor Constantine the younger the post of Pretorian Prefect of the Gauls, which meant actually the governorship of a great part of Europe, including Britain and Spain. In this luxurious home was born, in the year 340, the youngest child of the great Roman official, a boy named Ambrose, destined to be a noble and powerful worker in the Church of Christ. He was one of three children, the eldest of whom, Marcellina, nine or ten years older than he, was from her early youth dedicated in a special way to the service of God and the poor, though she did not leave her own home; and Satyrus, the other brother, was also remarkable for his sincere piety and blameless life. The three loved each other devotedly, and for nearly forty years they lived almost constantly together, in such peace and harmony as are not often seen even in a Christian household. When little Ambrose was about ten years old, his father died. The widowed mother and her children then returned to their own home near Rome, where we are told the boy was educated with the greatest care, his mother and elder sister taking the warmest interest in his upbringing. It is probable that Ambrose early showed signs of both talent and unusual strength and decision of character. A story is related about a swarm of bees flying over his cradle as a baby, even alighting on his face without stinging, and then soaring upwards to the sky, which was noticed by the father of Ambrose at the time as a sign of future greatness. Another story, which is more certainly true, is told of the visit to the family of a bishop, whose hand, according to the custom, was kissed by Marcellina and the other ladies present as he was bidding them farewell. Thereupon the boy Ambrose extended his own hand to his mother and sister to kiss, saying as he did so that he too would be a bishop some day. Marcellina reproved him for what seemed to her rather unbecoming boyish fun ; but the saying came true !

We seem to know a great deal about S. Ambrose, for much detail is contained in his own letters and writings, which were most carefully collected and arranged, about two hundred years ago, by two Benedictine monks, whose work is quite to be relied upon. Much of what makes him a very important figure in the history of the Church would perhaps be dull and uninteresting to you, though I hope you will care to read about it when you are older ; but I will try to give you some idea of his brave and fearless and yet most loving and sympathising character, by a short account of the principal events in his life.

He was not intended for the priesthood, but was trained to the law. In this he soon distinguished himself, and held some important posts, the last of which was that of magistrate for the province of Liguria. The city of Milan was thus under his governorship, and in 374, the Bishop then dying, Ambrose attended a great meeting assembled to appoint his successor, about which there was much discussion and disputing. While this was going on, a clear, sweet voice was suddenly heard calling out, "Ambrose, bishop; Ambrose, bishop." It may have been some little child who knew him by sight, and had heard some confused account of the reason of the meeting; or it may have been that some older person, wiser than they knew, had made the baby call out the words. The story reminds us of the choice of both S. Fabian and S. Hilary ; and as

F

was the case with them, so it was now. With one consent the cry was taken up, and though not even a priest at all, Ambrose was chosen. He did his best to avoid the honour, feeling himself unworthy of it, even concealing himself for some time in a friend's house. But when messengers were sent to Rome, and returned with the Emperor's full approval, Ambrose yielded, and immediately entered upon the preparation for his consecration.

Once set apart for his high office, he threw himself into it heart and soul. He gave up all his possessions to the care of his faithful brother Satyrus, to be by him employed for the Church and the poor, excepting only a provision for his sister Marcellina, in order that he might be free from worldly cares; he set himself to study those subjects which his sudden call had found him naturally not specially trained in; as he says of himself simply, "I had to begin to teach before I had begun to learn;" his house was open to all whom he could in any way serve or help; his time was so entirely occupied with his duties, and with meditation and prayer, that he would never be present at "banquets or great tables, and only entertained others with the greatest frugality." And even several years later, when his untiring energy and zeal had arranged and ordered things with regularity, S. Augustin complains that it was almost impossible ever to find the Bishop for a moment at leisure; "His only relaxation was the change from one laborious employment to another."

They were stirring and troubled times in which he lived. The twenty-three years of his "episcopate" saw the deaths

of five Roman emperors, three of them by violence, and
the overthrow of two usurpers. Two of these emperors,
the boy brothers, Gratian and Valentinian II., both of
whom were treacherously killed while still quite young, were
dear to the good Bishop as if they had been his own sons;
they looked to him for counsel and direction; for Gratian
in particular he wrote treatises at the young Emperor's own
request, and after Gratian's death his boy brother, Valentinian, followed S. Ambrose's advice, even as to the amusements and sports he might indulge in, and the plain fare
the Bishop counselled him to eat. It is told that Ambrose
mourned for these young brothers with bitter tears.

From the mother of Valentinian, for the young Emperors
were only half-brothers, came what were probably St.
Ambrose's sorest trials. She was the Empress Justina, an
ambitious and interfering woman, who had unfortunately
become what was called an "Arian"—a follower of the
false teacher Arius, who caused such terrible trouble in
the Christian world. Justina made many efforts to obtain
high Church appointments for her own friends, and re-
sented Bishop Ambrose's opposing her. She also tried to
seize by force two of the churches in Milan, and but for
the Bishop's extreme firmness, tempered with perfect gentleness and dignity, the whole city would have been convulsed
with religious disturbances, in which, no doubt, much innocent blood would have been shed. Yet this same Empress
always fell back on S. Ambrose when she and her son
were in any danger or difficulty, trusting, and not in vain,
to his generous and forgiving nature.

After the murder of Valentinian, the whole of the Roman Empire was reunited under the great Theodosius. He too was a close friend of the Bishop, to whom he looked up as his spiritual father. Theodosius was a sincere Christian, and a good and benevolent ruler, but he was hasty and violent in temper, and on one occasion this led him to commit a great crime. Several officers of the Roman garrison at Thessalonica were murdered by a mob enraged by a dispute with some of the soldiers, and on hearing of this suddenly, the Emperor was so indignant that he gave orders for a massacre of seven thousand of the citizens— men, women, and children—to avenge the insult. Ambrose was horrified when the news reached him of this cruel and wicked slaughter of innocent people, and, never backward or cowardly in righteous anger, he told Theodosius plainly how frightful had been his sin. For eight months the Emperor pleaded in vain to be admitted as usual to the services of the Church, but not till entirely and completely satisfied of his full repentance would the brave Bishop absolve and receive him. Theodosius died five years after this. It is said that he never afterwards passed a day without grieving for the one terrible blot on his life, and his attachment to Ambrose grew greater ever after.

" I have known no bishop worthy so to be called save Ambrose," was a saying of his ; and with his last breath he asked for his friend, and begged for his blessing on himself and his children.

Ambrose himself only lived two years longer. It seems probable that his ceaseless work, and his never in the

least sparing his own strength, wore him out before his
time, for he was but fifty-seven when he died, though he
writes of himself as already an old man. His dear brother
Satyrus died several years before him, and that this was a
sore grief to Ambrose we know by his own words. But
Marcellina lived longer than her brothers, and was with
the Bishop to the last: to her unselfishness and devoted
spirit this must have been a happiness, though when brothers
and sisters are linked together by the bonds which united
these three, death brings no real separation.

In the "Confessions" of S. Augustin we read his own
account of his friendship with S. Ambrose, and of the help
he obtained from the good Bishop at a time when his
mind was darkened by doubts and errors. It seems probable that it was not so much by the arguments and direct
teaching of S. Ambrose as by his personal influence—the
sight of his earnestness, his holy unselfishness, his honesty
and hearty faith—that S. Augustin was drawn closer to
Christianity. For S. Ambrose was not so much a great
scholar as a great and good *man:* he had, indeed, not
been trained in the study of theology; he was more a
liver than a preacher of the truth. Yet he was not perfect:
there are instances in his life where his intense zeal some-
what blinded him to thorough fairness: he once blamed
Theodosius for defending some Jews who had been ill-
treated by their Christian neighbours, but this was an
error of judgment. Never was he influenced by selfishness or self-seeking; and another story which tells how,
to ransom some captives carried off by the Goths, the

Bishop did not scruple to break up and sell even the sacramental vessels, shows how free he was from narrow-mindedness. "The Church has gold," he said, "not to store up, but to use for her children's need."

There is a Life of S. Ambrose, by his secretary Paulinus, which is not altogether to be trusted. Out of affection, no doubt, Paulinus adds many exaggerations which the Bishop himself would certainly have disliked. But the account of the saint's death is simple and touching. At the time his last illness seized him, he was writing on the forty-third Psalm; too weak to use a pen himself, as he had always done, he was obliged to dictate to his secretary, but when he came to the twenty-fifth verse he was forced to stop, and the work was never ended. There it is still, as it was left all those hundreds and hundreds of years ago—the two last verses unmentioned; reminding one of some ancient piece of embroidery such as I have seen, the needle still there, as it was run in for the last time by the gentle hand whose task was never completed.

His death was perfectly peaceful. He lay for some hours with his hands crossed, and at the end, having received the Blessed Sacrament for the last time, his faithful spirit fled.

"I have not so lived amongst you, that I should be ashamed to live," are among the last words recorded of him, when begged by his beloved flock to pray for his own recovery; "and I do not fear to die, because we have so good a Lord."

But a few months after S. Ambrose, died another saint,

also a great and conspicuous figure in the Church's history. This was Martin, Bishop of Tours. He was many years older than the Bishop of Milan, of whom I have just

S. Martin (*Martin Schoen*).

been telling you, for he was twenty-three at the time of S. Ambrose's birth. So he was fully eighty years of age when he died. His life is in almost every particular a contrast to that of S. Ambrose. Though principally known to us as a saint of great influence in France—indeed, "no prelate," we read, "ever made as deep an impression upon the heart and imagination of France, and of a considerable portion of Western Christendom besides"—he was not a native of that country. He was born at Sabaria, a town in what is now called Lower Hungary, and he was the son of pagan parents of no particular importance. Yet in some unknown way he himself had early become a sincere follower of Christ. So zealous and earnest was he, that while still a mere child he wished to leave his pagan relations and live like a hermit in the desert. It must have been a difficult position for a boy, and only his unusual character could have kept him safe and right in it. He does not seem to have angered his parents, and he succeeded in becoming a "catechumen," or pupil to some Christian teacher, in hopes of learning to be himself a priest one day. But this hope he had for some time to resign. At fifteen he was obliged, by his father's wish, to become a soldier, as the father himself had been, and this disappointment Martin bore well and patiently, for we are told that he so behaved in his new profession as to win the affection and respect of all about him. He never joined in anything wrong, yet he was so modest and lovable that he never appears to have given offence, or to have been accused of setting himself up above others. He was exceedingly charitable, so much so that he deprived himself of almost everything. One bitter winter's day when with his regiment at Amiens in France, riding out by the city

gates, Martin was met by a shivering, almost naked beggar.
Money the young soldier had none to give, it was all
gone already in helping others, for the season had been
exceedingly severe ; but do *something* for his suffering
brother man he *must*. So he threw off his own cloak, and,
drawing his sword, cut it in two, giving one half to the
beggar, and wrapping himself up again as best he could
in the other. Of those about him some laughed and
mocked, others seemed ashamed to have done nothing,
but that night a vision came to the young soldier. He
saw our Lord, clothed in the one half of the divided
garment, and heard His voice, saying, "Martin, who is
only a catechumen, hath thus clad Me."

And from this time the young man knew no rest till he
had been baptized and fully received into the Christian
Church. The desire of entering the priesthood had never
left him, but he had still to wait. At last he saw an
opportunity of quitting the army. Some extra pay was
offered to him as well as to the others, and Martin, knowing his own eagerness to leave, declined it, and asked for
his dismissal. This was met by a taunt of cowardice, for
fighting with some German invaders was then looked for.
"In the name of the Lord Jesus, protected only by the
Cross, I will thrust myself into the thickest squadrons of
the enemy without fear," was Martin's answer. But this
was not to be, for that very night overtures of peace were
received and accepted, and at last the soldier was free to
follow the vocation he was so sure was his.

He sought S. Hilary at Poictiers as his guide and adviser,

but even when instructed by him and approved of, he was too modest to accept any but the humblest position in the priesthood. He spent some time in journeying to his native Hungary, with the hopes of converting his own relations, and with some of them he succeeded. On his return he met with many delays and troubles, suffering cruel persecution at the hands of some of the Arian party at Milan. But at last he found himself again safely in his adopted country, where his friend Bishop Hilary gave him a small grant of land at Lugogé, near Poictiers, where in the most simple and humble way Martin founded what has since been noted in history as the first French monastery. Here, with some few companions and pupils, he lived for eleven years, employing all his time in prayer and teaching and works of charity, and in this retirement, no doubt, he would gladly have spent his life.

But true worth is not always left in the shade, even in this often misjudging world. The Bishop of Tours died in 371, and so great was already the fame of S. Martin's goodness, his wonderful holiness, and never-failing charity —charity not only of deed, but of word and of thought, "for he never judged others hastily, and always tried to interpret their actions in the best way"—that with one voice he was chosen to fill the vacant post. It was hard to persuade him to do so, but at last he yielded to the people's wish, and became their Bishop, though still keeping as much as he could to his habits of retirement. Two miles from the city he built a monastery where, though never neglecting his other duties, he passed a great part of his time; it is said that no priests were so esteemed as those who had been trained under him at Tours.

Three times in his life the Bishop had to leave his home for the Court of the Roman Emperor at Trèves. Once he undertook a mission to Valentinian (the father of the boy Emperors so cruelly murdered); twice we see him appealing to the usurper Maximus. His missions were always in some cause of justice or mercy, and his voice was always raised against tyranny or cruelty. He blamed the Emperor much for allowing a sect of Christians called "Priscillianists" to be severely treated, even though no one more earnestly regretted their errors; in this endeavour to prevent religion being made an excuse for injustice, S. Martin and S. Ambrose acted together, though it is not certain that these two great men ever met.

In his own diocese S. Martin worked unceasingly to spread the true faith, and he succeeded almost beyond his hopes. We are told that he had a charm of manner about him which few could resist—the charm of perfect sincerity, and of the most loving and self-forgetting sympathy, I think it must have been—love and sympathy for all mankind, pagan as well as Christian, for with, as we are told, "Christ ever in his heart," every human being for whom his dear Lord died was sacred and precious to him.

Many miracles are related as having been performed by S. Martin, but it would take too long to tell you about these, as it is difficult to draw the line at the exaggerations that have gathered round them. One, perhaps the most touching, is said to have occurred in his later years when, on a certain day passing through Paris, he met a leper, from whom every one was shrinking back in horror. S. Martin stopped and spoke to him kindly, and, not content with this, actually kissed him as he prayed for God's blessing on the poor outcast. And the very next day the leper, a leper no longer, came forward to give thanks publicly for his cure. No doubt whatever exists that, to quote the words of a great writer whom no one would accuse of exaggeration, "the believing prayer" of the saints "often received extraordinary answers, more often than might have been dared to hope for." And the very exaggerations tend to show that there must have been real ground for the belief in which they began. The personal influence of S. Martin was in itself wonderful, for he was not a very learned man, nor very great at argument. He kept his strength and vigour almost to the last, and died, surrounded by the friends who loved him as he deserved, on the 11th November, 397 A.D.

His name is familiar to us in the term "Martinmas," and also in that sweet echo of warm and sunny days which sometimes comes late in the autumn, often called "S. Martin's summer."

We remember this saint also on the 4th of July, when, about eighty years after his death, his body was "translated" or removed to a new tomb behind the altar of a splendid church at Tours, dedicated to him.

S. Jerome.

CHAPTER VI.

ABOUT the year 340 was born at the little town of Stridon, near Aquileia, in that part of the world now known as Lower Hungary, and not far, therefore, from the birthplace of S. Martin, a man whose name has always stood high in the ranks of the Church's most honoured sons, whose services to Christianity were, indeed, in one particular especially, of the greatest value. This was S. Jerome, who, like S. Ambrose, S. Augustin, and S. Gregory the Great, makes one of the four Latin fathers mentioned in our calendar. An immense collection of his writings has come down to us, in which are to be found a great many letters, written both to his own friends and to the numbers who demanded from him counsel or instruction. It is from these that we know the most about him, and the information is very full. Almost all the details of his life and character are in our hands.

But of these a very great part would not be interesting or useful to children, or indeed to people who are not called upon for very special study of these matters. S. Jerome took part in all the religious discussions and differences which, alas! about this time began to rage with unchristian violence within and around the Church. He was a very learned and studious man, so eager to defend the true faith that his zeal often outran his charity. Some of these discussions were on subjects of great importance, though others among them now seem unworthy of the labour and time spent upon them. And still more to be regretted were the bitterness and ill-will they called forth. Yet S. Jerome was neither jealous nor ungenerous; he was conscious of his own hastiness of spirit, and the history of the cordial friendship between himself and S. Augustin, which had begun by almost violent disagreement, raises our veneration for both these two great teachers still higher.

But before I go on to speak of the work, for which we have all such cause for gratitude to S. Jerome, I must give you a short sketch of his life.

He was the son of Christian parents; he was carefully educated, and when about seventeen was sent to Rome to complete his studies. In one of his letters he speaks of himself as having been rather an idle little boy. "I remember," he writes, "things which would make you laugh. I used to run in and out of the servants' rooms, thinking of nothing but my games, till I was dragged away from my aunt's lap to that grim old tutor." And as a youth in Rome he by no means gave himself up to study entirely. He seems to have been very fond of amusement, and amusement in the wealthy society of the great city at that day was full of dangers and temptations. But the young Jerome was not without some serious thought; he tells how he used occasionally to visit the catacombs, when the sight of the tombs of the early martyrs, his "ancestors"—"in the faith" which he professed, must have made him take himself to task. And his love of study also prevented him from falling far into idle or bad habits. Before he left Rome he asked for and obtained baptism, which at that time was often delayed till a young Christian was grown up.

Henceforth there was no faltering about him. He devoted all the powers of his vigorous mind to the study of his religion and to writing upon it. He also battled exceedingly for the spread of what is called "asceticism," which means a life of extreme self-denial, giving up all bodily comforts, eating and drinking merely what is absolutely necessary to keep oneself alive, dressing in the roughest garments, and sleeping on the hard ground. The question as to how far this sort of self-discipline is right is one which the wisest and holiest of our Lord's followers have found it difficult to decide. There are times in the world's history when the very severest measures seem called for against the terrible dangers of selfish luxury and love of ease and worldliness of all kinds. And that the "life in the desert" can never be pleasing in God's sight we dare not say, when we read of S. John the Baptist, so honoured by our Lord Himself, or when we think of the forty days of loneliness and fasting which even the Blessed Saviour sought as His own preparation. God has many ways of training His children. Our concern is not to judge others or mock at rules which may seem exaggerated or

G

unnecessary, but each and all to pray earnestly that our own heart and spirit may be taught what is the Father's will for us, that we may follow it.

And certainly, if ever there was a time when any extreme of this kind seemed called for, it was in these last years before the final destruction of the Roman Empire, when even Christians themselves were tainted and weakened by the selfish luxury and the contemptible effeminacy which made great Rome herself a victim to the wild, fierce, vigorous barbarians of the north.

It was in Gaul, where Jerome passed some time after his baptism, that he learnt much which impressed him for the rest of his life. At Trèves he met many Christians of distinction, and it was at this time that he copied for a friend two whole books of S. Hilary's. One of these was a Commentary on the Psalms, and it seems probable that this task helped to direct S. Jerome to what we cannot but consider the work of his life—the translation into Latin of the greater part of the Bible, both the Old and New Testaments, and the correction of such translations as already existed. The particulars of S. Jerome's labours belong more perhaps to a history of the Bible than to that of the Father's own life, and in this short sketch I have not space to tell you much about them. But it is interesting to know that to S. Jerome's Latin version of the Scriptures we owe our present English translation, and indeed most of the translations into other modern languages. He was not content with the Greek versions then existing of the Old Testament, for they varied so much from each other that it was impossible to tell which was correct; but with immense trouble and pains he learnt Hebrew and Chaldee, so that he could go to the original. It is almost amusing to read his account of what it cost him to acquire these languages; of "hissing and broken-winded words"—"the labour and difficulties I went through; how often I despaired and left off, and then began again." And then he adds, "I thank the Lord that I now gather sweet fruit from the bitter seed of those studies." And again and again he returned to the charge; up to the later years of his life he was still seeking lessons in Hebrew to perfect his knowledge. His translation of the New Testament was of course a less laborious task, as Greek, in which it was originally written, had always been familiar to him, and there were Latin translations already, which he partly used.

About the year 370 S. Jerome returned from France to Italy with his friend and foster-brother Bonosus, who had travelled with him. They went back to their own home, and for some years Jerome lived at Aquileia, near his native town, Stridon. At Aquileia he had several learned Christian friends, but his hot temper and want of consideration for others, if they disagreed with him whenever he himself was very eager about any subject, often caused trouble, and some years later we find him leaving his own country in consequence of some dispute, and travelling with Evagrius, who afterwards became Bishop of Antioch, and two or three other friends, to the Holy Land. At Antioch a fever attacked them; two of the party died, and Jerome himself was exceedingly ill. This illness seems to have had a great effect upon him, increasing his terror of a worldly life, and on his recovery he determined to become a hermit. He was now about twenty-eight. Hearing from an aged monk about the hermitages in the desert of Chalcis, in Eastern Syria, thither Jerome betook himself, and there he stayed for five years, leading a life of the greatest self-denial and severity, though not of idleness, for he wrote much during these years. But again he made himself enemies; his neighbours, the other hermits, accused him of unsound doctrines, and disputes came on. In 379 he returned to Antioch, sorry, he says bitterly, "to leave the desert, but not the monks." At Antioch he consented, though unwillingly, to be ordained priest, but with the real humility which so strangely underlay his proud and hasty temper, he would only accept the lowest position in the priesthood, and it is said that he never thought himself worthy to officiate at the celebration of the Holy Communion. From Antioch he went for a year to Constantinople, where he much benefited by the teaching of the great S. Gregory Nazianzen, who was then Bishop there, and with whom he seems to have been most happy. And in the year 381, fifteen years after he had left it, a mere youth, to travel in Gaul, the now famous and learned Jerome returned to Rome.

The three years he spent at Rome are full of interest. It was at this time that he made the friends from some of whom throughout the rest of his life he was rarely separated — the widowed Roman lady, Paula, and her

children. In the midst of the luxurious society of the
doomed city there were yet some righteous left. Another
saintly lady, named Marcella, with her sister and aged
mother, were the centre of this little Christian world, no
longer in fear of persecution, but sadly aware of the godlessness and wickedness around them. At their palace
the earnest and eager scholar was received with joyful
respect, and the Bishop of Rome, Damasus, also welcomed
him as a friend. These years were in many ways happy
ones, but they ended for Jerome again in trouble, for
which, it is to be feared, his own sharpness of tongue
was partly to blame. Paula had three daughters; the
eldest, Blesilla, already at twenty a young widow, and
seemingly more frivolous and worldly than her mother
and sisters, was, it may be said, "converted" by the influence of S. Jerome. She gave up the amusements and
foolish occupations she had cared for, sold her jewels for
the poor, studied under his direction, and by this change
gave great offence to her friends in Roman society. And
but a few months later the beautiful young woman died
of a violent fever, to the terrible grief of her family. S.
Jerome's whole heart and soul were filled with pity, and
his wise and true words were the mother's greatest comfort.
But many people in Rome were furious at his influence,
and even accused him of having caused Blesilla's death
by the changes his advice had made in her luxurious way
of living; and no doubt he brought this blame upon himself by the extremely severe, satirical, and even insulting
way in which he spoke and wrote against all worldliness

and selfishness, especially that of professing Christians. In the end the unhappy feelings stirred up made Jerome decide on leaving Rome for ever. He did so in 385, accompanied by his younger brother, Paulinian, who had now joined him for life, and a friend named Vincentius, and made his way back to Antioch. There the following year Paula and her second daughter, Eustochium,* already specially dedicated to a religious life, joined them. It is sad to read of the parting between Paula and the son and daughter she left behind. Indeed, it is rather difficult to think it was right of her to give up her home, but at this distance of time we cannot judge, and Paula must have felt called to special work for the Church. Separation did not lessen their family affection, for years afterwards her son sent her his little daughter to educate, and her daughter Paulina's husband, Pammachius, when his young wife died, wrote to her as to a mother.

The little party of friends, after visiting Palestine, settled at Bethlehem. There Paula founded a sort of convent, or "hospice," as it is sometimes called, where she and Eustochium were joined by other Christian ladies, and in the troubles which soon came on at Rome this place was a valued refuge for many. Besides their own occupations of teaching and charity, Paula and her daughter, who were both very cultivated women, were able to help S.

* This seems a curious name for a girl. It appears that her real name was "Julia," and that "Eustochium," which means in Greek "justness of aim," was added as a sort of affectionate name in her praise.

Jerome with his writings. They both died before him; the mother in 404, Eustochium fourteen years later, two years before the death of the Father himself.

This occurred on the 30th of September, 420 A.D. He was then a very aged man—eighty-four, if not older. The thirty-four years he spent at Bethlehem were passed by him in a large cave, near a monastery he had founded; even when feeble and infirm he never excused himself from the severe and extreme self-denial he had so preached to others. And his industry was unceasing, for besides the works on the Holy Scriptures I have told you of, he wrote a great number of commentaries, four books illustrative of the Bible, seven on Church history, and a quite wonderful number of letters. And think what "writing" meant in those days, when every line had to be copied and recopied with the greatest neatness, when there were no books to refer to, save other manuscripts, often terribly difficult to decipher. Ah! we little realise for how much we have to thank these grand old Fathers of the Church.

It is touching to read that the aged S. Jerome's last days were tended by the grand-daughter of his friend Paula —another Paula, the same who was sent to Bethlehem as a little child to be trained by her grandmother and aunt.

Few, if any, names in the annals of the Church are better known or more widely honoured than that of the great S. Augustin, Bishop of Hippo. To many not specially interested in the histories of other saints, *his* name is yet familiar, and this will always be so while Christian records exist. For, learned divine and theologian as he was, it is yet *the man himself*, in his own account of his character and life, that seems to come so close to us, with his loving heart and overflowing sympathy, his deep humility and perfect candour, his wonderful insight into human nature with its ever mingled good and bad. His "Confessions" is a book for all times and all nations. One feels that every word it contains is fresh from his own heart and soul. When you are grown-up men and women you will, I trust, read it for yourselves.

It begins with his first infancy, tells of his boyhood and self-willed youth, of the many faults and failings of his early manhood, his terrible struggles after better things, and longings, at last to be fulfilled, to attain to true peace of mind. And through all runs, like one sweet strain of music, sometimes plaintive, sometimes rejoicing, the story of his mother's love and patient devotion, love expressing itself in ceaseless prayers, answered in the end. It is from this "autobiography" that we know the most of this great man.

Aurelius Augustinus, to give his complete Latin name, was born on the 13th of November, 354, at the little town of Tagaste, in the province of Numidia, in the north of Africa. His parents, though not exactly poor people, were not rich or important; his father, Patricius, was a pagan, but his mother, Monnica, was a most sincere Christian, and it almost seems as if she had been of superior position to his father, for we read of her having been carefully brought up in a good home, and she seems to have suffered, though always patient, loving, and gentle, from her husband's violent temper and occasional rough ways. But in some respects Patricius was a good father. He spared no expense to give his son the best education in his power, for even as a child Augustin showed signs of talent and quickness as well as of strong and determined character. His mother loved him more than words can tell, but she loved him wisely. While agreeing with his father about the education of his mind, her greatest care was for his *character*. She taught him from his childhood all the truths of Christianity, and though they must often have seemed to fall on unheeding ears, they yet took deeper root than showed.

Augustin was a high-spirited, self-willed boy. He disliked learning as a child, and even later on he only gave his best attention to those studies which he took a fancy to. He was first at school at Tagaste, then at Madaura, a neighbouring town, from which he returned when he was sixteen, as his parents could not then afford to continue to pay for him. He brought home great praise for the progress he had made in some of his lessons, especially rhetoric, and his father was so pleased that he seems to have been foolishly indulgent to the boy, for during more than a year he wasted his time, spending it with wild and idle companions, regardless of his mother's warnings and distress. Yet his conscience, he says, was never altogether silent ; he knew he was doing wrong. At seventeen he went to Carthage (which, as you know, was then a very important town of the Roman Empire, in North Africa, and not so very far from Augustin's home) to continue his studies, and just about this time his father, to Monnica's great joy, became a Christian, though this joy was speedily mingled with sorrow, for soon after his conversion Patricius died. Now was the time for Augustin to have been his mother's comfort, and for him to have begun to return to her some of the devotion she had shown him. But, alas! it was not so; many more tears were yet to be shed by S. Monnica, many more days and nights to be spent in prayer for her son—he loved her fondly, but he grieved her terribly. At Carthage, though he went on with the studies he liked, and which he was too clever not to succeed in, his life was wild, extravagant, and riotous. Sad accounts of him reached the poor mother, who at this very time was denying herself to pay for his education. Yet through it all his conscience still spoke; he was miserable and restless, in turns trying to forget all good things, and then again seeking feverishly for light and finding none. He took up strange and false doctrines, he studied much by fits and starts, and his great talents made their way, so that while still a very young man he became famed as a teacher at his native place, where he returned to live.

But his return brought no happiness to his mother. He openly professed the false beliefs he had taken up, so that her heart was almost broken. Once, he tells us, she went, nearly in despair, to consult a Christian priest of great wisdom and charity. He told her that it was best at that time to leave the young man alone; he was too proud and self-willed to listen to counsel. But Monnica persisted, crying bitterly, so that at last the good man exclaimed half impatiently, " Go your way, and God bless you : the child of such tears will not be suffered to perish," and looking upon these words as a prophecy, the faithful mother felt comforted.

It would take too long to relate all the history here. Now and then it seemed as if Augustin was on the very brink of changing, and once in particular, when a dear friend of his, a friend from childhood, died, he seemed in his grief to be indeed "feeling after God ; " but again and again the dark clouds of unbelief, the even darker and blacker fogs of selfish sin and wrong-doing, shut him out from heaven and holiness.

When about twenty-seven, Augustin, by this time more and more unhappy and dissatisfied, discontented with his position at Carthage, where he had spent the last few years, made up his mind to try his fortunes at Rome. This was sorely against his mother's wishes; she dreaded the luxury and godlessness of the great city for him ; she could not bear the idea of his going so far. In her anxiety she left her home and went with him to the seaport whence the ship was to sail, begging him to return with her. Then he was guilty of a mean and cruel sin, which he afterwards bitterly repented : he pretended to give in to her, but said he must go on board to say farewell to a friend. S. Monnica waited for him in a little chapel by the sea, dedicated to the good S. Cyprian, waited and waited, till at last the miserable truth became too plain—her son had deceived her ; he had actually sailed ! I scarcely think the much-tried mother had ever shed as bitter tears as fell that day in the lonely oratory on the African seashore.

At Rome, soon after his arrival, Augustin fell ill of a severe fever; in his delirium he was constantly going over his desertion of his mother. He recovered, and did not seem much changed, but doubtless this illness worked with other things for his good. He met with disappointments at Rome; happily so, for it led to his accepting an offer to go to Milan instead, as a teacher of rhetoric. And at Milan at that time was the great and holy Bishop Ambrose. Now began at last a real turn for good in the life of Augustin. Hitherto he had often sneered at and despised the Christian teachings; they were "too simple" for a mind trained in the profoundest human learning. But even intellectually he could not despise S. Ambrose. He went to hear him preach, he tried to have private talk with him, which, however, the Bishop, probably from wise motives, did not overmuch encourage, ever kind and friendly though he was. Some ground was gained, however, and when, two years after their miserable parting, his mother, alone and unprotected, came across the sea, braving storms and perils in calm trustfulness for his sake, Augustin was able to tell her that at least he had given up for ever the false and wild faith, "Manichæism," as it was called, which had wrought him such mischief. Henceforward his studies seemed to lead towards light; even the noblest of the pagan writings changed, as it were, in colour to him; they began to strike him as full of longing and yearning towards *something* higher, towards truths which their great authors had not, in God's providence, in this life been permitted to learn. And to Augustin these truths had been at his very door ! Since babyhood he had been taught and guided and prayed for.

But he *would* not accept what was waiting for him. And this, several thoughtful writers on S. Augustin point out as one great lesson of his life. He made himself think he could not believe, but in reality his difficulties were more those of soul and spirit than of mind. "It is to the heart that God first reveals Himself." It is to "the pure" that the "seeing Him" is promised. And Augustin was sinful, and did not try to be better; his spirit was proud, and he did not pray to be made humble. So that the things which are revealed to babes were for long hidden from the wise and learned man.

The actual story of the day which he looked upon as that of his full conversion shows this very clearly. He had been much impressed by the visit of a young friend, himself a convert to Christianity, who told him of the faith and devotion of a community of Egyptian monks. The contrast between these men and themselves struck Augustin and another of his friends named Alypius, then living with him, sharply. "Why can *we* not believe like them ?" they asked. And later that day, when sitting in his garden alone, pondering over his sore distress, as he had done so often before, an answer seemed to come. A voice, like that of a child, sounded at a little distance, saying, "Take up and read." "It may have been only some boy or girl at play," says S. Augustin ; but he obeyed it. And the verse on which his eyes first fell as he opened the New Testament seemed sent on purpose. Yet it was perhaps not exactly what a human teacher would have chosen for him. It was a simple command to be *good*, to give up selfish sin, and in the strength of the Lord Jesus Christ to follow in His steps. And from that moment Augustin obeyed, and his conflict and misery were over.

Nothing can be more touching than his account of the happy life he and his mother now spent together. It was not for long. She lived to see him, the man of thirty-three, with two other friends, baptized at Milan by the holy Ambrose. They were preparing to return to their own African home, when at Ostia, where they were resting on the way, the sweet and saintly Monnica died. She was not yet old, only fifty-five, and her illness was a sudden one—a fever. But she had felt that death was near. S. Augustin tells us of a conversation they had together one day at Ostia, and somehow one fancies it must have been a Sunday afternoon, sitting at the window overlooking a garden. They talked as sometimes, though rarely, the dearest friends do talk—of the mysterious blessedness of the future life; of that unspeakable "seeing of God" He Himself has promised to His pure in heart. And S. Monnica's beloved face seemed to her son as if transfigured with unearthly radiance when she told him that she felt as if her work on earth were over. She died within a week.

His grief, like all the other feelings of his vehement, though no longer uncontrolled nature, was overwhelming. But he had many consolations. Among them, I cannot help thinking, must have been some words of his mother's —among her last—in which, "with great endearments and affection," she assured him "that never had she heard my mouth utter harsh or reproachful sound against her." Think of that, dear children; through all his fits of temper, all his terrible self-will, *never* had he spoken roughly to his mother.

With the death of S. Monnica ends her son's own story of his life. But there is another biography of him by his friend Possidius, and other details of S. Augustin's later history are to be found among his own writings, which are very numerous. I have lingered long over the first half of his story because it is so interesting, but in reality it was only after its close that begins his career as a great figure in the roll of the saints—as a Father in the Church.

He returned to Tagaste a year after his mother's death, and there he founded a sort of community of Christian friends desirous of study and self-improvement in holy things. But he was not long allowed to remain in retirement. His great talents made him known and sought for, and a visit to the neighbouring city of Hippo ended, after much doubt of his fitness on his own part, in his being ordained priest, and afterwards consecrated bishop there. For nearly forty years, till his death in 430, he laboured unceasingly and unflaggingly. His influence spread far beyond his own part of the world; Christianity has never had a more valiant champion. And he had much to do. Divisions in the Church were many; attacks from without were not wanting. Any proper account of the warfare against error and wrong which he specially waged would be impossible in this short sketch, and also very difficult to explain to you.

S. Augustin's house at Hippo was a home for all young Christian students; all his private means were spent on others; he lived frugally and simply; but still, in his way of dressing, the service of his table, and such arrangements, there was care and neatness, and no exaggeration or affectation. He would never allow in his presence *any* unkind words to be said of the absent. The visits he paid were to the sick, or sorrowing, or friendless, and in his sermons his only aim was that he might interest his hearers and be understood by them, unmingled with any desire to show off his own learning and eloquence. One of his most important books, that called "The City of God," written at the time when the taking of the great city of the world was making men feel as if the universe itself were tottering, is "one of the noblest works the ancient Church can boast of." And in it there is no narrow-mindedness. Human society, life in the "cities of men," need not, should not, be opposed to that citizenship of the future, for which, fallen and sinful as we are, we may yet hope, if we remember that this world is no true or lasting abiding-place. This is the spirit of the book, and it was wonderful that the brave-hearted saint could write thus encouragingly, when we take into account the terrible wickedness of the civilised world of his times.

S. Augustin died peacefully, though surrounded by conflict and bloodshed. For the troops of the northern invaders had by this time pressed on even to the African

The Vision of S. Augustin (*Murillo*).

shores. He was aged and weary, for much care and labour, many vigils and frequent fasting, had been his portion. He had prayed that, if in God's providence his beloved Hippo must fall into other hands, he, infirm and old, might pass within the gates of that better city, whose blessedness he had meditated upon so often ; and his prayer —no cowardly one, he had indeed fought his fight—was granted. His thin white face, shining "as it had been the face of an angel," surrounded by the friends whom up to the last he had gently begged to leave him alone that he might prepare for death more perfectly, his eyes from time to time turned to the walls where hung, copied out by his desire, the seven penitential Psalms, Augustin, great saint and master—great penitent, as he would have described himself—"fell asleep." This was on the 28th day of August, A.D. 430.

His works were collected together by the Benedictine monks, in one edition of eleven large volumes, at the end of the seventeenth century. In England we often speak of him by the pleasant and more homely name of S. *Austin.*

The picture on the preceding page, called "The Vision of S. Augustin," refers to a dream he relates. At the time that the saint was writing one of his learned treatises, he dreamt that he was walking on the seashore and there saw a little child digging a hole into which he said he meant to empty all the waters of the ocean. When Augustin told him that it was impossible, the child replied that it was not more so than for a human being to hope to understand the great mysteries of God.

CHAPTER VII.

S. Britius, November 13, A.D. 444.—Lammas Day, August 1, Fifth Century.—S. Remigius, October 1, A.D. 533.—S. Benedict, March 21, A.D. 543.—S. David, March 1, A.D. 544.—S. Leonard, November 6, A.D. 559.—S. Machutus, November 15, A.D. 564.

THERE is very little to tell about S. Britius, or "Brice," as he is sometimes called. But what there is, is interesting, as it carries us back to S. Martin of Tours, and his great work in France. Britius was one of S. Martin's pupils at his monastery of Marmoutiers, near Tours. Indeed, Britius was probably unusually privileged, for some accounts state that he was under the care of the good bishop from his infancy, his parents being poor people, and unable to educate him. But if this were so, S. Martin's kindness met for long with nothing but disappointment and ingratitude in return. Britius gave him great trouble by his disobedience and folly, and showed so little fitness for the religious life, that S. Martin was frequently urged to send him away. But the bishop, besides the power, almost amounting to prophecy, of foreseeing the future which several of his biographers tell us that he possessed, had certainly the gift of reading character. Through all the young man's violence and rudeness—for it is even related that he was one day overheard calling his benefactor "a fool," S. Martin perceived underlying good.   He bore with perfect patience the mockery which Brice sometimes even ventured upon to his face.   "If Christ endured Judas," he used to say, "why should I not bear with Brice?"   And when the fit of passion was over the young priest used bitterly to repent and beg for forgiveness.

One day S. Martin foretold to him that better things were in store for his future, but that sore trouble and suffering must also be gone through for his purification.   The bishop's words were literally fulfilled.   Ere he died he had the happiness of seeing Britius so changed that with one voice he was chosen as S. Martin's successor.   But the "reaping of the whirlwind" had yet to come.   Several years later, the old stories of his misdeeds were raked up and exaggerated by jealous mischief-makers, so that the bishop was obliged to leave his home, and though held blameless by the best judges, of any conduct unfitting him for his post, he had to spend seven sorrowful years in exile and loneliness.   But he meekly accepted his punishment, declaring that he had deserved it.

At last the Bishop of Rome, Sixtus III., interfered in his behalf, and as the see of Tours was again vacant, Britius returned, and was welcomed by his people.   He fulfilled his duties conscientiously and wisely for seven years, dying well advanced in age on the 13th of November 444, more than forty years after the death of the saint who had been to him more than a father.

S. Britius is the last saint of the fifth century, whose

name is in our calendar; but before going on to the next
—across an interval of nearly a hundred years, I must
explain to you the meaning of a festival enjoined to be
kept on August 1, and which had its origin in the fifth
century.   This is what is called "Lammas Day."   The
word "Lammas" comes from "Loaf mass," and the day
was kept as a feast of thanksgiving for the first new wheat
of the year.   Bread made of that wheat was offered and
blessed in the chnrches; the service was looked upon as
a very solemn one, and after the usual Latin prayer of
blessing, ending with the words, " Per Christum Dominum
nostrum," was added, "Through whom Thou, O Lord,
dost ever create, sanctify, vivify, bless and bestow on us
all these good things.   Through Him and with Him, and
in Him, is to Thee, God the Father Almighty, in the unity
of the Holy Spirit, all honour and glory."

Lammas Day has another memory attached to it.   It is
also a festival in honour of the miraculous deliverance of
S. Peter from prison, and though this actually happened
a little before Easter, it is commemorated on August 1,
because on that day in the fifth century was dedicated at
Rome the church of "S. Peter ad vincula," where were
kept chains, believed to be the very ones which fell off the
apostle at the touch of the angel.

The life of the next saint on our list, S. Remigius, or
Rémi, as he is called in French, covers nearly a century.
It was a century which saw great changes in Gaul, of
which, though descended from Roman ancestors, he was
a native, being born at Laon about the year 435.   The

ancient inhabitants of Gaul were by this time much intermingled with the tribes from the north, who had over-
thrown the Roman power and made themselves masters
of the Gauls themselves.   And though the changes had
been helped by force of arms, they were not altogether
brought about by violence.   The new-comers adopted, to
a great extent, the manners and customs as well as the
language and names, and gradually the religion of their
southern homes, and the event which gives its greatest
distinction and interest to the life of Remigius was the
baptism at his hands of Clovis, king of the Franks,* which
took place on Christmas Eve in the year 496.

Of Remigius himself we do not know very much, for,
long as he lived, he left almost no writings, and some of
the later accounts of him are evidently not to be trusted.
But it is certain that he was both a holy and earnest
Catholic, and also " a man of ability and force of character."   He was of high birth, and his father, Emilius, was
the owner of large estates, on which the family lived as
became their rank.   Rémi was the youngest child, and
his mother, Celinia, is said to have brought him up with
special care, intending him for the priesthood.   He did
not disappoint her hopes, but more than met them, by
retiring for a time by his own wish to a life of solitude to
prepare himself for his work.   A pretty story is told of his

* " At the time of his conversion Clovis was the only sovereign who
professed the orthodox creed. . . . Hence the kings of France derived
the title of ' Eldest sons of the Church.' "—Robertson's " History of
the Christian Church."

election, when only twenty-two, to the bishopric of Rheims. He was very tall and handsome, and it is said that he was standing among the other clergy in the great church there, when a ray of sunshine, " smiting through a small clerestory window, fell on and illumined his face." And this was taken as a sign of his fitness for the post, even though he was below the proper age. He occupied it for more than seventy years.

King Clovis, though a pagan after the northern kind, was married to a Christian princess—Clotilda, of the Burgundians. From the first her most earnest efforts were directed to the conversion of her husband. He allowed their eldest child to be baptized, and even though it died in infancy, and Clovis half believed that this was in consequence of its baptism, Clotilda persuaded him to yield again to her wishes when a second son was born.

" I thank God," she had said, at the death of her first baby, " who has thought me worthy to have a child ready to be called to His kingdom." And when the second boy fell ill, and seemed dying, she kept her trust, and prayed that he might recover, which he did.

Nothing, however, prevailed with Clovis, till once when his army was all but routed in a battle with another of the wild barbarian tribes, the Allemanni, in a sort of desperation he turned for succour to the name he had often heard on his wife's lips. And his courage revived, the tide turned, and his troops conquered. His prayer had been that of an ignorant and unenlightened man; the conversion which followed it can scarcely be described as a very *spiritual* one, but still it would be very wrong to doubt its *sincerity*. And there is no doubt that the strength as well as the earnestness of S. Remigius was most powerful in its influence.

Some rather touching incidents are told of Clovis in connection with the bishop. One is well known. S. Rémi, when instructing him in the Christian faith, one day read to him the story of our Lord's sufferings and death. The half-civilised chieftain glowed with indignation.

"Oh, if only," exclaimed the King, with boyish wrath, "if only I could have been there with my Franks!"

And on his baptism day, when in honour of so great an occasion, and anxious to impress him as much as possible with its joyfulness, Clotilda, with the help of Remigius, had arranged that not only the church itself, but even the roads leading to it should be beautifully adorned and decorated, Clovis seemed awestruck, and asked, with the simplicity of a child, "If this were already the kingdom of heaven which they had promised him?"

"No," the bishop replied; "but it is the beginning of the way thither."

With the King were baptized his two sisters and more than three thousand of "his Franks."

Two or three letters of S. Rémi's have been preserved, which are thought by several authorities to be genuine. One of these, sent to Clovis just before he marched against Alaric, king of the Goths, in 506, is a model of wise and good advice.

All that we know of this saint seems mingled with the

history of the Frankish king, and Rémi himself is almost forgotten in the greatness of the work he helped to achieve. In this, I think, there is something that reflects rather nobly on the saint's own character. He gave no thought to what the future would say of *him ;* he cared only that God's work should be done.

We have no particulars of his death, but it is supposed to have taken place on January 13, 533, many years after that of King Clovis. He is, however, commemorated on October 1, because on that day, A.D. 852, his body was re-buried in a new tomb at Rheims, where he has always been greatly and specially honoured.

There comes before us now a striking figure. His very name reminds one of the picturesque mediæval times, over which, though he little knew it, his influence was to spread so widely—S. Benedict !

He was the great founder of the order of monks which bears his name, and the real originator of the numberless branches—among them the monks of Cluni in the tenth century, the Carthusians and the white monks of the eleventh, the Grey Brothers of the twelfth, and the Trappists of the seventeenth—which all acknowledged his system as their real root.

Do you wonder, children, that we should be taught by the Church to reverence as a saint one whose life-work was of this kind? For monks and hermits are often nowadays spoken of with contempt, or at best with a sort of mild pity —it is seldom that they are really admired and venerated. Yet this is not the spirit in which they are looked upon by

S. Benedict (*from an engraving by Wierx*).

wise and thoughtful people. Even putting on one side the
holiness and goodness of their lives, and the wonderful service that their prayers and example rendered to the cause
of Christianity in those troublous times, these unselfish men
deserve the gratitude of all the present civilised world for
other reasons. But for their care and the safe protection
of their monasteries, we should have lost half, if not all the
links with ancient learning we now possess; history itself
would have been almost impossible to trace; many of the
beautiful arts and gentle refinements of life might have
perished altogether.

S. Benedict's own story will best show what must always
be considered his greatest services—those he rendered to
religion, and to what flows from it, true goodness of life.
He was born at a time when, as I told you in the chapter
about S. Augustin, the world was in a most sad state. The
northern tribes kept following each other as it were in great
waves, waging war not only on the nations they had first
come to conquer, but on such of their own race as they
found in possession before them; the old pagan religion of
Greece and Rome had indeed all but disappeared, but for
a time it almost seemed as if Christianity too were to be
lost in the terrible confusion. For the Church was as a
house divided against itself, so invaded was it by "heresy,
schisms, and divisions;" a great part of Europe where the
faith of Jesus Christ had once been carried had fallen
back into new barbarism, and Roman society, even such
of it as was professedly Christian, was godless and wicked
beyond description. Benedict was the child of a noble

Italian family; by his mother's side he was the last representative of the lords of Nursia (Norcia) in the Duchy of Spoleto. He was sent, with the best intentions no doubt— for an old and trusted nurse, called Cyrilla, went with him— as a mere child, to Rome for his education. There he stayed some years; but as he grew into a youth, old enough to realise the godlessness of the society about him, and shocked at the wickedness of his college companions, he took a strange resolution for one so young. He determined, like Christian in the "Pilgrim's Progress," to fly from the world altogether. He rushed away from Rome to a place called Subiaco, fifty miles west of the great city, where, in a gorge among the wild and lonely hills—a branch of the Apennines—he met a monk, to whom he told his troubles. This monk, Romanus, sympathised with him, and helped him by giving him a hair shirt and a coat of skins; with these the young hermit settled himself in a cave, completely dark, except for one opening to the sky. And there, boy as he was, he lived alone for three years, his only visitors the rough shepherds of the district, who at first took him for some new kind of wild beast, till by his efforts to teach them and do them good they came to look upon him as already a saint. His only food was a portion of the scanty fare of Romanus, which the monk used to lower down to Benedict in his cave, by a rope with a bell at the end. We are not told what the young recluse's family thought of his mode of life, but it seems likely that they saw that it was a case in which they should not interfere. For the nurse, Cyrilla, followed him and found out where he was, and then probably returned to Nursia with news of him. He was certainly not forgotten; some years later his twin-sister Scholastica, already a nun, moved to a convent, which she had chosen on account of its nearness to his monastery.

For before long it became clear to S. Benedict that the founding of a new order of monks, of a higher and better kind than had yet been, was to be the work of his life. His first experience helped to show him the faults and imperfections of the monasteries already in existence, for, at the request of some monks struck by his character, he became their head. But he found them so undisciplined and irregular, so far from his model, that his reproofs made them angry, and they tried to poison him in a cup of wine, which it is said broke to pieces on his making the sign of the cross over it. He left them with what seems but a mild rebuke, and returned for a time to his cave. He was not, however, to be long left in solitude. Year by year the fame of his wisdom and holiness spread, and disciples flocked around him, eager to learn and to copy his example, till at last his cave was but the centre of twelve small monasteries, each large enough for twelve monks. They came from all sides; they were of all races, "clergy and laymen, Romans and barbarians, victors and vanquished," but among them the dearest to his heart, those with whom he probably felt he could do the best work, were young boys sent to him to be trained and educated. For they had their lives before them; they could, and many of them did, influence enormously for good the world so sorely in need of pure and holy example and precept. Thirty-five years did Benedict pass in this way at Subiaco; then came troubles. Jealousy and envy sent mischief-makers to turn the hearts of his young pupils, his "children," against him, and S. Benedict saw that for their sakes he must go elsewhere. Taking them with him, leaving the elder monks who needed him less, he travelled many miles in search of a new home. He found it on the summit of a mountain, "standing, with a town and stream at its base, on the borders of what were formerly Latium and Campania, nearer to Naples than Rome." There he founded the monastery of Monte Cassino, of world-wide fame, with which his name is principally associated. There, taught by his long experience, his ever-increasing unselfishness and holiness of spirit, his intense earnestness to do good, he brought to perfection his system. There was no exaggeration or unreality in his teaching: much of it— for example, his "twelve rules of humility"—might be rules for all; he respected and encouraged study and learning. He, like S. Austin, disliked extremes and affectation, and desired his monks to eat sufficiently, and to be ever ready to show hospitality. His young pupils were taught to work actively out of doors when not at study or devotions. A neighbouring hermit, who, by chaining himself painfully by one foot to a rock, thought he was acting in a most praiseworthy manner, was reproved by S. Benedict for so doing. "Brother," he said, "if thou be truly a servant of Christ, His love should constrain thee, not an iron chain."

There are many stories of S. Benedict, anecdotes of his generosity, his great discrimination, his trust—once during a terrible famine he gave away all but one day's food, assured that God would provide for the morrow, as He did —his undaunted courage, when called upon more than once to face the fierce and cruel Goths. These incidents are full of interest, but intermingled with miracles, which it takes time to sift. But I cannot leave out the beautiful and touching story of the Abbot's last days.

His sister Scholastica had taken up her abode in a convent near him. His one great "treat," so to speak, of the year was a single day which he allowed himself to spend with her. He used to walk down the mountain side towards the valley where she lived, Scholastica meeting him half-way. The very spot, some say, is still known. There came one year the appointed day—it must have been in February—the brother and sister spent it together at her convent ; never had they more enjoyed their precious hours, or held "sweeter converse." They had their evening meal together, and towards its close Scholastica, with a sudden impulse, begged her brother to spare her a few hours longer. " Do not leave me to-night," she said ; "let us go on talking of heaven as we have been doing."

But Benedict was startled at such a thought.

" It would be impossible," he said ; "for no reason could I leave my monastery for a night."

Thereupon Scholastica, none the less gentle and loving that she was a saint of holiness, yielded for once to a feeling of disappointment. She put her head down on the table and burst into tears, and as she wept she prayed. And almost at once a clap of loud thunder was heard, and before they could believe their ears a furious storm was raging around them.

"God pardon thee, my sister," said the Abbot, dismayed. "What hast thou done?"

But Scholastica was not distressed.

"God was more indulgent than thou, my brother," she replied, with perhaps a gentle smile. "Thou canst not now leave this shelter to-night."

So her wish was granted: they talked together till morning.

A very few days after this, S. Benedict, gazing out of the window of his cell, had a wonderful vision. It seemed to him that a dove flew past him, upwards to the sky, cleaving its way with its pure white wings through the heavens till they closed upon it. And he knew that his sister's spirit had passed into Paradise.

He could not mourn or grieve, he could only praise God and rejoice. Perhaps he knew what was to follow. Forty days later the twin brother and sister were together again. For a sharp short fever attacked S. Benedict, and he knew his end had come. Scholastica, by his wish, had been laid in a tomb in his own chapel. Thither at the last he had himself carried by his faithful disciples, and leaning by the open grave at the foot of the altar, he, strengthened by the Holy Viaticum, died as he had wished, as he had felt became a true soldier of the Cross, *standing*.

His beloved monastery, as he had foretold, was destroyed

by the Lombards more than thirty years after his death. But his work lived. It lived in the hearts and souls of men, helping to keep alive the knowledge and love of God through the darkest times; it lives still, for true holiness can never die.

The name of S. David, whom we commemorate on the 1st of March, seems so familiar compared with many others of our Black Letter Saints, that it is difficult to realise how very little we know about him, though he is the patron saint of our own Wales, and has left us the legacy of the old cathedral dedicated to him in the quaint village—for "town" it cannot be called, even though it is a "city"—of the same name on the bleak far-off Pembrokeshire coast. Even the date of his death is uncertain, some writers placing it in 544, others not till 601. Many agree that he was born about 462, but even among these some keep to 601 as the date of his death, maintaining that he lived to the age of a hundred and thirty-nine, which is *not* probable. He was the son of a prince of Keretica, now Cardiganshire; he was born where he died, at his own St. David's, then called Menevia. He seems to have been intended for holy orders, for he was carefully educated, first as a child by his mother Nonna, or Nonnita, and as a boy by a Christian priest named Iltutus or Iltyd at a college near Cowbridge. Thence he was sent for ten years to study under a great teacher named Paulinus, himself a disciple of the famous S. Germanus of Auxerre, at a place. called Ty-Gwyn in Caermarthenshire. While under Paulinus' care, David was ordained priest, and when he left Ty-Gwyn he went back to

I

his own home, and there straightway, almost on the spot where now stands the cathedral of St. David's, he founded a monastery. This was evidently the wish of his life ; for years afterwards it was with the greatest difficulty that, on the recommendation of Paulinus, he was forced from his retirement to give the help of his "holy eloquence" at a great council assembled in Cardiganshire to put down the heresy of Pelagius. David had to attend the council, but his success in speaking there brought about the very thing he would most have dreaded. He was elected bishop, or "primate of the Cambrian (Welsh) Church." This was in the days of the hero king, Arthur. David's wishes were yielded to by King Arthur on one point ; he allowed him to move the seat of the primacy from Caerleon on the Usk to his own beloved Menevia.

Of the personal life and character of S. David we have little record. He left no writings, though he was highly esteemed as a preacher. But this much is certain, that notwithstanding his love of retirement, he proved a most zealous and hard-working prelate ; "he informed by words and instructed by example," and we cannot but admire the self-denial which reconciled him to passing his life so differently from what he had planned it. Perhaps, after all, it was what he was best suited for, for as an abbot his rule had been extremely severe and less judicious than that of S. Benedict. It might have ended in unwise exaggeration. He died on the 1st of March, probably in the year 544, active and busy to the last, too busy to concern himself about leaving any records to tell of his life or his work.

For it was a sore struggle that the Church in Britain and her servants were at that time engaged in—"a struggle almost for life"—against " a fiercer paganism than that of Rome."

There is a pretty legend about one of S. David's monks, Modemnoc, who was to go as a missionary to Ireland. Modemnoc had charge of the monastery bees, and they were so fond of him that they followed him on board ship, and would not leave him. At last he was obliged to return to ask the saint's consent to taking them with him. David blessed them, and bade them go to their new home in peace. In this way honey was introduced into Ireland, where hitherto bees had never prospered.

The custom of a leek being worn on S. David's Day is sometimes thought to have reference to the very meagre fare of his monks, but this is not certain.

S. Leonard, " patron of prisoners," was a young Frankish nobleman at the court of Clovis. Some say that he was one of the three thousand baptized at the same time as their sovereign, other accounts state that the King was his godfather at a later date ; but whichever of these was the case, all agree that he was taught and directed in religion by the good S. Remi. He took so much to heart the bishop's instructions, that notwithstanding the urgent desire of Clovis that he should remain at his court, Leonard decided on quitting it for a life of devotion and self-denial. He spent some time at the monastery of Micy, near Orleans, but desiring a still more solitary retreat, he chose a forest near Limoges, where he built himself a little oratory.   Here he lived after the manner of hermits of his time, his food wild herbs and fruit, his time alternately devoted to prayer, meditation, the active succour of the sick and suffering, and occasional exhortation and preaching in the neighbouring churches ; and after a time, as so often

S. Leonard (*old fresco*).

happened, he was joined by others, moved by the same longings after a holy life as had influenced himself, to whom he could not refuse his help and sympathy.   So that by degrees his forest hut became the centre of a community.   He encouraged no idleness ; all who came to

cast in their lot with him were expected to work, both for
their own needs, and for those who were unable to work
for themselves. For some reason which we do not know—
possibly in his early days he may have seen sad sights
which impressed him—Leonard's heart was especially
drawn to " prisoners and captives." Whenever it was possible he visited such unhappy sufferers, using his utmost
endeavours to obtain, when deserving, their release, and
also to instruct them in religion. He died, dearly loved
and venerated, on the 6th of November 559.

S. Machutus, though a Welshman by birth, born towards
the end of the fifth century, belongs more to France than
to England. For though educated in his native country,
he was forced by the troubles there, at the time of a rebellion against King Arthur, to take refuge in Brittany.
There he found himself among a kindred race, and there
he spent his life. He stayed for some time in what was
then called the isle of Aaron, the spot on which now
stands the town of S. Malo, where there lived a famous
hermit named after the brother of Moses. Then Machutus,
or Malo, went to Luxeuil to see a monastery there, and
this journey led to his being chosen Bishop of Aleth, a
town on the mainland near S. Malo. He lived there forty
years; but at one time a party was formed against him by
some of the petty Breton princes, and he was obliged to
leave. With a company of his monks he took refuge at
Saintes, where the Bishop received them kindly. Before
his death his ungrateful flock repented, and begged him to
return to them, for they had suffered many troubles in his

absence, and missed him greatly. He was too true a Christian not to forgive, so he consented to their request. He spent several years in his old home, but died on his way to Saintes, where he seems to have wished to end his days. He was then a very old man. Some accounts state that he did not die till 627, which would make him more than a hundred years of age, and it is certain that the simple and abstemious life of many of these ancient saints, as well as their calm and quiet spirit, did tend to long life, much more than the luxury and restlessness in which so many people now spend their time. S. Malo is one of the saints about whom many pretty *animal* stories are told. It is said that one day a little bird laid its eggs in his cloak, which he had thrown down, and when he found them he would not have them disturbed till the mother had hatched her fledglings. It is also told that he tamed a wolf, so that it worked for him like an ass. Evidently he was both gentle, forgiving, and gracious.

CHAPTER VIII.

𝕾. 𝕲regory the 𝕲reat, March 12, A.D. 604.—𝕾. 𝕬ugustin of Canterbury, May 26, A.D. 604.

"**S.** GREGORY THE GREAT, Bishop of Rome."
This is the first of our saints distinguished by a "surname" in his honour, and the only one on the roll to whom the adjective "great" has been applied. It would never have been so by his own wish, we may be sure. The man who in his youth renounced all worldly rank and high position; who, disappearing for a short time from his fellow-citizens, was next seen by them in the roughest and coarsest of monkish garments, instead of pacing the streets "in robes of silk covered with jewels;" the man who turned the palace of his ancestors into a monastery, and tended with his own delicate hands the beggars who crowded for relief to the hospital at its gates—he who, in hopes of escaping the high dignity for which he believed himself so unfitted, hid for days in a forest cave whither he had been carried concealed in a basket; he who, to the last, asked for no prouder title than that of "Servus servorum Dei"—he was not one to have cared for praise and fame even after death.

But he was a "great" man, and he was a "saint." His humility only makes him the greater and the holier.

Distinction and honour were no new things to Gregory.

He was born of an ancient and illustrious Roman family, and, as the son of the rich senator Gordianus, he was appointed, while still quite young, "prætor of Rome." The great city was fallen and sunk; no longer the capital of the Empire, but carelessly governed from a distance by the rulers, whose real interests were all in the East, where, at Constantinople, they held their court, Rome was now the scene of endless troubles and misfortunes. The Lombard tribes were always threatening at her gates; the government on the spot was in feeble and often treacherous hands; "storms and inundations" added to the miseries of "war, famine, and disease." Worst of all, the Church herself was torn by factions, schisms, jealousy, and party spirit of every kind. Can we wonder that Gregory, when he had at last to yield and accept his election as Pope, did so with "bowed head and weeping"—despairing, as he says himself, "of guiding into port this old and shattered ship, leaking on every side, with which God has charged me."

But it was God's charge, and as such S. Gregory ever viewed it, never relaxing in effort, never wavering, never resting, even when so racked by pain that he could scarcely stand, and often so depressed and dispirited that he—and not he alone, for most religious minds of the time thought the same—could not help believing that the end of the world was at hand.

It is, however, often darkest before dawn. S. Gregory's life and work were the beginning of better things.

Even as their city governor the young man had gained the hearts of the Roman people; they must have been thankful to have some one honest and unselfish, really anxious for the public good, in those days of unscrupulous extortion, and it was as the servant of God that Gregory was thus conscientious : even before especially devoting himself to the religious life, the Divine Spirit was the director and guide of his heart and actions.

But it was not for long that the young prætor was happy in his post. At that time the monks of S. Benedict were established in Rome, their monastery at Monte Cassino having been destroyed, and they were S. Gregory's dearest friends. He grew more and more to long for the life of seclusion, and at last he made the break, giving up every tie to society ; and on the death of his father, which occurred about that date, he spent all his possessions in founding seven monasteries, and in ministering to the poor—a tremendous proportion of the Roman inhabitants in those days ; among S. Gregory's daily pensioners were even many of the nobility, reduced by misfortunes to the point of starvation.

The new monk carried his own self-denial too far. He worked too hard, fasted too often, and kept more vigils than his strength could stand. And he only discovered his mistake too late, for his health was injured ; the rest of his life was passed in almost constant suffering.

The first interruption of his retreat came in 577, when the Pope, Benedict I., persuaded him to be ordained deacon, so that his services might be employed as one of the seven "cardinal deacons" of Rome. One year later, Benedict having died, the new Pope, Pelagius II., sent Gregory on an embassy to the Emperor Tiberius at Constantinople. His mission had to do with the election of Pelagius, and he was also directed to beg for help against the Lombards. He stayed a few years at Constantinople, and while there he met Leander, Bishop of Seville, who remained one of his dearest friends till death.

On his return to Rome, Gregory obtained the Pope's leave to make his home at his own monastery of S. Andrea, of which he was now chosen abbot. The few years that follow—till A.D. 590—seem to have been the happiest and most peaceful of his life. It was during this time that occurred the well-known incident of S. Gregory's passing through the market-place, and there observing some fair-haired, fair-skinned boys exposed for sale as slaves. On being told they were "Angli" and pagans, he replied that such outward beauty should be matched by inward grace, for they looked like "Angeli." And the interest thus awakened made him at once entreat the Pope to send a band of missionaries to the distant island of Britain, whence the poor young captives had been brought, he himself volunteering to lead them. The Pope consented ; the mission was arranged, and started. But at three days' journey from Rome the little party was overtaken by special messengers from Pelagius, instructed to bring back Gregory, if needs were, even by force. A tumult had broken out in the city when it was discovered by the inhabitants that their dearly-loved benefactor had left them, and the Pope was obliged to recall him. Gregory consented to return.

In 589 A.D. the plague broke out at Rome. The Abbot

of S. Andrea's was, as might have been expected, the foremost in the army of help and succour of every kind. He preached daily also, and he arranged a solemn procession of penitence, in seven divisions, starting from seven parts of the city, each chanting a litany as it went. These came to be known in later days as the "Greater Litanies," and were sometimes called "the black crosses," from the mourning clothes and banners used by the chanters. It must have been a strange and wonderful sight—a whole city, as it were, in visible repentance—repentance only too sadly called for. The Pope, Pelagius, was one of those who died of this fearful pestilence, and then came upon S. Gregory the sore trial I have told you of—that of being chosen as his successor.

This was in 590 A.D. S. Gregory was then about fifty.

The fourteen years of his pontificate were years of incessant labour, labour of so many different kinds, much of it requiring such consideration and clear-headedness, such tact and energy, that one wonders how a single man, and that man an almost constant sufferer, and one whose nature was peculiarly nervous and sensitive, could overtake it all. For, besides the usual duties and responsibilities of a bishop, S. Gregory had to manage the Papal property, which had now become important. The greater part of this wealth he distributed to all in need, living himself most simply, though receiving daily at his table the many thankful for his bounty. As a "landlord" he was most careful to see that none of his tenants, farmers or peasants, were in any way oppressed or unfairly treated. The state of confusion and terror in which Italy was then plunged added greatly to Pope Gregory's difficulties. In the midst of his spiritual cares for his people, he had to see that they were guarded from invasion and still greater ruin than had already overwhelmed Rome, and even from constant danger of death itself. It was through his negotiations that any sort of terms were come to with the Lombard tribes, and that a time of peace was secured. Theodelinda, wife of the Lombard King Agilulf, was a Christian, and a faithful friend of S. Gregory's. With her help he obtained some influence over Agilulf, nor was his object only to secure peace. He was earnestly anxious to convert these northern pagans, and never lost an opportunity of missionary work among them.

Within the Church herself Gregory's task was a most difficult one. The Bishop or Patriarch of Constantinople took upon himself a new and unauthorised title, that of "Universal Bishop." Clearly foreseeing what this might lead to, Gregory, humility in person where he himself was concerned, but zealous for the dignity of his office, struggled for years against the encroachment. In the plainest words he stated that such a position was to be claimed by no man. He would never accept it himself, nor consent to it for any other. This courageous firmness brought upon him much ill-will, and, besides gaining that of the Eastern bishops themselves, it interfered with the friendship which had formerly existed between him and the Emperor Mauritius. This Emperor was, with all his family, cruelly put to death by a wretched usurper named Phocas. And almost the only cloud which dims the pure and holy lustre surrounding the name of S. Gregory arises in connection with this Phocas. For once, Gregory allowed his anxiety for the welfare of his sorely tried flock and the interest of the Church to lead him out of the straight path of sincerity. He wrote a flattering and respectful letter to the new Emperor, a letter which could not have expressed his true feelings, as he well knew the cruel, brutal, and godless character of the tyrant.

While earnestly anxious for the internal purity of the Church, most plain-spoken in his reprimands of those who deserved them, strict and almost severe in the absolute self-forgetfulness he taught to both his clergy and his monks, S. Gregory was yet strikingly distinguished in those early times, when zeal was often only another word for intolerance, by his wide-minded charity and gentleness towards those who were not Christians. "Conversions wrought by force can never be sincere," he wrote once, when directing the gentler treatment of Jews who had been sharply handled. Yet this gentleness went hand in hand with the most ardent missionary spirit. He wrote often and earnestly to persons of position in France and Spain, to help and encourage all efforts at conversion in those countries, and kept up friendly relations with the Frankish and Visigoth rulers of those countries. His interest in Britain, the country of his little "Angeli," never slumbered ; but of this I shall be able to tell you more when we come to the life of S. Augustin of Canterbury.

S. Gregory left many writings, among them an exposition of the Book of Job, a treatise on the pastoral office, a great many sermons, and, perhaps the most interesting of all, a collection of nearly a thousand letters, written to all sorts of persons, in all sorts of places.   He was not a very learned man, having studied neither Greek nor Hebrew, but he was exceedingly thoughtful, intelligent, and acute.   He rendered valuable service to the Liturgy, putting into form one large and important part of it ; and even more associated with his name is the Church music, to which he gave great time and attention, collecting and revising the ancient voluntaries, and adding to them new chants, as well as both the music and words of several hymns.   He founded at Rome a school for sacred music, and in his last years, when too ill to leave his little room, he used to have the choir-boys with him for practice.   As late as the ninth century, a monk of Cassino, "John the deacon," writes of having seen the couch on which S. Gregory lay, and the whip with which he "menaced" (I am sure he never went further than this) his little pupils.

There are, as might be expected, many legends about this great and remarkable saint.   One of them I will tell you, as it has been represented in pictures under the name of the "Supper of S. Gregory," and you might some day see one of these.   In the days when Gregory first became a monk, there came one morning, begging for food, a poor shipwrecked sailor.   The monastery stores were exhausted, and having no money left either, Gregory gave the man a little silver basin, the last thing of value he possessed.   It had belonged to his mother.   Years and years afterwards, when the monk had become Pope, it was his custom to feed twelve poor men regularly at his own table. One day casting a glance around, he saw there were *thirteen*.

"Who is the extra guest?" he asked his steward. The steward counted in his turn. "I see, Holy Father, but twelve," he replied. When the meal was over, S. Gregory addressed the stranger, and asked who he was.

"Dost thou not remember," he answered, "the poor man to whom thou gavest thy last possession—the silver porringer? I am he. My name is Wonderful, and for my sake God will refuse thee nothing thou askest."

Then Gregory saw that his visitor was no mere mortal guest. But he disappeared, and to no eyes but his benefactor's had he been visible.

In pictures S. Gregory himself is often painted with a dove on his shoulder. The reason for this is that after the saint's death, his friend, "Peter the deacon," had a vision of the Pope writing, with a dove whispering into his ear, which was interpreted as signifying the inspiration of the Holy Spirit.

Pope Gregory took an interest in sculpture and painting, as well as music. His views on these arts in connection with religious worship were very wise; and a letter of his on the subject exists, in which he reproves a bishop who, in fear of idolatry, had caused some sacred statues to be destroyed. Among other advice he reminds him that "painting is often to the ignorant what books are to the learned."

S. Gregory died on the 12th of March, A.D. 604.   He had always suffered much in health, but the last years of his life were "a kind of martyrdom," from the disease now known as rheumatic gout.   To the end he worked unweariedly, but he longed for rest, and death came to him as a welcome friend.   He was not a very old man; some accounts make him only fifty-five, but it is more probable that he was about ten years older.   At the little town of Gemignano in Tuscany there is a small chapel in the cathedral, on the walls of which are painted scenes from the life of a humble saint scarcely heard of elsewhere, but so associated with the great Father of the Church whom I have been telling you about, that it seems natural to relate here her simple story.   She was a peasant girl, named Fina, poor and unknown, but of singular holiness.   She was very beautiful, but extremely modest, and while still quite young she was so crippled by paralysis or rheumatism that for years her life was spent lying on one side, unable to move. To comfort her, she was told of the long and cruel sufferings of the brave and patient Gregory; and, though six centuries and a half had passed since his death, the thought of him became to the poor child a source of certain strength and support; she felt as if he were to her a dearly loved and venerated friend.   As time went on, her troubles increased, for her poor mother died, and Fina was left to the mercy of the neighbours.   They were kind, but had not much time or money to spare, and often she had to lie for hours and hours alone in her hut, untended and unnourished. Even the mice and rats sometimes ran over her.   She could not move a hand to drive them away. No existence one has ever heard of could be more desolate. But her head was unaffected, and her heart and spirit grew more and more pure and holy. She never murmured; she was always gentle and loving, and trying to think of anything she could do for others. And at last one night, as she lay alone, she had a vision. She saw S. Gregory, his face illumined by no earthly radiance, standing by her. "Dear child," he said, "on my festival Christ will give thee rest." And so it was. On the 12th of March, A.D. 1253, she died. Across all those centuries the example of the saint had shone out for the strength and comfort of a poor little ignorant peasant girl.

Of S. Augustin of Canterbury, as he is usually called to distinguish him from his namesake of Hippo, we know personally very little. The interest of his life to us consists in his work in our own country. He was one of the monks of S. Gregory's monastery of S. Andrea, at Rome, also, it appears, a close personal friend of the great Bishop; and it is certain that Augustin must have been possessed of special missionary qualities, as well as of sincere holiness and peculiar devotion to the cause of religion, otherwise he would not have been chosen by the Pope to lead the band of forty on their errand of evangelisation. It is at the time of his thus being distinguished that we first hear of him. This was in the year 596.

Since the incident of his own attempted journey to Britain, Gregory had never forgotten the far-off island to which his thoughts had been directed by the three fair, flaxen-haired children in the slave-market. And as soon as he was able to do so, he planned an effort for this country's conversion. This was not confined to sending his forty-one Benedictines; a letter exists of S. Gregory's to one of his priests in Gaul, directing him to purchase any "English" youths that might be offered as slaves, and to have them educated in the Christian faith, so that they might afterwards be sent back to teach their fellow-country-men. It was probably by means of his correspondence with Gaul that Gregory was so well informed about the state of Britain as to be able to choose a good time for his mission.

Ethelbert, King of Kent, had married Bertha, daughter of Charibert, the Frankish King of Paris. Bertha was a Christian; she had taken with her to her new country Liudhard, a French bishop, as her religious director. She had now been married nearly twenty years, and though she had not succeeded in actually converting her husband, she had won his good-will for her religion, to which many of his subjects had given in their allegiance. This encouraged her and Liudhard to write to Gaul for help. And their appeal reached to Rome.

Augustin and his band started, and got as far as Aix, in Provence. There, unfortunately, they listened to terrifying accounts of the wild and savage nation they were about to visit. Augustin, it appears, was not himself so discouraged as his companions, but he could not prevail with them, and either by their wish, or in real perplexity, he retraced his steps to Rome to ask leave to give up the attempt. But their chief was not one to sympathise in faint-heartedness. Back came Augustin, fortified in his own spirit, and supported by S. Gregory's strong and inspiriting letters. And at last, all dangers safely passed, the little troop landed safely on the English coast, at Ebb's Fleet, near Sandwich. It was, indeed, no small matter to have come so far—we in these days cannot in the faintest degree picture to ourselves what such a journey really meant. And the courage which had overcome the fears and misgivings only too natural, considering the certain danger and the unknown risks, calls for our admiration.

And this great mission succeeded as far as first attempts of the kind can do. It is true that, in one sense, it was not the first conversion of England, for the ancient *British* Church had existed from very early times. But the gradual occupation of the country by the Anglo-Saxon tribes, driving the Celtic inhabitants ever farther and farther into the extremes of Wales, Cornwall, and the North, had, as far as England was concerned, almost made an end of Christianity. There were still remains of what had been. The first service held by S. Augustin and his companions was in a little church just outside Canterbury, dedicated to S. Martin, and dating from the time of the Romans, where Queen Bertha, through all the years of her faithful endeavours, had been wont to pray.

The missionaries, as soon as they arrived, begged for an audience with King Ethelbert, which he, prepared no doubt by the Queen, granted at once. He only made one condition—that the meeting should be in the open air, for he was still enough of a pagan to dread sorcery or magic on the part of the new-comers. The spot chosen was an open space near Ebb's Fleet; thither the King and his attendants repaired, crossing the Stour to the Isle of Thanet, and thither came slowly up from the shore in solemn procession, chanting a Litany of prayer for success and blessing, headed by one bearing a long silver cross, and followed by a banner representing "the Great King, our Lord Jesus Christ," Augustin and his forty monks. It must have been a striking scene, even apart from its intense interest for the Catholic Church through all time. Augustin himself, tall of stature and noble in presence, the central figure, at once impressed Ethelbert. For the King bade them all be seated, that they might the more conveniently deliver their message. The interview ended favourably. Without making any rash promises for himself, the Saxon ruler granted to the missioners full power and freedom to prosecute their work, and safe quarters in a temporary abode in the Stable-gate at his royal town of Canterbury. There the innocent simplicity of their daily lives, the heavenly sweetness of their teachings, aided by their earnest prayer and fasting, won their way; numbers came daily to be baptized, and on the Feast of Whit Sunday, June 2, A.D. 597, the King joined himself to these. And on the following Christmas day more than ten thousand of his subjects were baptized at one time.

Before long, Augustin, following the instructions of S. Gregory, crossed over to France, there to receive his own

consecration as bishop.   On his return, a permanent home
was given to him by Ethelbert, in Canterbury, on the
site of the present Cathedral.   An ancient British church,
desecrated in later times by having been used as a Saxon
temple, was restored to Christian use, and dedicated to
S. Pancras, and beside it was founded another monastery,
of which "Peter the deacon," one of Gregory's most
esteemed monks, became abbot.

This same Peter, with another brother, Laurence, had
already been sent to Rome to report the good news to
their beloved Bishop there.   By letters still in existence
we read how overjoyed he was at these tidings ; indeed,
his hopeful nature now saw no difficulties in the way of
a speedy and complete conversion of our island.   For it
was, of course, impossible for him to know in how unsettled a state it still was, nor did he look for any troubles
between his clergy and those of the still existing British
Church.   He sent back the messengers with fresh helpers,
and loaded them with everything his kind heart could
think of, to cheer them in their banishment and to adorn
their newly founded churches—books, beautiful vestments,
and sacred vessels, the "pallium" of an archbishop for
Augustin himself, and letters of fullest sympathy and wise
counsel.   It is by some of these letters that an idea has
been given rise to that Augustin was inclined to be
haughty and proud-spirited.   For S. Gregory warns him
against "pride and vainglory," and reminds him that all
his success was the gift of God and by His grace.   It
would be uncharitable, however, to take these friendly

words of counsel as words of reproof. Still, it seems probable that Augustin was inclined to be hasty, and his commanding presence may have added to the impression of haughtiness which he gave. This was unhappily the case at a meeting appointed between the new clergy and the ancient British bishops, which ended very badly. S. Augustin had come prepared to meet them half-way on the points of ritual and other observances as to which they differed, his great desire being that the two Christian bodies should unite for the conversion of the Saxons. But he gave offence to the Britons, by not rising to meet them when they arrived, and the breach was never healed. Augustin is said to have spoken bitterly and angrily when he found them obstinate in refusing to come to agreement, and some writers even maintain that he uttered words of prophecy against them which were fulfilled some years later by a terrible massacre of the monks of Bangor by the Saxons. But this is quite unlike all we are told of Augustin's real character, which was charitable and tender, "knowing no other weapon against sinners than prayers for their conversion." And had he lived to see it, he would sincerely have rejoiced at the good work still to be done by the Celtic Church in the Christianising of Northumbria and Mercia.

Nor had he been trained to any narrow-mindedness or ungentleness. Such were not S. Gregory's ways. His letters of counsel are full of charity, and what, even in religious matters, one cannot but call "good sense." His missionaries were told to stand out for no hard and fast

line in smaller matters; they were left at liberty to choose
for their new liturgy whatever appeared "pious, religious,
and right;" they were to remember that "things are not
to be loved on account of places, but places on account
of good things;" that their efforts were to be patient and
steady, since one that would "mount to the highest must
do so by steps, not by leaps."

After his one failure—that of coming to a brotherly
understanding with the British clergy, S. Augustin returned
to Canterbury, where he spent the rest of his life. He
was spared to see the whole of Ethelbert's kingdom converted, new bishoprics erected at Rochester and London,
a cathedral dedicated to S. Andrew at the former place,
and a church dedicated to S. Paul at the latter.

On May 26, but two months after the ending of S.
Gregory's sore sufferings, his dear friend and brother,
Augustin, died. We do not know his age—he may have
been much younger than the great Bishop—nor any particulars of his death. The two had never met since their
last consultation in Rome, when Augustin, discouraged and
perplexed, returned there for direction. But in death they
were not long divided, and the disciple could meet his
master again with joy, having spent his life in the work
entrusted to him to do.

CHAPTER IX.

S. Chad, March 2, A.D. 672.—S. Etheldreda, October 17, A.D. 679.
—S. Lambert, September 17, A.D. 709.—S. Giles, September 1,
(about) A.D. 724.

IT will not be often now, in continuing the history of the
saints of our own Prayer Book Calendar, that we shall
need to leave England. From the time of S. Augustin of
Canterbury our island has its own distinct Church Chronicle;
and the lives of the Saxon saints, of several of whom I have
now to tell you, are interwoven with those of the earlier
Christians of Britain, those of the ancient Celtic Church,
which, through all the confusion and disturbance of those
tumultuous centuries, had yet never ceased to exist. The
great recorder and historian whom we have to thank for
the clearer knowledge of the times we are now entering
upon, Bede, the venerated and saintly writer, will soon
come before us himself. We have to thank him not only
for his accounts of the Church in his own times, but for
the light he throws back upon these dim and hazy records
of the first Christianity of these islands, and for the full
justice he does to the work and devotion of the Celtic
priests, even though his own thorough sympathy and approval lay with the teachings of S. Gregory's missionary

monks and their successors.   Not that the two schools—
if we may call them so—of Christian training were really
opposed to each other.   The questions on which they
differed, of which the most important was the right date
for keeping the festival of Easter, seem to us now matters
which might have been easily settled.   But they did not
prove so ; strong feelings were aroused on both sides, and
it is therefore the more pleasing when, notwithstanding
this, we find members of each party ready to speak well
of the other.

The life of S. Chad brings before us very distinctly the
state of the Catholic world of Great Britain at that time.
He was himself of Saxon birth, one—the youngest, probably—of four brothers, Cedd, Cynebil, and Celin, all of
saintly life and character.   Yet, though Saxons, these
brothers were trained and educated in the British Church,
Chad himself partly at the monastery of the holy Bishop
Aidan, at Lindisfarne, partly in Ireland, at a place with
the strange name of Rathmelsigi, where, Bede tells us,
he gained the friendship of another young Northumbrian
Saxon, named Egbert, a man of extreme beauty of character
and life, with whom he loved to study, and whom he never
forgot, though they did not meet again in later life.   The
elder brother of Chad (or Ceadda, as he is sometimes
called), Cedd, had founded a monastery at Lastingham, in
Yorkshire.   In the year 664 he died of the plague.   On
his deathbed he appointed Chad to be his successor.   In
the few years that follow, to his own death in 672, is com-
prised all the real interest of Chad's life.

He had not long been abbot at Lastingham when he was
summoned thence by King Oswi, of Northumbria, who
desired to make him Bishop of York. Oswi himself belonged to the Celtic, or, as it is frequently called, the
Scottish Church, but his queen and his eldest son Alfrid,
also a ruling sovereign—as his father had made over to
him the kingdom of Deira—were strongly attached to the
Roman views. A great council had been held at Whitby
shortly before the death of Cedd, which only ended in the
two parties becoming more divided, Colman, the Bishop of
Lindisfarne, and several others of the Celtic Church, with-
drawing to Scotland altogether. Cedd, it appears, accepted
the Roman rules, but it seems probable that his brother
Chad, owing perhaps to his long residence in Ireland, kept
firmly to the views in which he had been educated ; and this
may have been one reason why King Oswi was so eager
to make him bishop. It was a mistaken eagerness, for at
the very time there actually was already a bishop of York
—Wilfrid, a zealous and active priest of the other party.
This Wilfrid had gone to France for his consecration, not
desiring to have it at English hands, and had delayed his
return, which gave Oswi the opportunity of putting Chad in
his place. Some writers have blamed Chad for accepting
it, but his after conduct shows he did not do so from any
ambitious or selfish motives. He was consecrated by a
bishop of Wessex, Wini, who joined with him in the service
two British bishops.

The new prelate won the admiration of all by his blameless and devoted life. He took S. Aidan as his model,

following in everything the simple and humble bearing of the priests of the Celtic Church. He travelled about, like the apostles, on foot, all over his diocese, teaching and instructing alike "in the towns, the villages, the castles, and the cottages," studying whenever he had leisure, doing good to all, welcome everywhere. It is disappointing to read that this beautiful and useful life was interrupted. For, after a time, Wilfrid returned home, and though he seems to have behaved considerately, retiring at first to a monastery at Ripon, the gentle Chad was not long left in the post he filled so well. At that time there came to Canterbury a new archbishop, Theodore by name, a native of Tarsus, a learned and energetic man. Though a foreigner, he speedily made himself acquainted with every particular of his new work, visiting all parts of England himself. When he reached Northumbria he heard the history of the two bishops, and after inquiring into it, he decided in favour of Wilfrid, reproving Chad for having accepted the dignity, and even throwing doubts on his consecration having been according to rule.

S. Chad's reply was, like himself, full of the dignity of true humility. "If thou judgest that I have not duly received the episcopate," he said, "I willingly resign it, for, indeed, I have never thought myself worthy, though, for obedience' sake, I accepted it."

Yet it must have been a harsh trial, for he was no longer a young man, and had he been less truly holy much bitterness of spirit would have been only natural. Theodore, himself a generous-hearted man, was touched by his submission. He would not allow the Bishop to give up his rank, but confirmed it in so far as he thought that the consecration had been irregular, and after a space of retirement at his own Lastingham, Chad was appointed bishop of the Mercians, and fixed his abode at Lichfield. We are told that on his new appointment the Archbishop insisted on Chad's taking more care of his health, and allowing himself a horse for his more distant journeys ; and, finding the submissive saint inclined to be obstinate where self-denial was concerned, Theodore with his own hands lifted him on to his horse, "so holy a man did he esteem him."

It shows, indeed, how strongly marked must have been S. Chad's saintly character, how almost perfect his lovableness, that in so short a time he should have made a lasting impression on so many. For he only lived two years and a half in his new see, and the whole of his influential life, as abbot and then bishop, only covers a space of eight years, yet his quaint, uncouth name has always been loved and reverenced in England. No fewer than thirty-one churches are dedicated to him, among them the first church ever built at Shrewsbury. There are several graceful legends about him, but the most beautiful story I can tell you is the account of his death, related by the Venerable Bede, which we have no reason to consider only a legend. A deadly fever, or an illness of the kind, had broken out in the neighbourhood, but the Bishop himself was quite well, when one day a monk named Owini, much esteemed by S. Chad, and who had followed him from his Yorkshire monastery, had a strange experience. Owini wás alone, working in a field or garden near the little oratory where the Bishop was praying, when suddenly a sound of voices fell upon his ears, voices such as he had never heard before, such as it is but seldom given to mortal ears to listen to, angelic voices "singing most sweetly and rejoicing, like happy visitants coming down to earth from heaven." The beautiful sounds seemed to float along overhead, till they were just above the oratory. Thither they appeared to enter, and for a short space there was silence. Then, as if their mission were accomplished, the voices rose again, from the roof of the sacred building, wafting upwards, heavenwards, till "their inexpressible sweetness" was lost in the distance. Amazed and overawed, Owini stood gazing; in a few moments he saw the oratory window opened, and the Bishop beckoning to him to come near. "Go quickly to the church," he said, "and fetch the Brothers hither, and do you return with them."

When they were assembled, S. Chad exhorted them in beautiful and touching words to continue in all good and faithful practices, as he had taught them; above all, like the aged St. John, he repeated what was truly the keynote of his own life, "Love one another." "For the day of my departure," he explained, "is near at hand. The beloved guest who used to visit our brethren has come to me to-day, and has been pleased to call me from this world." Then, asking for their prayers and blessing them, he dismissed them, "sorrowing." But Owini stayed behind.

"I beseech you, father," he said, "to tell me the meaning of the wonderful music I heard."

"If you heard it, my son," Ceadda answered, "tell it as yet to no one. The voices were those of angels who came to call me away to the heaven I have always loved and longed for. In seven days they will return and take me with them."

So it proved. The Bishop fell ill the next day, and on the seventh he died.

"His holy soul," says Bede, "as we may well believe, was carried by the angels to the eternal joys above."

Then he goes on to speak of S. Chad's many good deeds and sweet qualities. One of his habits was always to pray when a storm arose ; the more violent the storm the more earnest were the saint's supplications ; "entreating the Lord's mercy on all mankind," praying "that we may never deserve the stroke of His anger."

"It is no wonder," says Bede, "that he gladly looked forward to the day of his death, or rather to the day of the Lord, whose coming he had always so looked for."

S. Etheldreda, who is commemorated on October 17, is the last woman among our Black Letter Saints. Though last, or at least latest, she was not *least* among them ; in one sense, indeed, she was the greatest, for she was what no other of these holy women had been—a queen. And she was great in more real ways than this. She was truly holy, earnestly self-denying, and devotedly charitable. Yet in reading the history of her life it is impossible to deny that she did wrong in more than one instance, or at least that she made some very great mistakes, and that in endeavouring to put these right she was not just or fair to others. Her story brings before us, as you will see, some

S. Etheldreda (*from an ancient Saxon miniature*, A.D. 980).

of the characters we heard about in the life of S. Chad. For, though much younger than he, she died only seven years after him; like him, too, she was of Saxon family,

one of four sisters, as he was one of four brothers, and her
sisters were all good and Christian women. She was the
third of the fair daughters of King Anna of East Anglia;
her mother was a sister of a well-known saintly woman,
Hilda, Abbess of Whitby; her father and grandfather were
both holy and devoted men. So from her birth she was
reared in a saintly atmosphere, and it is not surprising
that while still quite young she made plans of consecrat-
ing herself to a specially religious life. But she was very
beautiful, and it does not seem as if she had been able
always to keep up to her own ideal, for long, long afterwards she spoke of having loved to adorn herself with
necklaces and jewels, and of having yielded to feelings of
vanity. All such girlish weaknesses, however, she quickly
outgrew; but, considering what she believed to be her
" call " in life, it is surprising to find that she early married.
Her husband was a prince of a Saxon colony near her own
home, named Tombert. He loved her devotedly, but seems
to have been of a gentle and yielding nature, and allowed
his beautiful wife to live the life of a nun rather than
that of a princess. He died two or three years after their
marriage, and all might now have been well had Etheldreda
not made the grave mistake of marrying again, contrary to
her own wishes, to please her relations, who much desired
the alliance, as it was with the son and heir of the powerful
Oswi, King of Northumbria. Her new husband, Egfrid,
was not only young and wealthy and attractive, he was,
we are assured, pious and God-fearing. So that, having
married him, Etheldreda's duty was plain—she was bound

L

to make him a good wife, and to help him, when before
long he became king, to fulfil the heavy responsibilities of
a ruler.   She did not see things in this light.   On the contrary, her only idea of serving God was to do so by a life
entirely out of the world and severed from all family ties.
King Egfrid was less yielding than Prince Tombert, though
when at last Etheldreda asked leave to go altogether to live
n a convent, he gave a kind of stormy consent.   Another
person was to blame for her going so far as this.   You remember Wilfrid the Bishop of York, whose long absence
in France King Oswi took advantage of to put gentle S.
Chad in his place?   This Wilfrid was a great man ; he
did an immense amount of good in his long life, which is
full of interest to read, but he did wrong with regard to
Etheldreda and her husband.   For King Egfrid, knowing
the Bishop's powers of persuasion, and how much the
Queen respected his judgment, asked him to prevail upon
her to return home to her royal and wifely duties.   But
Wilfrid's feelings were all in favour of her becoming a nun,
and he secretly allowed her to make her vows, while letting
the King think he was acting on his side.   *This* was wrong,
for double-dealing from any motive is wrong, and wise and
Christian writers who have told the story do not hesitate
to blame Wilfrid, great Christian teacher and missionary
though he was.   No doubt he thought Etheldreda really
intended for the life of seclusion and separation from the
world, and so she probably was.   For when at last, the
King's vain endeavours to win her back all having failed,
she founded a convent on lands of her own, left her by her

first husband, nothing could have been more holy and consistent than her life. "Its traces went deep into the memory of the Anglo-Saxon Christians, triumphing over time and human forgetfulness beyond that of any other woman of the race."

The Isle of Ely, where she made her home, was at that time really an island, "a waste of rushes and water," out of which rose the little bright green spots, where were the villages and farmsteads. To get from one to another, boats were required. There were the remains of one church, which, with the help of her brother, King Aldulf, Etheldreda restored, and beside which she built her convent. Here she was joined by her sisters, Sexburga and Ermenilda, and other relations, for this family seems to have been a very united one, and together they passed their time in devotion and useful work. Numbers of girls were sent to the Abbess Etheldreda to be educated, for the teaching of the young was one of the special charges of the Saxon convents in those days, and one of the benefits for which perhaps posterity has not been grateful enough. It is easy to pass our judgments upon these cloistered lives, even to mock at them as idle and selfish— though it was rarely in these early times that they deserved such reproach—but it is *not* easy to say what the Christian world, even of our own days, would have been without them. And if their religious fervour seems to us "exaggerated," remember that the same was said in other words of some whom Christians have long learnt to look up to as their leaders; if, in some ways, these holy men and women were more "childish" than we, they were also more "child-*like*," in the sense which God requires the very wisest and most learned of His people to be so. We have grown too accustomed to the teaching which seemed to them—but a generation or two separated from the fierce northern warriors whose idea of heaven was of never-ending drinking of wine out of the skulls of their enemies—so wonderful, so truly a "Gospel," that all else beside it lost importance; and because they were so much in earnest compared with us, we think ourselves wiser than they, forgetting that there is a "wisdom" which is "foolishness," and "things" we are inclined to call "foolish" which "God hath chosen to confound the wise."

Etheldreda did not live to be old. She died of one of the diseases of those times which the old chroniclers are content to describe as a plague. In the last days she suffered much from her throat, which had to be cut by a surgeon, clumsily enough, no doubt. The bodily sufferings of even the saints had none of the comforts *we* now have when we are ill, dear children; but she bore all with angelic patience, dying in full summer time, on the 23rd of June 679. Her festival is kept on October 17, because on that day, several years later, her body was reburied in a new and more beautiful tomb.

Not very many years ago part of a cross was dug up at Ely, and, by the inscription on it, it appears to have belonged to one placed there by "Owini," the same Owini who heard S. Chad's angelic summons. This Owini was originally a nobleman of Etheldreda's own household, and it was when she left her court for ever that he joined the Lastingham monks. He was a most earnest and holy man, devoted to the young princess from her babyhood. It is supposed that after his bishop's death he returned to end his days near his dear lady.

S. Lambert of Maestricht, as he is generally described, seems to have been one of those saintly characters of whom his biographers have nothing but good to tell. And the history we possess of him is quite to be trusted. It was written by a deacon of his own church, not many years after the Saint's death. Lambert was the son of rich and noble parents; his family had been Christians for several generations. He was most carefully brought up at home, and then confided to the care of Theodard, Bishop of Maestricht, to be by him instructed for the priesthood. He is described as "wise and amiable," "stately and handsome, loving, pure, and humble," and he in no way disappointed the hopes of his parents and his old tutor, by whom he was much beloved. He was only twenty-one when Bishop Theodard was cruelly murdered by some lawless chieftains, who had already plundered his church; and young as he was, Lambert was chosen to succeed to the empty episcopate. For some time all went well. The youthful bishop was full of zeal and devotion, and he seems to have had by nature a cheerful and energetic character, which, strengthened and purified by Divine grace, made of him a model priest. He was courageous too, never afraid of reproving wrongdoers, though tender and encouraging to the truly penitent. He was a favourite

with the King, Childeric II., which is one of the few things
that can be said in this prince's favour. But when Childeric was assassinated, in 673, and succeeded by his
brother Theodoric, a new "maire du palais" used his influence to depose the good young bishop, and to put in
his place a most unworthy man. Lambert withdrew to
the monastery of Stavelot, where he spent seven years.
Perhaps he felt that this was useful discipline, for the important post he had held so young might have tended to
spiritual pride. At all events, he acted as if he thought
so; for he behaved with the greatest humility, submitting
to authority in everything, like the youngest novice. One
winter night, when rising for prayers, he accidentally let
drop his sabot, or wooden shoe. The sound re-echoed
through the darkness and stillness, and reached the ears
of the Abbot. Perfect silence was the order for these
hours; and a sharp reproof was sent out, directing that
whoever had made the noise must go and pray before the
cross in front of the church as a punishment. It was
freezing weather. Next morning, when all assembled for
matins, one was missing, and the Abbot remarked it. He
was told that the brother he had ordered out to pray had
not yet come in.

"Fetch him in," said the Abbot, and the penitent was
recalled, covered with snow, and almost dead with cold.
To the good father's horror, he recognised the bishop.
Thereupon he fell on his knees, asking pardon for his
mistake.

"Ask God's pardon," was the reply, "for thinking you

need mine. Should I not be content to endure suffering and cold, as S. Paul did, if so I may better learn to serve God?"

The appointment of the well-known "Pepin d'Héristal" as "maire du palais" caused the recall of Lambert to his bishopric. He returned with new energy and ardour to his beloved home. His labours were not confined to his own flock; he did much as a missionary, working up through the countries now called Belgium and Holland to the very confines of Friesland, where the ground had been already broken by another enthusiastic Christian priest, the Anglo-Saxon Willibrod, afterwards Bishop of Utrecht. Among some barbarous tribes, in a terribly savage, marshy district of Belgium called the Campine, S. Lambert was wonderfully successful. He used to sit down in the fields, surrounded by the people, teaching and comforting them, like a true follower of his Master.

His death was sad, yet it was a noble one, and has been considered by the Church as placing him in the rank of martyr. Two of his relations had taken upon themselves, without his knowledge, to punish some misdoers who had plundered his church by killing them. The times were rough and lawless, and it is not to be wondered at that the friends of S. Lambert could not tamely bear injury to one so loved and revered. But the misplaced zeal ended in worse trouble. The relations of the murdered men set upon the bishop and his young kinsmen, when they were on a journey, resting for the night at what was then a mere hamlet, and is now the town of Liege. When the assassins were seen approaching, S. Lambert's companions made ready for defence. But he bade them sheathe their swords.

"You have been guilty," he said. "Your sin must now be expiated;" and his influence was so great that he was obeyed. He laid himself down upon the ground, his arms extended in the form of a cross, and there, defenceless, he awaited the end. It soon came: the ruffians, untouched by his meekness, ran him through with a sword, killing also his kinsmen and all his attendants. Another reason has sometimes been given for this wicked murder, but the best authorities believe this account of it, and it agrees with what is known of S. Lambert's character.

He was murdered on September 17, A.D. 709. He was first buried at Maestricht, but afterwards removed back to the spot where he died. And there, in later years, over his tomb rose a church dedicated to his memory.

Of late all the Christian world has heard and thought so much of the heroic devotion of one whom we may truly call a saint of our own days—the priest and missionary of the lepers—that it is a little disappointing to find that S. Giles or Egidius, who is distinguished in our calendar as the "patron" of these most unfortunate sufferers, had no special connection with them. He owes his associa- tion with lepers to the fact that in 1117 Matilda, wife of Henry I., founded a hospital for leprosy "without the walls of London," "under his invocation." The neighbourhood, though certainly no longer "without the walls," in which stood this church, still bears the saint's name as the parish of St. Giles. The reason why he was chosen by the Queen to give a name to her undertaking tells us something of his character. He was renowned as the patron saint not only of lepers, but of cripples and beggars, "of all driven by

S. Giles (*Lucas van Leyden*).

misery into solitude, like the wounded hart." For he was himself in spirit a thorough "solitary," gentle and compassionate, and the earliest part of his history which we can really trust relates how a king of the Goths hunting one day in the forests near the Rhone on its Mediterranean side, chased a hind till the creature took refuge in a cave. The king entered and found the pretty hind protected by a white-haired hermit, whose shoulder had been wounded by the arrow intended for the animal. This was late in the seventh century.

What had been the former history of the hermit is very uncertain, but it seems most probable that he was a Christian Greek, who, in his intense desire for solitude, left his own country and travelled to France, where he first settled near Arles, and afterwards, when the king found him, in Provence. His holy conversation made a deep impression on his visitors, and the king begged him to leave his cave and accompany him to his court. It is uncertain if he did so for a time, but all authorities agree that before long he accepted a gift of land, on which he founded a monastery of the Benedictine Order, famous in after days as the "Abbaye de St. Gilles." It was destroyed during the Saracen invasion, at which time it is supposed that he and his monks took refuge with Charles Martel at his court of Orleans. But it was restored in time for the old man to return there, and there to die when more than eighty years of age. As was probably the case with several other saints of whom we actually know but little, we are led to believe that his personal life and character must have been marked by beauty and lovableness, of which the details have been lost, otherwise it is not possible to explain the devotion so long and lastingly shown to their memory. Every county in England, except Westmoreland and

Cumberland, has churches dedicated to S. Giles; there is also the old cathedral of Edinburgh, of which city he is the tutelar saint.

S. Giles died on September 1, 720. Almost his last words are said to have been those of the blessed Simeon, "Lord, now lettest Thou Thy servant depart in peace!"

Part of the Church at Jarrow, containing Bede's ancient chair.

CHAPTER X.

The Venerable Bede, May 27, A.D. 735.—S. Boniface, June 5, A.D. 755.—S. Swithin, July 15, A.D. 862; translated, 971.

THE story of the life of the next saint on our roll—that of the great and learned scholar, Bede or Beda, known to all ages by his special title of "the Venerable," is a singularly pleasing one—a rest and refreshment to the spirit even to think of. It is like a strain of sweet though solemn music heard through the clang and clamour of those turbulent times; it is like coming upon an old garden shut in by high walls in the midst of the turmoil and confusion of a great city. Yet it was not in any sense a selfish life of calm repose; in the words of one of his modern biographers, "an existence more completely occupied than his it would be impossible to imagine." Nor were its beauty and harmony only owing to outward circumstances; they were far more the result of his perfectly disciplined character, of his wonderful simple-mindedness and absence of vanity and self-seeking, above all, of his entire submission to God's will, and to the guidance of His Holy Spirit. He was a man of great gifts, gifts consecrated from the first to the noblest service; there seems never to have been any struggle or perplexity in his life; from earliest childhood he was gradually prepared and fitted for the lasting and useful work he was to do.

We do not know who were the parents of Bede, even though we have the whole facts of his life from the time he was seven years old. He was born A.D. 673, and in the year 680 he was sent for his education to a neighbouring monastery at Weremouth (near Newcastle). This monastery, as well as one but a short distance from it—at Jarrow—had been founded by Benedict Biscop, a Northumbrian nobleman, who had become a monk, and devoted all his time and possessions to the service of the Church. The little boy Bede was confided to his care, being sometimes at one of the monasteries, sometimes at the other. At the early age of nineteen, " his great piety and endowments being considered to supply his want of years," he was ordained deacon. His first guardian, S. Benedict Biscop, had died the year before. It is probable that Bede owed much to this good and holy man besides his religious training. For S. Bennet, as he is often called, had made no less than five journeys to Rome, always on some service of the Church, or for some benefit to his beloved monasteries. He was a man of taste and culture of every kind—he had studied architecture at Rome, and brought from abroad, glass for the windows, and all the most beautiful adornments he could procure for his church, and he had also, for those days, a wonderful library. Besides all this, S. Bennet took great interest in Church music, and had engaged at Rome a musician named John the Chanter, who came back with him to

instruct the monks in singing and ritual. Eleven years
under such a master help to explain Bede's wide-minded
intelligence, which strikes his readers as the more remarkable, since it is known as a fact that he never travelled
farther from the banks of his own river than to the city
of York, and that only shortly before his death. His
whole life was spent in the peaceful monastery, which
must have seemed to him the only home he had ever
known. Yet few, very few, names of those early times
are more famed ; it is doubtful if any authors of any age
are more admired and trusted than this gentle and learned
Saxon monk, and to judge by the way he is always spoken
of by other writers of his own time, as a man he was loved
and honoured by all with whom he had anything to do.
He seems to have passed through life without arousing
any ill-will or enmity.

At thirty—A.D. 702—he received the order of priesthood. This is really the only *event* to be noted in his
history, with the exception of his visit to the court of
King Egfrid at York in 734, only the year before he died.
The real dates of his life, had he written it, would have
been those of his numerous works. He has left a list of
these. It contains a great many commentaries on the
Old and New Testaments, a large collection of letters on
important subjects, lives of the saints, a martyrology, a
book of hymns, several scientific works, and several books
of instruction for the young. He also translated some
of the Scriptures into Anglo-Saxon. But the most important work of all was his " Ecclesiastical History," a

book in which was collected "nearly all the knowledge of his times;" a history so truthful and accurate, so clear and careful, so free from exaggeration and gentle in spirit, as to be a model of its kind and of lasting value, not only to the learned, but to all intelligent minds.

Besides his writings, Bede left a great boon to his country in a school at York, which he was the principal means of founding. He had much at heart the instruction of the young, and loved teaching, for which he was certainly well qualified, for he was acquainted with most of the great Greek and Latin writers, he knew some Hebrew, and had studied "grammar, rhetoric, arithmetic," as well as all the natural sciences, including that of astronomy, which he had access to, and he was well read in poetry.

The story of his last days and of his death is a familiar one, but it will bear telling once more. He was not a very old man, only sixty-two, when he began to suffer greatly from asthma, which, about Easter in the year 735, became much worse. But he went on with his usual work till the day before that of the Ascension, May 26, "joyous and happy," as was his wont. On that morning he was dictating his translation into English of the Gospel according to St. John, when he told his secretary, a young monk, to write quickly, for he felt his strength going. The monk wrote on, then said to him—

"Dearest master, there is still one chapter wanting. Will it be grievous to you to continue?"

"It is no trouble," he answered; "but write fast."

After a while, however, he asked another monk, Cuthbert, from whom we have the whole account, to fetch a box in which he kept some small treasures which he valued much, and when Cuthbert had done so, and at his request summoned the priests of the monastery, S. Bede distributed his little gifts among them as remembrances of him. They were some peppercorns, some incense, and a few little handkerchiefs.* As he gave them he spoke lovingly to each friend in turn, begging them all to be mindful of him in their prayers, and when he saw them weeping, censured them by saying gently that "his time was come "—" I long to be with Christ, to see Him, my King, in His beauty."

Towards evening he went on with his dictation.

"But one sentence more, dear master," said the boy secretary, adding in a moment or two, "now it is finished."

"It was well said, it is finished," the saint replied. "Raise my old head in your arms "—he was lying on the floor, opposite his little oratory—"that I may look once more at the happy, holy place where I was wont to pray, and that sitting thus, I may sing to the glory of the Father, and of the Son, and of the Holy Ghost."

Thus he did, and as the last word of the "Gloria" passed his lips, his spirit fled. This was on the 27th of May 735.

At the old church at Jarrow, recently restored, is still shown the spot—the little sanctuary—to which S. Beda's dying eyes were turned.

* One of the words in the original, "Oraria," is by some translated "rosaries," supposed to be the kind made of strings of *beads*, and thus to have been the origin of this word.

In sharpest contrast to this life of holy calm stands out that of S. Boniface, the martyr Bishop of Mainz. He was born the very year that the little Beda was sent to the monastery which was to be his home for life, and like him, at the same early age, that of seven, he too was confided to an abbot to be brought up and educated among his monks. Young as he was, this was done, we are told, at his own request, granted with some reluctance by his parents. They were of noble birth, living near Crediton, in that part of the kingdom of Wessex which is now the county of Devon. The boy was sent first to a monastic school at Exeter, and before long to Nutsall, or Nutcel, near Winchester, and at the monastery there, he remained till the age of thirty, when he was ordained priest, having gained already great eminence among his brethren for his diligence and devotion, his gifts as a preacher, and his intimate knowledge of the Scriptures. But Winfride, for such was his baptismal name —that of "Boniface" being added to it later—was not intended to spend his days like S. Beda in the peace and quiet of the cloisters. He had a very different "call;" his spirit was fired with missionary enthusiasm, and he could not rest till he had joined the band of devoted workers under Willibrod, across the northern ocean in savage and heathen Friesland.

He obtained his Abbot's consent and started. But it was at a bad moment. Radbrod, king of the Frisii, was at war with Charles Martel, and violently persecuting the Christians; there was no foothold for new missionary enterprise. Winfride returned to Nutcel, but a year or two later he set out again, this time with a more organised plan of action. He went first to Rome, where he was warmly received by the Pope, and furnished by him with letters approving of his intended mission work. Thus armed, Winfride, as soon as the winter was over, crossed the Lower Alps into Bavaria, where he stayed some little time busying himself in trying to revive the Christian Church there, which had fallen into a very dead and half paganised state, and then went on into Thuringia, where he found the same sort of efforts much called for, as well as the more distinct missionary labour of fresh conversion. But he had hardly settled to his work in Germany when news came of the death of Radbrod, and Winfride, whose special interest in the Frisians had never slumbered, thought it his duty to join the great Willibrod in the far north. With him he laboured unceasingly and with great success for three years, but finding that Willibrod wished to make him his own successor in the bishopric, and shrinking from the responsibility, Winfride parted from him, and returned to Thuringia, thence working northwards into Hesse, and everywhere meeting with encouragement.

The year 723 saw Winfride again at Rome, this time with a report of excellent success. Pope Gregory II. conferred on him the rank of bishop, though not appointing him to any special place, thus leaving him free to work wherever he thought best. It is generally thought that it was at this time Winfride added the name of Boniface to his own Saxon one, and it is as Boniface that he is generally known. He did not linger long at Rome, but recrossed the Alps to Hesse, full of new ardour. He had need of it, for already many of his converts had fallen back, making a strange religion for themselves by mingling their old pagan rites with their new worship. At Fritzlar, near Geismar, Boniface dealt a severe blow at the heathen superstition. There stood an ancient oak, dedicated for ages to the pagan "Thor," and believed by his worshippers to be under supernatural protection. Followed by all his clergy, the missionary bishop on an appointed day met the assembled pagans at this spot, and with his own hands felled the huge tree, which came crashing to the ground, splitting into four pieces, "leaving a great patch of light in the green leafy vault, through which the sun fell on the triumphant Christian prelate."

This courageous deed, simple as it was, had a powerful effect on the ignorant Thor-worshippers, and enormously increased S. Boniface's influence over them. With the wood of the oak he built a chapel in the forest, which he consecrated to S. Peter. Conversions followed in great numbers, and so wide a field of missionary work began to open out that S. Boniface wrote to his old English home for help of various kinds. His requests were generously responded to. Great numbers of priests and novices joined him, to work and to be trained for work. Many women too came over from England, mothers, sisters, and relations of the priests already on the ground, women of high birth and delicate breeding, fearlessly eager to take part in the great cause. Among them were a mother and daughter, named "Kunihild" and "Berathgrit," who settled in Thuringia; a lady named "Thecla," who took up work at Kitzragen; another named "Walpurgis," the sister of one of Boniface's most esteemed companions, who joined her brother. For a very pleasing feature of these early times was the brother-and-sister affection so often deepened and sanctified by Christian devotion. It is lovely to think of these girls, as many of them were—beautiful and refined—helping and strengthening their brothers, often doubtless consoling and encouraging them when dispirited or over-worked, adding a grace and charm to the vigour and energy of the ardent missionaries such as even the fierce pagans themselves could not resist. For, we are told, "even the ferocious Germans, who had hitherto delighted but in war, knelt meekly at the feet of these gentle teachers." Among them I must not forget to mention Lioba, the cousin of S. Boniface, who is described as "beautiful as the angels, charming in speech, learned and wise." Nor must we leave out the story of one of the Bishop's most faithful followers, a youth named Gregory. It was on S. Boniface's journey from Friesland to the south that he first met this Gregory, then a boy of only fifteen. The missionary priest, not yet a bishop, stopped one night at a convent near Trèves. There while the guests were at table a young kinsman of the venerable Abbess was employed to read aloud to them in Latin a lesson out of the Holy Scriptures.

"You read well, my son," said the missionary; "but do you understand it?"

The boy replied that he thought he did, but it proved that he had difficulty in translating into his native language, so the priest took the book and explained it to him.   His clear words and impressive manner so touched the young Gregory that he begged leave there and then to follow Boniface as a disciple.   With some difficulty—for the visitor was a perfect stranger to her—he got the Abbess's consent, and from that time Gregory became as his own son to the great teacher.   He lived many years after the death of S. Boniface, dying as abbot of a monastery at Utrecht, loved and respected.

In the year 738 Boniface made his third and last visit to Rome, where Gregory III. was now Pope, and where the victorious missionary was received with the greatest honour.   He was now both archbishop and legate, with the fullest authority as such that he could have.   Besides the monasteries and convents dotted about Germany wherever there was a chance of success, he had founded four bishoprics in Bavaria, and after the death, in 741, of Charles Martel, who, though a professed Christian, was far from a consistent one, his work became both wider and less interfered with.   The sons of Charles Martel, Carloman and Pepin, were thoroughly at one with him. Carloman himself became a monk, and when, in 751, Pepin was crowned king, which he had long been in reality, though in name only *maire du palais*, it was from the hands of the missionary primate alone that he would accept his consecration.   It would be difficult and bewildering to give the details of all S. Boniface's work.   Besides the Bavarian bishoprics, he founded four other very important ones at Würzburg, Eichstadt, Bamberg, and Erfurt;

also the great monastery of Fulda in the wild forest of Buchenau, which, grounded on the same Benedictine rule, became for Germany what Monte Cassino was for Italy. And we must remember that all these were not only centres for Catholic instruction, but actually centres of civilisation. Without their softening and regulating influence, the greatest rulers, the bravest generals might have struggled in vain to establish discipline and order amongst the lawless mass of barbarian tribes. For it was not merely the *name* of conversion, the nominal acceptance of Christianity, that satisfied this true evangelist. Holy baptism, in his teaching, was but the gate of entrance to the new life. "Sin," he said, when addressing, in the simplest language, some of the recently baptized, "must be renounced in deed as well as in intent." "You must love God with all your heart, with all your soul, and with all your strength, and your neighbour as yourself." "Fear none but God, but fear Him always."

Some years before the end of his labours, S. Boniface was able to reckon that he had made a hundred thousand converts: it was enough to have filled with pride a spirit less disciplined, less self-forgetful, less ready to look upon himself as but an instrument in God's hands. And his watchfulness over his flock was untiring. Nothing we read of him is more admirable than his constant calling to mind how easy it is for converts to fall away, how unwearied must be each pastor's labours, how incessant his prayers, if the true *life* of the Church is to be maintained.

It would have seemed fitting and gracious that this long

career of eager and untiring service should have known some space of repose before its end. Already, when but a little past fifty, Boniface writes of himself as if his years and labours were telling on him. In a letter to a dear friend in England, the Abbess Eadburga, when asking her to send him copies of certain parts of the Scriptures, he begs that they may be written plainly, "because of my old eyes." *
Strong and indefatigable as he had been, the year 753 must have found him infirm and wearied, for he was now seventy-three. And this year we find him, with King Pepin's consent, appointing his valued friend and helper Lull or Lullius, an English monk at Malmesbury, who had come over to him, as his successor in the bishopric of Mainz, and a letter is still preserved in which, writing as a father might do who knows his days are numbered, he prays Fulrad, the royal chaplain, to use his influence in favour of his immediate clergy : " Priests appointed in various places, monks teaching little children, old men who have laboured long with me. . . . For all these I am full of anxiety, lest at my death they be scattered . . . and lest the people on the heathen borders should fall away from the love of Christ . . . and my clergy in those border lands suffer much. Bread they can obtain, but not clothes . . . let me know if my request can be granted, that I may have some assurance for their future."

It was granted, and then having set his house in order to

---

* In the same letter he asks for a copy of the Epistles of S. Peter " writ in letters of gold, that the Holy Scriptures may be reverenced and honoured before the eyes of the pagans."

the best of his ability, the old Christian soldier set off on his last campaign. He must strike another blow for Friesland before he died. With a few chosen companions, among them Gregory of Trèves, now a man of forty-six, luggage, of which the principal contents were three of his best loved books, an altar-cloth, and a shroud, he journeyed northwards, till he reached the east of Friesland, where he began his missionary work in the usual way. And at first all was promising. Some already Christian tribes received the party gladly, and new converts came forward to receive baptism in sufficient numbers for a special day to be appointed for a large confirmation. It was to take place on a summer's day, June 5, on the banks of a river—the river Burde, near the town of Dockum, where the missionaries had pitched their tents. It was the eve of Whitsunday.

That morning saw a different sight from the solemn service so joyfully hoped for. A horde of armed savages, enraged by the bishop's success among their countryfolk, and greedy for the treasure which they imagined he and his friends possessed, rushed down upon the band of devoted men. The aged saint came forward, standing at the door of his tent, and calmly commanded that no resistance should be made, no useless blood shed by the Christians, whose number was a mere handful compared with their enemies.

"Let us not return evil for evil," he said; "the long expected day has come. Strengthen yourselves in the Lord ... put all your trust in Him." He was obeyed, and the savages, more merciful than the persecutors of the civilised

Roman days, killed their defenceless victims quickly.   S. Boniface stretched himself on the ground, laying his venerable head on one of his precious books, the cover and leaves of which—it was the " De bono mortis " of S. Austin —were stained with his blood.   Ages afterwards it was still to be seen at his own monastery at Fulda, where his remains, and those of one of his martyred companions, were afterwards buried.   His body, it is said, was wrapped in the shroud he had brought with him.   For the savages, disappointed in the booty they had expected to find, turned murderously on each other, and the wild onslaught was soon at an end, so that the trembling Christians of the country were able to gather reverently together all that was left of the martyred saints, and to succour the few, among them Gregory, who had escaped with life, unwillingly enough we may be sure.

S. Boniface, or Winfride, as Englishmen cannot but love to call him, left few writings, for, though a man of culture and learning, his time, as we have seen, was incessantly occupied in active missionary work.   But his letters are both important and interesting, throwing considerable light on his day, full of wisdom and good sense as well as of holy zeal, genuine humility, and gentleness.   But he was also firm and strong, in word as well as in deed, fearless in reproof, even of the great ones of the earth.   Fifteen of his sermons are also extant.   They are simple in style, practical, and impressive.

The ninth century, as you have read in your histories of England, was one of terrible troubles in this country, owing to the repeated Danish invasions. A great part of the efforts that had been made by wise and holy men to spread religion and knowledge seemed to be undone. The monasteries, libraries, and schools throughout the country were destroyed; for long it must indeed have appeared as if our poor island were really fated to fall back, time after time, into heathen barbarism.

There are but few names that stand out brightly through the dreary years preceding the reign of the great and good Alfred, the heroic and saintly king who was truly the saviour of his unhappy land—among these few that of Swithin of Winchester has been deservedly remembered. And though there is no actual record of King Alfred's having been directly under his care and influence as a boy, it is almost certain that he was so, for S. Swithin was the tutor and guardian of Ethelwulf, the father of Alfred, and constantly with him in later life as his most valued counsellor and friend. King Ethelwulf died in 857, Swithin not till 862, so that the young Alfred must have been as much as thirteen at the time of the good priest's death, old enough certainly for a child of his thoughtful and intelligent nature to have profited by such companionship. Some writers believe that, on the first journey to Rome of the little Alfred, he was under the care and escort of S. Swithin.

The saint's early years were passed in happier times than his later ones. He was born about 801 A.D., during the reign of Egbert, while England was, comparatively speaking, at peace. Very young he was sent to the monastery of Winchester, there to be educated for the priesthood, into which he was ordained when between twenty and thirty. His character was singularly holy. He was unselfish and unambitious, in no way elated by his great influence over his pupil Ethelwulf, yet never afraid of standing out bravely and firmly, in his direction of this well-meaning but weak sovereign.

One of the first acts of Ethelwulf's reign was to make Swithin Bishop of Winchester. This was in the year 836. But even in this important position he remained humble and self-forgetful. Like the old Celtic monks, he loved to visit the different parts of his diocese walking and barefoot, clothed in the simplest monastic garments, and careful lest this very simplicity should have any look of affectation, he often travelled by night, that he might be unseen. But while self-denying to the extreme for himself, he was full of thought for others. He built not only several churches, but almshouses for the aged and helpless, and also bridges, of which very few existed in those days. He took a great interest in Church music, which he dearly loved, and was unwearied in his charity and care for the poor.

This good man went to his rest on July 2, A.D. 862. "As he lay a-dying," we are told, he begged his monks "not to bury him in the church, but in a humble place where the feet of passengers might tread and the rain of heaven fall upon him." For his heart was full of love for his kind. His wish was carried out. But more than a hundred years afterwards, a Bishop of Winchester, named Ethelwold, transferred the saintly bones to a rich shrine within the cathedral church, and it is on the day this

"translation" took place, July 15, that we commemorate
him. A century later they were again removed to a tomb
in the church, which still exists, and there they yet lie
" under a broad stone east of the choir in the presbytery."
It is noteworthy that the shrine of this holy and humble-
minded man, as indifferent to fame or honour for himself
in death as he had been in life, should be one of the very
few undoubtedly genuine tombs of the early saints still
existing for Christian veneration.

The old saying, which you have all heard, of the weather
on S. Swithin's day being a prophecy of what we shall have
for forty days to come, has never been satisfactorily explained. There is probably some truth in it, in so far as
that just about that time there is often a change from wet
to fair or fair to wet weather. But no one can tell what
gave rise to it originally. I cannot help thinking that the
feeling he expressed about liking that the rain should
fall on his grave may have drawn attention to the state of
the weather at the time of S. Swithin's first burial, for all
through the thousand years and more since he said them
his simple words have never been forgotten.

Richard II., with his three protectors, S. John the Baptist, S. Edmund, and S. Edward the Confessor. (*From an ancient diptych now at Wilton.*)

CHAPTER XI

S. Edmund the Martyr, November 20, A.D. 870.—S. Edward the Martyr, March 18, A.D. 978, translated June 20, A.D. 980.—S. Dunstan, May 19, A.D. 988.

THE story of Edmund, the young martyr king, is in great part historical, though with this is mingled, as is almost always the case, a good many details which strictly speaking must be called "legendary." But all that is of real interest regarding him we are justified in believing to be true; it would be carrying caution too far to do otherwise. For all writers agree in their descriptions of his beautiful character, his straightforward manliness and bravery, his unusual thoughtfulness for others and forgetfulness of self; his love of justice, his practice of mercy; all springing from and centering in his devotion to the service of God. In reading about him it is impossible to doubt that from his earliest years he had drunk deeply at the source of all true goodness, the inexhaustible fountain of "the grace of our Lord Jesus Christ."

Edmund was only fourteen when he was chosen king of the East Anglians. The crown did not become his by direct inheritance, for though of royal descent, as his father belonged to an English-Saxon kingly family, Edmund was not nearly related to his predecessor, Offa, who, wishing to end his days in peaceful devotion, retired to Rome in 855, appointing his young kinsman to be his successor. King Offa must have had great discernment to see in the boy the promise of the noble qualities Edmund showed as ruler; a better choice could not have been made. Edmund was crowned by Humbert, Bishop of Elman, or Helmham, at Sudbury on the Stour, on Christmas Day; a beautiful day for the reign of a true king to begin. While he was still very young, writes the monk Asser or Asserius,* " he already showed forth in his countenance what was afterwards manifested by the Divine will, for the boy with his whole powers trod the path of virtue, to end as the Divine Goodness foreknew, in martyrdom."

For fourteen years he reigned, a father to his people. His kingdom was tributary to that of Wessex, for since the year 802, when the whole of England was united under Egbert, those of the provinces of the former Heptarchy still existing under separate names had to acknowledge the King of Wessex as their head. Before Edmund's time there had been bitter war between East Anglia and Mercia, in which the churches and monasteries had been terribly destroyed. It was one of the first cares of the young King to restore them. He also regulated and amended the laws, and personally inquired into the concerns of his people, discouraging flattery or falsity of any kind, earnestly striving after " a

---

* Asser or Asserius, a monk of great learning in the reign of King Alfred, by whom he was much esteemed. He wrote the life of Alfred, which is really a history of the times.

right judgment in all things." He was rewarded by the
devoted love of his people and the friendship and respect
of his contemporaries. During his reign East Anglia was at
peace with the rest of England. And among all his many
duties Edmund found time for study. He is said to have
learnt by heart the whole of the Psalter, so that he might
never be without it. The habit of committing valuable
knowledge to memory was much more practised in those
days of scarce and cumbersome books than now, when we
can buy a perfect edition of both the New and Old Testaments for a few pence; and in some ways it is to be
feared we have lost by the change. What can be so easily
obtained is not always valued as it should be.

These happy years ended sadly. In 870 there came a
fierce Danish invasion headed by two brothers, Hincmar
and Hubba. There is a legend, but almost certainly *only*
a legend, that they bore special ill-will to the king from
a false belief that he had treacherously slain their father,
Ragnar Logbrod. But that they were under this impression is disproved by the fact that they had actually already
spent some months as peaceable settlers under Edmund in
East Anglia, when their fierce restlessness made them set
out northwards on a tour of pillage and massacre through
Northumbria and Mercia, returning by the fen country to
Suffolk. There, in the very kingdom where they had been
hospitably received, mad with carnage, furious against
Christianity and its teachings of peace and love, they met
King Edmund and his army at Thetford. The battle,
though fierce, was not decisive, but Edmund, realising that

N

his little force could not resist the fast increasing Danish hordes, and unwilling to shed uselessly not only the blood of his own people but that of the very pagans who were his foes, disbanded his troops, and with a few followers calmly awaited the renewed onslaught in his castle of Framlingham. There overtures of safety for himself were made, provided he would abandon his people and abjure his faith. On his refusal to do either he was taken prisoner and, loaded with chains, carried before the barbarian general in his tent. Again the Danes tried to tempt him by promises and threats. "We can kill you," they howled.

"I can die," he quietly replied.

And he did die, though not till after tortures as cruel as even his holy courage could endure. Beaten and scourged, his mangled body, like that of the Italian Sebastian, was made a mark for the arrows of his tormentors, till at last their ferocious rage was satisfied, and they ended his sufferings by beheading him. To the end his voice was heard in prayer and praise. Bishop Humbert, who had remained King Edmund's spiritual director since his coronation, shared his martyrdom. The body of the saint was carried away by his Christian subjects and secretly buried; his head, flung by the heathen into a thicket in the forest, was discovered many months afterwards, and laid in its place in the humble grave. Eventually the remains of S. Edmund found a resting-place at Bedricsworth in Suffolk, where they were finally buried in the eleventh century. A monastery already existing at Bedricsworth became the great abbey of Bury S. Edmunds, so called in remembrance of the martyred king, though the word "Bury" has nothing to do with his being interred there; it is only another form of "burgh" or "borough."

No shrine in England has been more visited and reverenced than that of S. Edmund; for several centuries the kings of England made a practice of retiring there to pray for protection and blessing. Indeed, the impression left by the life and death of the young King shows how great and lasting can be the *personal* influence of a noble and holy character.

On the 20th of June we commemorate the "Translation" of S. Edward, king and martyr. Two years before this date, on the 18th of March, 978, this young sovereign was treacherously murdered. He was only seventeen years old. His history is doubtless well known to you; I think all English children have listened to it with sympathy and indignation. How the sweet-natured, generous lad, whose life under the wise guidance of Dunstan seemed so full of high promise, in the very act of knightly courtesy was stabbed from behind by the orders of the stepmother, wickedly jealous for her own son, whom poor Edward had always treated with the greatest kindness and affection. But secular history has little time to spare for those prematurely ended lives, which leave not much visible trace after them, though tradition has handed down to us a bright record of the boy-king's character. He was holy and devout in spirit, modest, unselfish, and charitable, one of God's own children; "early ripe," we must believe, for a better world than this, where true goodness has so often in one form or another to suffer martyrdom.

A great figure now comes forward in the roll-call of our saints. A great man, and like most such, at one time and in many ways a sorely misjudged one. Dunstan, Archbishop of Canterbury, statesman, reformer, scholar, artist, friend and director of seven sovereigns, more than all, saint and man of God, stands out conspicuously indeed. His remarkable character, his eventful life, deserve much study and thoughtful consideration. The little I am here able to tell you of him I can only hope may lead you to read and inquire further for yourselves.

His story has been written by many, but unfortunately nothing of his own remains; no writings of any kind, not even a letter. It would be impossible here to mention all the sources from which our knowledge of him, knowledge immensely increased and corrected of late years, is derived. And with the real facts concerning him is mixed up a quite astonishing amount of legend and exaggeration, not altogether to be wondered at, as you will understand when you hear something of his character and the curious, half poetic, half fantastic strain of extraordinarily vivid imagination, united in him to the most practical qualities.

The earliest biography of S. Dunstan is in some ways the most interesting, though in itself of no literary merit whatever. But it was written almost immediately after his death, and is the work of an unknown priest, who mentions himself only as "B.," and a great part of it, the author says, he had heard from the archbishop's own lips, when he sat of an evening instructing the boy pupils whom even in his old age he gathered about him in his home at Canterbury. Of these pupils the priest "B." was one.

Dunstan was born about the year 922. His parents were related to the royal family, and were people of culture and refinement as well as of sincere religious principle. His home was in a romantic neighbourhood, near Glastonbury, in the river-formed "island of Avilion," as it is called in poetry, the "Avalon" of the Romans. Legends innumerable cluster round this spot, the site, according to some, of the first Christian church in Britain—"a frail and humble erection, made of the branches of the forest trees and the wattled reeds of the marsh," by S. Joseph of Arimathea and his missionary band, the envoys of S. Philip to the heathen land across the sea. A century later, so runs the story, a second mission from Rome found the forest sanctuary still existing, and whether or not there is any truth in these very early traditions, it is certain that they were sufficiently credited to invest the spot with a holy repute. In Dunstan's childhood a party of Irish pilgrims settled at Glastonbury, hallowed to them by yet another legend, according to which their own S. Patrick had died and been buried there. A church of some kind was certainly existing early in the tenth century, around which lived in their own houses the clergy both married and unmarried, of whom the Irish priests were in every way the most learned and distinguished. To help out their scanty means these strangers received as pupils the sons of the well-to-do neighbouring families. And hither, to Glastonbury, Heorstan and Kynedritha, the parents of

Dunstan, brought their son, a little boy of nine, to receive instruction in classical learning, in writing, illuminating, carving, and music ; above all, in religion and theology. For from his birth they had in their hearts dedicated the child to the priesthood.

All accounts agree in describing him as a clever, precocious, highly strung, and delicate boy. The romantic associations of Glastonbury no doubt thrilled his imagination, and a too eager desire for knowledge forced his faculties still further. We are not surprised to hear of strange dreams and poetic visions, of sleep-walking, and finally of a severe and well-nigh fatal attack of fever. This illness is sometimes thought to have been in part the result of the rough and cruel treatment he received from companions of his own age at the court of King Athelstan, when on a visit there under the care of his kinsman Athelm, the Archbishop of Canterbury. The boy genius gained great favour with the grown-up people at the palace, especially with the ladies, who were delighted with his cleverness at designing for their embroidery, and the King himself took pleasure in his playing on the harp. But his accomplishments aroused the jealousy of the other young men and boys about the court; he was accused of practising magic, thrown into a muddy pond, where he was nearly drowned, and priest "B." tells a piteous tale of how the boy crept out to the edge and sat there shivering, while some sympathising dogs from a neighbouring farm did their best to comfort him, "showing me," his biographer relates, in Dunstan's own words, "more true kindness than human beings by the friendly wagging of their tails."

Banished for the time from court, not sorry, one would think, that it was so, Dunstan now went to the house of another kinsman, Alphege, Bishop of Winchester, who received him kindly. The bishop's whole influence was directed towards making Dunstan a monk; he saw that the young man was unusually gifted, and he wished to enlist him as an ally in the great cause of the reform of both the monastic orders and the priesthood, which he himself had much at heart. But for some time Dunstan resisted; he did not feel sure of his own vocation for the religious life. Another serious illness, however, seems to have changed his views, and on his recovery he presented himself for ordination, and at the same time accepted the monastic vows according to the rule of S. Benedict. It seems probable that it was at this crisis in his career, though some place it later, that Dunstan spent some time at the French Benedictine monastery of Fleury, where he must have had ample opportunity of studying and practising the rule in its entirety. His enthusiasm was thoroughly aroused. On his return to England he sought his old home at Glastonbury; there he made a little cell, five feet long by two and a half wide, and just high enough for him to stand .in upright, where he ensconced himself with full intention of passing his life as a hermit. He was still a very young man, delicate in health, almost morbidly imaginative, and tremendously in earnest; it was not to be wondered at that he again became a dreamer of dreams and "see-er" of strange visions, for his natural energy was repressed by the endeavour after a life for which he was not fitted, and the great reputation of sanctity which began to make his advice sought from far and near must have added to his own mistaken belief in this special vocation.

A vocation he undoubtedly had, and a work to do which no one else could have done as well. But it was not in the hermit's cell that his life was to be spent. He must have had a great deal of common sense as well as enthusiasm, for after a time we read of his occasionally leaving his corner of the abbey to visit congenial friends, from one of whom in particular, an aged lady named Ethelfleda, he accepted good advice. Her affection for him was almost like that of a mother, and continued till her death. In her last days he was of much comfort to her gentle and holy spirit, and a touching story is told of a beautiful vision vouchsafed both to her and himself of the "mystic dove," the blessed "comforter," promised to all Christ's children.

Ethelfleda seems to have foreseen and prepared the mind of Dunstan for a probably increased and wider sphere of work. And shortly after her death came a summons to the court of Edmund—Edmund the magnificent, who had now succeeded his brother Athelstan—which the monk obeyed. But his first connection with the king did not prosper. In some way he offended Edmund, and the king seems to have been glad to dismiss him from court by making him superior of the monastery of Glastonbury, which post just then became vacant. Now followed for Dunstan a period of great and congenial activity. His means were much increased by the property of Ethelfleda, which she had left to him, and he devoted everything he possessed to the restoration, or rather reconstruction, of his abbey. It was a noble piece of work, work designed and carried out by men who prayed as they laboured—who worked for love and devotion—the result was such as no paid and hireling toil and skill could ever achieve. Nor was the new abbot's attention confined to this part of his charge. He introduced the Benedictine rule in its greatest purity into his monastery, and in this his monks seconded him, for even before his reform Glastonbury was in a much better state than the other religious houses of England. And now it became a model for all to follow, a nursery also for training pupils to carry on the work elsewhere. Dunstan has been blamed by some for his strong objection to the marriage of the clergy. But whatever may be the opinions of other wise men at other times on this question, there is no doubt that he was then in the right. The English priesthood was at a low ebb; it was often looked upon as a mere provision for the sons of the better classes, and as a kind of *family profession*, to be embraced as a matter of course, with no thought of individual fitness or "vocation." So terrible a danger called for stern measures. Yet Dunstan behaved with humanity and consideration to the *already* married clergy and their families.

On the birth of Prince Edgar, in 944, Dunstan, even now only twenty-two years old, was recalled to court, King

Edmund having apparently outgrown his annoyance, and impressed doubtless by the unmistakable talent and strength of his young kinsman. Now begins what may be called Dunstan's public life. In those days it was constantly the case that a great churchman was chosen to take an important part in statesmanship, it was in fact a necessity that it should be so, and happy was that kingdom where, to the wisdom, learning, and culture of which the leading ecclesiastics were almost the only possessors, they added the disinterestedness of a truly public spirit and fervent Catholic unselfishness. Odo, Archbishop of Canterbury, and Thorketal, Chancellor of England, were Dunstan's colleagues as councillors of the King, and though he became speedily the ruling spirit, all three worked together wisely and successfully. There was much to do, for the repeated Danish invasions had unsettled and demoralised the country. But by vigorous measures further mischief was checked, and Danes already in the country were encouraged to mingle and intermarry with the Saxons, so as gradually to become part and parcel of the nation. And as these most pressing difficulties were by degrees disposed of, Dunstan turned his attention to the state of the Church and the monasteries, sorely in need of reform. This reform, unflinchingly persevered in through incessant difficulties and amidst innumerable outside cares of state, was the real life-work of S. Dunstan.

In 946 Edmund died, murdered at one of his own state banquets by an outlaw named Leof. He was succeeded by his brother Edred, the Witan or great national council passing over the late king's sons on account of their extreme youth. The perfect confidence and friendship existing between Dunstan and the thoughtful and serious-minded young king must have made the few years of his reign about the happiest of the great churchman's public life. The retirement of the good old chancellor Thorketal left his post open, and by the king's wish Dunstan accepted it. Every good measure which he proposed was eagerly seconded by Edred; together they and Odo the archbishop planned and laboured for the welfare of the kingdom, themselves setting the useful example of godliness and unselfishness in high places, so that, as we are told by the old chronicler, in Edred's reign "the palace became a school of virtue."

But Edred was another of the "early ripe." He had always been fragile in health, and in 955 he died. The reign of his nephew, the frivolous and childish Edwy, brings us to that part of the history of S. Dunstan in which he has been so unfairly judged. It would be wearisome to go into the details of the contradictory accounts of Edwy's reign, and of Dunstan's conduct to the young king. It is one of those pages of history of which the *facts* have been disregarded in order to serve prejudice and party spirit, and it has only been of late years that the truth has been arrived at. There is no doubt that Edwy was a giddy and pleasure-loving youth, very open also to flattery. Perhaps his uncle's court was too grave and dull for him and his young brother Edgar, and it is quite possible that Edred had made the mistake of

bringing them up too severely, so that when at sixteen
Edwy succeeded to the throne, his first and principal
thought was that he would now be free to amuse himself.
A worldly-minded and ambitious woman, a cousin of his
own, with her lively and frivolous daughter Elgiva, became
his greatest friends, and when Edwy was only seventeen
he was drawn into a marriage with this girl. Such a marriage was sorely against the wishes of both Dunstan and
Odo the archbishop, as their great desire was to influence
Edwy for good. And indeed it was not a properly lawful
alliance, as in those days cousins were not allowed to
marry. At the great state banquet in honour of his coronation, Edwy, getting tired of the long formal feast, left
the table and his guests in a rude and impertiment way,
and went off to laugh and chatter with these two ladies.
Terrified at what might be the consequences of such
behaviour, Dunstan and Odo forced the foolish boy to
return to the banquet, even, it is said, pulling him along
by the arms. This offence was never forgiven by Edwy
and still less by Elgiva, and not long after both the archbishop and the abbot were banished from court by her
influence. Dunstan withdrew to Glastonbury. But not
content with what she had done, Elgiva sent down troops
to plunder the monastery, insulting the abbot at the same
time by making the king ask for an account of all the
money that had passed through his hands as chancellor.
Dunstan treated this demand with dignified silence, and
soon after set sail for Flanders, by this step evading the
further persecution, not improbably to end in death, which

his enemies were preparing for him. A wild time followed in England. Edwy deprived the monasteries of all their possessions, scattered the monks, and even ill-treated his own mother because she remonstrated. It must have been bitter news for Dunstan in his banishment to hear of this undoing of his life-work. At last the foolish young king was startled into his senses by a revolt in Mercia headed by his brother Edgar, and in a battle which took place he was severely beaten. He seems at last to have recognised his folly, and when Dunstan, summoned by Edgar, returned to mediate between the brothers, Edwy submitted to his advice. Elgiva and her mother were banished from his court about the time of the rebellion. It is not certain what became of them, but a story still to be found in some histories, of Dunstan's cruelty to the revengeful beauty, is quite unfounded, for at the time of her falling out of favour with the king he was absent in Flanders.

The kingdom was divided between the brothers, but Edwy only lived one year after this, dying in 959. His story is a sad and pitiable one, for he might have been a useful and respected sovereign. On his death the Witan, or great national council, elected Edgar as his successor, and decrees were passed in favour of the restoration of the monasteries, which had so sorely suffered. For Edgar, though far from a good man, was wise enough to recognise in the Benedictines his best friends, and to follow the counsels of their great head in everything concerning the nation. In 962 Dunstan was made Archbishop of Canterbury, a dignity which he had little desired, but which he came to see that he must accept, if his influence was to continue.   One story relates that this conviction was impressed upon him in a dream. He made a journey to Rome, in order to have his appointment confirmed by the Pope, or in other words to receive the "pallium," or archiepiscopal mantle.   The sixteen years of Edgar's reign were prosperous ones for England, though there can be no doubt that not the king but his great counsellor was to be thanked for this.   The country was entirely at peace during this time, the laws were revised and improved, many smaller statutes being passed, which we may be sure were for the good of the English people, though some seem curiously trifling. Busied incessantly as he was with the affairs of government, Dunstan was obliged to leave church concerns a good deal in the hands of the two bishops of Worcester and Winchester, Oswald and Ethelwold, who being quite of accord with him, thoroughly carried out his wishes, especially with regard to the reform and extension of the monasteries.   You must remember what the monasteries really meant in those days, in order to understand the importance of this.   They were not only the centres of religious life and learning—they represented all the *education* of the time; without them small lasting improvement could have been made in any way.   For after all, our English forefathers before the Norman Conquest were but a generation or two removed from barbarism, and the constant coming in among them of the Danish tribes, which went on for so long, made the struggle between civilisation and savagery still harder. Dunstan was never found wanting in straightforward courage, though this at one time, as you have seen, had cost him dear. Wrong-doing he rebuked in both the king and his courtiers; he once punished Edgar, who richly deserved it, by inflicting a penance which lasted for seven years.

Edgar died in July 975. His death was the signal for the outburst of troubles, greatly caused by his own sin. You remember the story of the young King Edward so foully murdered by his stepmother? This woman, Elfrida by name, was Edgar's second wife, and the way in which he married her was very wicked, for she had a husband living when the king was first attracted by her beauty, and there is little doubt that Edgar murdered him so that Elfrida might be free. She was thoroughly bad. Her great ambition was that her own son Ethelred, though only a boy of seven, should ascend the throne, and we have seen that in the end she succeeded, though her success brought her little happiness. But before making up her mind to murder her stepson, she tried other means, which but for Dunstan would have put Ethelred in his brother's place. At this time, and for many years before and after, there were almost constant disputes between what are called the "secular clergy," in other words priests, but not monks, and the monks, many of whom were also priests. The secular clergy were very lax and self-indulgent in many cases, looking upon their sacred calling as a mere profession or means of livelihood. The strict discipline and devoted self-denial of the Benedictines shamed and annoyed the secular priests, and there was always a strong party among them ready to do the monks an ill turn. With this party the Queen allied herself, promising the priests power and advantages of every kind should her son—in reality herself—obtain the sovereignty. A great council was held, in which the claims of the brothers were discussed; the eloquence and reasonableness of the archbishop gained the day for Edward, and he was crowned on the spot. But the secular clergy were not yet satisfied to submit. Other councils were held, in which questions of church discipline and rule were intermingled with the dispute as to the succession. Dunstan, true to his colours, never wavered on any point as to which he had made up his mind, and at the last of these councils his firmness made a still greater impression on his opponents by the help of a curious accident, which was looked upon as supernatural. The beams of the flooring gave way, and every one present was more or less injured, save only the archbishop and his supporters, whose part of the room remained solid. But the cause of the young king was after all only gained in appearance, for the very next year witnessed his murder. A foul deed: "To the Angle race," says the old chronicler, "was no worse thing done than this since they first sought Britain."

With the death of Edward, Dunstan's public life came virtually to an end. He could not refuse to crown the boy Ethelred as the rightful successor, nor was the child himself in any way responsible for his brother's murder. The wretched Elfrida, overcome with remorse, had withdrawn to a nunnery, and it is said that before her death Dunstan, satisfied of her repentance, gave her absolution. But it was a bad beginning for a new reign, and we read in history that every gloomy forecast was fulfilled. Fresh incursions of the Danes brought back the old horrors of massacre and pillage; there was no longer a strong and faithful steersman at the helm, and the king was one of these weak and vacillating monarchs who seem almost a greater curse to their people than are even unscrupulous tyrants.

And Dunstan was now old; he had always been physically delicate, and he had worked "with the strength of ten." It was but fitting that his last years should be spent in the retirement of devotion and spiritual contemplation, which, had he been a less conscientious man, he would never have quitted. And even now he was active. His preaching attracted hearers from all parts of the country, and it was to these last years of his life that the Church is indebted for the canons and regulations which are both edifying in themselves and interesting to historians and antiquaries.

We have a touching account of his last days. He preached on the festival of the Ascension, May 17, 988, with even more than his usual earnestness, his subject being the Incarnation and the Atonement. Then after the consecration of the Eucharist a sort of fervour of holy zeal came over him, and he spoke yet again, reminding his people of our Lord's blessed promise, fulfilled on the Day of Pentecost, praying earnestly that His Spirit might de-

scend on each one of them. And as he prayed his face
" seemed to shine and dart forth rays of light."

He died two days later ; on a Sunday morning early, as the
sun was rising, his brave and faithful spirit entered into rest.

He was buried in his own cathedral of Canterbury, in a
spot he had himself chosen. There, five hundred and ten
years later, his remains were identified, resting where they
had been laid under his monument on the south side of
the high altar—at peace in death, though his life had been
one of almost incessant anxiety and struggle.

Several traits told of S. Dunstan show that he loved
children. He liked to have his boy pupils about him even
in his last days, and it is said that in earlier life he knew
personally every little scholar in the monastery school at
Glastonbury. There is a story too of his having a dream
when away from the abbey, in which he saw one of these
children borne upwards in the arms of angels. Soon after
a messenger coming over to him with tidings, the abbot
asked if all at Glastonbury were well.

" All," replied the monk who had been sent.

" What, *all?*" repeated S. Dunstan.

" Yes, all but one little fellow who has died," was the
reply.

"God rest his happy spirit ; I saw him carried heavenwards," the abbot replied.

His own spirit seems indeed to have been often more in
heaven than on earth. In one of his dreams or visions he
learned a beautiful "antiphon," which he wrote out when
he awoke and taught his choristers to sing.

CHAPTER XII.

S. Alphege, April 19, A.D. 1012.—S. Edward the Confessor, died January 5, A.D. 1066, translated October 13, A.D. 1163.—S. Hugh, November 17, A.D. 1200.—S. Richard, April 3, A.D. 1253.— O Sapientia, December 16, Holy Name of Jesus, August 7, early in the fifteenth century.

ALPHEGE OF CANTERBURY, archbishop and martyr. The last martyr in the roll of our saints, and one whose claim to the holy title was at one time disputed. But when you have heard his history, you will, I am certain, agree with the judgment of S. Anselm, that he who dies "for righteousness and charity" is indeed a Christian martyr.

Alphege, or Elphege, as his name is sometimes spelt, was the child of rich and noble parents. They were good people, too; they brought him up carefully, and gave him the best education to be had in those days. But, though they were Christians, their faith—that, at least, of his mother—was not firm enough to rejoice in the boy's decision, while still very young, to renounce the world and devote himself to the religious life, for we read that she shed bitter tears when she heard it, and used many entreaties to dissuade him. But the young man, or boy, as he probably was at that time, stood firm.

He lived for several years in the monastery * of Derherste, in Gloucestershire. From there he went to Bath, where, according to some accounts, he spent some years as a hermit, becoming renowned for his wisdom and good counsel. It is certain that he became later abbot of the monastery at Bath, and it is there we find him when, in 984, at the age of thirty, he was chosen by S. Dunstan to be Bishop of Winchester. As a monk S. Alphege's whole endeavours had been directed to the reform and improvement of his community, into which had crept many abuses and much want of discipline. We read that "he used to say that it would have been much better for a man to have stayed in the world than to be an imperfect monk, and that to wear the habit of a saint without having the spirit was a perpetual lie, and an hypocrisy which insults but can never impose upon Almighty God." He carried this same spirit into his new office, being a model of consistency and self-denial, united to what in such characters is often more rare —infinite gentleness and kindness to others. "He was no less remarkable for charity to his neighbours than for severity to himself." And in practical care for others, that

* "To avoid confusion I have used the words 'monastery' and 'convent' in their modern sense throughout. But in fact a 'convent' is nothing more than a Latin name for an association of *persons* who have come together to live for a common object. The monastery was the common dwelling-place, the convent the society of persons inhabiting it. This is shown in the formula used when a body of monks or nuns execute any corporate act, such as buying or selling land. 'The Prior and Convent of the Monastery of the Holy Trinity at Norwich,' 'The Abbess and Convent of the Monastery of S. Mary at Lacock.'"— *A Mediæval Monastery*, Rev. A. Jessopp.

active work for their material needs which is one part (though in common talk it is often spoken of as if it were the whole) of Christian "charity," the good bishop was eager and untiring. He gave so much to the poor himself, and pleaded for them so earnestly, that it is recorded that "during his time there were no beggars in the whole diocese of Winchester."

After twenty-two years of this holy and busy life came, in 1006, another call to Bishop Alphege. The archbishopric of Canterbury became vacant by the death of Alfric, and Alphege, though reluctantly, agreed to fill it. Stormy times and a stormy close to his useful life were before him. Already while only Bishop of Winchester he had done good service to his country by his mediation with the Norwegian, Olaf Tryggveson, whom he had induced to promise to King Ethelred never again to invade England; but in an invasion by the Danes in 1008 the part of the holy Alphege was changed. It was not again to be that of a peacemaker, but of a hero and a martyr.

As archbishop, as in his former less exalted positions, his consistent humility and fervent charity endeared him to the whole English Church. "He wept for the sins of all; and for the salvation of all he daily offered the life-giving Sacrifice." There was but one thing more he could do for his people, to give his own life; and when the time came he gladly gave it.

The new onslaught of the Danes began in 1008; a terrible time for England was the result of it. Ravaging, plundering, burning, massacring, on they came, till, in the year 1011, they laid siege to Canterbury itself, and after a valiant defence of twenty days, during which time the courage and spirits of all had been kept up by the Archbishop's holy words and ministrations, the invaders at last got into the city. Alphege, who while there was yet time to escape had refused to do so at the price of deserting his flock, hearing of the fearful slaughter which was accompanying the enemy's march through the streets, could not bear to remain quiet, but in spite of all remonstrances rushed out to try what he could do.

"Turn upon me rather than upon these innocent ones," he cried; "I have reproached you for your cruelties; I have fed, clothed, and ransomed your captives."

They did turn upon him; he was seized, beaten, kicked, and barbarously ill-used; then thrown into a dungeon where he lay for several months. But a pestilence breaking out among the Danish troops, they bethought them that it might be the vengeance of Heaven for their behaviour to one whom even they, savage and heathen as they were, knew to be holy. He was released, and entreated to help them. Nor did they ask in vain. His prayers and ministrations were ready, and by degrees the plague disappeared. Some sense of gratitude seems to have touched even these brutal hearts. At a council which they held, it was proposed that he should be set at liberty— it is said that Thorkell, one of their leaders, did his best to save him; but in the end they yielded to greed and covetousness, and demanded for him a ransom of three thousand pounds of silver. This he refused to levy, knowing that the lands of the Church in these troubled times were already sorely over-taxed, and saying that, even if the money could be got together, he would not allow to be spent on him that which he called "the patrimony of the poor."

So they carried him back to prison, till on Easter Sunday, which that year, 1012, fell on the 13th of April, they had him out again, and renewed their demands, alternating them with threats and menaces of torture and death. Again, and with increased firmness, he refused, adding that the only gold he could give them was that of the true wisdom of the living God. Then, their patience exhausted, they fell upon him. Like the first Christian martyr, he, the last of our English list, was stoned; like him, too, S. Alphege "prayed our Lord to forgive" these, his cruel foes. And dying, though not yet released from his agony, he raised himself a little from his couch of stones and murmured these last words recorded of him: "O good Shepherd! O incomparable Shepherd! Look with compassion on the children of Thy Church, which I, dying, recommend to Thee." And the sight of his slow torture touched one heart, that of a Dane whom the saint had but recently baptized. With his battle-axe he "clave S. Alphege's head, so that he sank down, and his holy blood fell on the earth and his holy soul he sent forth to God's kingdom."

He was buried first at S. Paul's, and eleven years afterwards translated to his own cathedral at Canterbury, on which occasion King Canute, the Danish sovereign of

England, but himself by that time a Christian, showed reverent honour to the saint's remains.

Just thirty years after the martyrdom of S. Alphege, the throne of England, which since the death of Ethelred in 1016 had been filled by Danish usurpers, was again ascended by a Saxon prince, Edward the Confessor. The story of his life and that of his reign are, of course, a part of English history. You have all read of his early exile from his own country, in consequence of the Danish successes; how he was brought up at the home of his beautiful mother, Emma, "the flower and pearl of Normandy," remaining there even when her marriage with Canute had made the Danish king his stepfather; and how, therefore, when in the end he was recalled to England, he was more like a foreigner than a native prince. But much of the beauty and real goodness of King Edward's character is touched upon but lightly in secular history, or passed over altogether; and when he is spoken of as "a saint," it is often in a tone of disparagement, as if holiness of a high order were by no means a desirable thing for a ruler. And it is true that as a king, Edward made some grave mistakes; but for these, not his *saintly* qualities, but rather a certain amount of weakness and narrowness in his character, and above all his foreign education, are to be blamed. Too little is said of his earnest desire to do his very best for his people by making justice and mercy the rule and guide of his actions. "While he sat as a king on his throne," says the Abbot of Rievaulx, in his account of him, "he was still the father of orphans, and the judge [or protector] of widows. . . . For he esteemed all that he had as not his own, but as belonging to all." What higher praise could be given to any sovereign?

And after all, though no exalted place as a ruler has ever been accorded to the last (if we leave out Harold's brief sovereignty) of our Saxon kings, his mild sway succeeded in securing for England the blessing which, under more brilliant monarchs, many nations have yearned for in vain—that of peace. For, with the exception of a short war with the usurper Macbeth to restore the rightful king Malcolm Kanmore to the Scottish throne, and some fighting against the Welsh, the English nation was undisturbed throughout the four-and-twenty years of the Confessor's reign, though internally the disputes between the king and the powerful Earl Godwin—disputes caused in great part by Edward's injudicious partiality for foreigners—at one time threatened to involve the country in civil war.

King Edward's name has always been associated with an improved code of laws, both for the priesthood and for the laity, to which he is believed to have given great attention. It is probable that many of these laws were really framed on those of King Alfred, which during the Danish sovereignty had fallen out of use. There is no doubt that Edward was most zealous to reform and strengthen the Church, but he made the great mistake of filling all the important posts with foreigners—an evil in every way, as it lessened the affection of the people for their spiritual leaders, and also tended to increase the authority and influence of Rome over the English Church

He built and endowed many churches and monasteries, of which the noblest—Westminster Abbey—though added to and in part rebuilt, still remains as a monument of his religious zeal. We are told that he had a peculiar love and admiration for the two apostles, S. Peter and S. John. To the former of these he dedicated the grand abbey, and the consecration of the completed building, which took place on "Childemas," or Holy Innocents' Day, 1065, is touchingly connected with the end of the gentle king's life. For when the day to which he had looked forward during the fifteen years the abbey took to build at last came, Edward was too ill to assist at the ceremony. And before it was over he was dead. His closing hours were full of peace and Christian joy. "Seeing the queen," we read, "weeping abundantly, he said to her, 'Weep not, for I shall not die but live, and, departing from the land of the dying, I believe that I shall see the good things of the Lord in the land of the living.'" And so, "in the faith of Christ and with His sacraments, and in the hope of His promises, he departed from the world, an old man and full of days.

This was on January 5, 1066, the Eve of the Epiphany. He was buried in the church he had founded, and there his bones remain to this day.

Edward the Confessor was the first king who practised what was at one time believed to be a miraculous power of healing possessed by the sovereign. That his *prayers* were never wanting for any of his subjects, from the greatest to the humblest, who desired them, we may well be assured. He was blessed with a very sweet temper, but a story is told which for once brings him into sympathy with such of us as find it difficult to be calm and gentle under provocation. His one great amusement was hunting, and on a certain occasion, when a poor peasant had unluckily come in his way "by upsetting the standings by which the deer are driven into the toils," the king actually lost his patience so as to swear at him, exclaiming, "I will give you just such another turn if ever it comes in my way." That such a display of temper was most rare in him is probably the reason of its being recorded. For, says his biographer, Aelred of Rievaulx again, " a singular sweetness appeared in his countenance . . . his words had a certain dignity and hilarity . . . he would be now aweing, now soothing; at one time instructing, at another consoling." "He conducted himself," says another chronicler, William of Malmesbury, "so mildly that he would not injure by a word even the meanest person."

We revere his memory, not on the day he died, but on the anniversary of the translation, nearly a hundred years later, of his remains to a new tomb in the abbey, in the reign of Henry II., by S. Thomas (à Becket), then Archbishop of Canterbury.

Hugh of Avalon as he was by birth, Hugh of Lincoln as he has come to be called in the history of his adopted country, is a character of whom, as man, as priest, as saint, it is delightful and refreshing to read and to think. "The model bishop," as he has been called, he seems indeed to have been a model in everything.

" Utterly fearless ; of keen intellect ; of playful humour ;

S. Hugh presenting a votary (*from a picture in the Boisserée Gallery*).

an ascetic without sourness; devoted to spiritual things,
but a shrewd observer of secular things; a hater of evil, but
full of love to every form of suffering," it would be difficult
to find a flaw in this noble man.

His history is an interesting one, and we have it in full,
written by a monk of his own Carthusian order.

He was the youngest child of a noble family in Bur-
gundy; his home was Avalon, near Grenoble. His mother
died when he was only eight years old, and his widowed
father, already an elderly man, gave up his estates to his
older sons, and retired himself with little Hugh to a religious house in the neighbourhood. Here his one con-
solation and occupation was the training of the boy, whom
from the first he desired to consecrate to the special service
of God. The old man's hopes were not disappointed. He
died when Hugh was nineteen, having been cared for by him
as by the tenderest and deftest-handed of daughters, happy
in the certainty of his son's undoubted vocation—a vocation
so unmistakable that already at this early age Hugh was ordained and at his post as an earnest and eloquent preacher.

But when no longer tied by his father's need of him, the
young priest sought for a sterner life. He joined the
brotherhood of the Carthusians, in the monastery on the
Great Chartreuse, founded fully a century earlier by S.
Bruno of Cologne. The Carthusian order was, and still is,
one of the strictest monastic rules. In those days the
brothers were as much hermits as monks. Hugh lived in
a cell apart, clothed in the coarsest garments, eating no
more than was absolutely necessary, and that of the plainest,

spending such time as was not devoted to prayer and contemplation in study and in the transcribing of valuable manuscripts. Besides this, the young brother took upon himself the entire care of an aged and infirm monk. He could not have lived without some one weak and suffering to tend !

So passed ten years. Hugh was strong and vigorous, physically and mentally. But he was training for a wider sphere. There came from the king of England to that far-off, solitary monastery, the request for a " picked man," the best they had, to be prior of the religious house at Witham, in Gloucestershire, which Henry II., at that time in the fervour of repentance for his treatment of S. Thomas of Canterbury, desired to found afresh after the Carthusian rule ; and notwithstanding his reluctance to accept the office, Hugh's vow of obedience to the superiors of his order obliged him to do so. He left his beloved retreat among the " pine-clad heights of the Alps, towering up to perennial snow," for the unknown England, where the rest of his life was to be spent. A very short time was enough to show the wisdom of the choice—his manliness and vigour soon established excellent discipline among the brethren, while his geniality and unselfishness won their affection.

" To him that is faithful in little " comes often in God's providence the call to higher things. Five years at Witham saw the close of S. Hugh's work there. For in 1086 King Henry, struck with tardy remorse for his neglect of the see of Lincoln—which for some years had been kept vacant while he enjoyed its revenues—determined to take steps towards the election of a bishop. The choice fell on Prior

Hugh, greatly, it is said, to the king's delight, for he had learnt to know the Carthusian well and intimately during his rule at Witham, as Henry frequently hunted in that neighbourhood. And to know Hugh, even for the "wayward" Henry, was to love and respect him. The prior, as before, was sorely unwilling to leave his post and to accept greater responsibilities—a reluctance constantly to be met with, even in our own days, in the noblest, most conscientious men; he only yielded, finally, to the command of the prior of the Great Chartreuse, to whom a deputation was sent from England asking him to exert his authority in the matter. And thus, though a foreigner, Hugh of Avalon became Hugh of Lincoln, one of the best beloved and most revered of our English prelates.

He was about forty-six years old when he was consecrated bishop. He filled the see of Lincoln for fourteen years, years which saw the death of Henry, the short nine years' reign of Richard the Lion-hearted, and the accession of the crafty, mean-spirited, and treacherous John. But Hugh, courageous, single-minded, and devoted to the highest service, did his work and upheld the dignity of his office undisturbed by these changes. It is said that there is little to record of the history of the diocese during his rule, because all went well, thanks to his admirable administration. "He gathered round him men of prudence and wisdom to advise with him on affairs of the see; he appointed none to the care of his flock but clerks of a modest and quiet spirit, however highly others might be recommended by their interest or learning." And when duty called him to make a stand against injustice or oppression he was always ready.   More than once it fell to his share to rebuke the sovereign.   On one occasion, soon after his consecration, he excommunicated the chief forester on account of his tyrannical cruelty to some of the tenants. Henry's anger was great, but the bishop kept firm, and though he might have won favour again by consenting to give a stall of his cathedral to a nobleman whom the king wished to enrich, he would not do so, replying that church appointments were for priests, not for courtiers.   In the end Henry gave in, convinced of S. Hugh's right judgment. Richard Cœur-de-lion the brave prelate also opposed in wrong-doing, by preventing the levying of an unjust and oppressive tax in his diocese, and again he triumphed, gaining not only his cause but the increased friendship and respect of the king.   "If all the bishops in my realm were like that man," said Richard, "kings and princes would be powerless against them."

To strength and courage was united in S. Hugh a truly Christ-like, tender, and loving gentleness.   All that was weak or suffering was sure of his affection : he visited and ministered to the most painfully afflicted lepers, always saying that it was a privilege to do so.   The poor, the sick, and the dying were never forgotten by him ; he would put any other work aside if called to perform the last rites for the very humblest.   And so simple and self-denying was he that even as bishop he but little changed his way of living from the old Carthusian days.   He was often seen carrying stones with the masons employed in building the

transept and choir which he added to Lincoln Cathedral—
building done under his own loving direction, "exquisite
work, so pure and beautiful that it has scarce any to sur-
pass it in England." And patient and cheerful as he was,
we read of his thanking his clergy for "bearing with" his
temper, which he describes as often "hot and peppery!"

Little children and animals loved the good bishop, and
flocked around him without any shyness or fear. There is
a pretty story of a swan which he made a practice of feed-
ing, and which, though fierce to others, was perfectly tame
and gentle with him. Every spring S. Hugh used to retire
for a while to a lonely and quiet place for prayer and meditation, about the same time at which the swans went away
to the wider waters of the fens, returning again a little later
in the season to the palace moat. It was noticed that the
creatures came back for two or three years just before their
friend, so the country people about looked out for them as
a sign of S. Hugh's coming home, and for long after his
death there lingered a belief that some day he would return
again with the spring-time and the swans. We can fancy
how they watched for him—the simple-hearted peasants,
and the little children, for whom he had always a kind word
and smile. And how his own pet swan, who used to push
its long neck into the bishop's wide sleeves with little cries
of welcome, must have missed him!

For on a sad November day in the year 1200 they
brought him home in his coffin, to be buried, as he had
desired, in the cathedral he had learnt so to love and care
for. The story of his death is sweet and touching, and I

P

wish I had space to tell you about it in detail. He was sent on a mission—of peace, you may be sure—to Normandy by the king, and when it was completed he allowed himself the delight of a visit to the old monastery up among the mountains which he had quitted nearly twenty years before. He was getting old now, and he had never spared himself—perhaps the journey had been too much for him —he fell ill of what was then called "a quartan fever" in London, on his way home, and on the 17th of November he died, calmly and peacefully, with many tender words of comfort to his weeping friends, while the chorister boys of S. Paul's were singing the "Nunc dimittis," his failing voice joining in, till it faded into silence and "peace."

We have come now to the last saint, last in the sense of latest, of our English Calendar—Richard de Wyche, Bishop of Chichester; Richard of Chichester, as he is generally called. Of the character and history of this good and able man, "who by a life of unobtrusive devotion to his pastoral work earned for himself the title of saint," we possess fuller accounts than of many whose names are more famous, for there are two biographies of him written very shortly after his death.

He was born near Worcester in the year 1194, and early sent to a good school, being in all probability intended by his parents for the priesthood, or at least for some minor post among the many kinds of "clerics" then in England. But family troubles, consequent on the death of his father, summoned him home, and here we have the first glimpse

of the self-denying spirit which distinguished him through
life. He gave up his studies, and, to help his brother,
devoted himself to the rough and hard duties of a farm-
servant, so earning the other's gratitude that after a time
he gave up his little property to Richard, saying he deserved to possess what he had saved from ruin. But not
long after, when the younger brother's prosperity brought
him the offer of a rich and beautiful young wife, some feelings of jealousy seem to have made the elder man repent
his gift. He need not have feared; he was in generous
hands. Richard restored everything, even expressing his
hope that his brother might win the young heiress, while
all he asked for himself was liberty to return to the life he
had only given up at the call of duty. His conduct must
have secured to him his brother's lasting affection, for much
later in life we find them again together.

Richard studied first at Oxford, then in Paris, where at
one time he was so poor that it is related of him and the
two companions with whom he lived that they could only
go out to the lectures in turns, having but one coat among
them. They ate nothing but bread and porridge. Richard
must have profited nevertheless by his studies, for he soon
after returned to Oxford, where he took his degree. Thence
he journeyed to the then famous university of Bologna,
where his abilities attracted so much notice that various
flattering proposals of worldly advancement were made to
him, all of which he refused. And after seven years spent
in Italy he came home again to Oxford, where he accepted
the Chancellorship of the university, though not for long,

as he was chosen by Edmund, Archbishop of Canterbury, to hold the same office under himself.

Those were sadly troublous times for the English Church. King and pope—Henry III. and Gregory IX.—were doing their best to ruin and despoil it utterly, sometimes in unison, sometimes pitted against each other, agreed but in selfish grasping and plundering. The clergy were so occupied in defending or attempting to defend their rights and property that they had little time for anything else. Yet it was a great age, too—it was the age of the "Coming of the Friars," those wonderful mediæval apostles, whose enthusiasm for Christ and Christianity did more for the world and for us all than will perhaps ever be fully realised.

Richard's attachment to the staff of the archbishop brought him into no smooth waters. And he was not the man to desert a friend in adversity. In 1240, Edmund, worn out by a hopeless struggle, in which, for peace's sake, he had yielded almost more than his conscience approved, seeing that the Church was "daily trampled on more and more, despoiled of its possessions and deprived of its liberties, became weary of living," and, accompanied by his faithful chancellor and a few other attendants, crossed over to France and took refuge in the Dominican monastery at Pontigny; where, for the few months of life that remained to him, "he gave himself up uninterruptedly to prayers and fastings." On the death of this dear master Richard removed to another Dominican monastery at Orleans, where, after further study of divinity, he was ordained priest. Returning to England, he was again

appointed chancellor to the Archbishop of Canterbury,
Boniface of Savoy, the queen's uncle, a very different man
from the devout and ascetic Edmund. Boniface had lived
the gay life of a courtier, was daring, unscrupulous, and
violent, yet at the beginning of his episcopal career he
seemed "not disinclined to care for the interests of the
Church," and, on the death of the Bishop of Chichester,
he joined with Grosteste, Bishop of Lincoln, in nominating
Richard for the vacant see. Henry, however, had desired
the appointment for a favourite of his own, and even
though the pope—by this time Innocent IV.—approved
of Richard, and himself consecrated him, the king seized
every opportunity of heaping insult and abuse upon the
new bishop, so despoiling him of his revenues that Richard
was actually indebted to the charity of friends for his lodg-
ing and daily food, and for the loan of a horse on which to
ride about through his diocese. But his energy and cheer-
fulness were undaunted, and in time Henry was obliged to
give in, and to restore the property of the bishopric, though
"in a ruinous and impoverished condition." The unselfish
and generous nature of Richard made the best even of this .
state of things. He gave away everything it was possible
to spare to the poor and needy of his flock, insisting to his
brother—whom he had made his steward—that he wished
for no luxuries of any kind, and causing him to sell the
plate so that there might be more to give. " Brother,
dear," he said, "whilst Christ is suffering in the person of
His poor, we have no need of gold and silver. We can
eat off common crockery as our father did before us."

If I had space, I could tell you several touching anecdotes of this good bishop, as generous and gentle to the weak or suffering as he was firm and inflexible against wrongdoing or injustice. His holy and useful life ended all too soon, for he was only fifty-six when he died, falling ill at Dover while on a tour of preaching. His death was of a piece with his life, full of noble faith and cheerful courage. Among his last words were these: "Thou knowest, Lord, how willing I should be to bear insult, pain, and death for Thee; therefore have mercy on me, for to Thee do I commend my spirit."

His tomb is still to be seen in Chichester Cathedral, though the silver shrine which formerly held his remains was carried off by the orders of Henry VIII. at the time that he pillaged and destroyed so many sacred places.

There are two minor festivals of later origin than any saints' days in our Calendar. The first of these, kept on the 16th of December, is called " O Sapientia," from the opening words of the first of a series of responses called the "Greater Antiphons," which used to be sung shortly before Christmas. And on the 7th of August we have the festival of the "Holy Name of Jesus," observed since the beginning of the fifteenth century, in special honour of that Name which, in the words of the ancient prayer for this day in the Sarum Use,* God

---

* From Cutts' " Dictionary of the Church of England." " The particular mode of celebrating Divine service in any country, diocese, or church is called the 'Use.'" Osmund, Bishop of Salisbury (Sarum), in the eleventh century instituted a Use which for long was followed over nearly all England.

has " made to be loved by all His faithful ones with the highest affection of sweetness."

And this day closes, historically speaking, our Black Letter Calendar—a calendar full of interest and edification, though we miss in it many holy names we have elsewhere learnt to love and venerate. Of some of these, at some future time, I would like to tell you, for among them there are not a few closely connected with our own branch of the Catholic Church, and several belonging to those wonderful earliest days of Christianity, of which, it seems to me, no true-hearted follower of our dear Lord can ever hear un-moved.

ALPHABETICAL INDEX.

S. AGATHA, 20.
,, Agnes, 59.
,, Alban, 45.
,, Alphege, 211.
,, Ambrose, 79.
,, Augustin of Canterbury, 145.
,, Augustin of Hippo, 103.

S. BEDE, 173.
,, Benedict, 121.
,, Blaise, 69.
,, Boniface, 178.
,, Britius, 115.

S. CHAD, 154.
,, Cicely, 40.
,, Clement, 7.
,, Crispin and Crispinian, 42.
,, Cyprian, 29.

S. DAVID, 129.
,, Denys, 38.
,, Dunstan, 196.

S. EDMUND THE MARTYR, 191.
,, Edward the Confessor, 216.
,, Edward the Martyr, 195.
,, Etheldreda, 159.
,, Enurchus, 74.

S. FABIAN, 17.
,, Faith, 48.

S. GEORGE, 54.

S. Giles, 168.
,, Gregory, 135.

S. HILARY, 77.
,, Hugh, 219.

S. JEROME, 95.
,, John ante Portam Latinam, 5.

S. KATHARINE, 67.

S. LAMBERT, 165.
,, Laurence, 24.
,, Leonard, 131.
,, Lucian, 44.
,, Lucy, 56.

S. MACHUTUS, 133.
,, Margaret, 65.
,, Martin, 87.

S. NICHOLAS, 75.
,, Nicomede, 4.

S. PERPETUA, 9.
,, Prisca, 36.

S. REMIGIUS, 117.
,, Richard, 226.

S. SWITHIN, 187.
,, Sylvester, 73.

S. VALENTINE, 37.
,, Vincent, 62.

PRINTED BY BALLANTYNE, HANSON AND CO.
EDINBURGH AND LONDON.

A Catalogue of Works

IN

THEOLOGICAL LITERATURE

PUBLISHED BY

Messrs. LONGMANS, GREEN, & CO.

39 PATERNOSTER ROW, LONDON, E.C.

Abbey and Overton.—THE ENGLISH CHURCH IN THE EIGHTEENTH CENTURY. By CHARLES J. ABBEY, M.A., Rector of Checkendon, Reading, and JOHN H. OVERTON, M.A., Rector of Epworth, Doncaster, Rural Dean of Isle of Axholme. *Cr. 8vo. 7s. 6d.*

Adams.—SACRED ALLEGORIES. The Shadow of the Cross —The Distant Hills—The Old Man's Home—The King's Messengers. By the Rev. WILLIAM ADAMS, M.A. *Crown 8vo. 5s.*

The Four Allegories may be had separately, with Illustrations. 16mo. *1s. each. Also the Miniature Edition. Four Vols.* 32mo. *1s. each;* in a box, *5s.*

Aids to the Inner Life.

Edited by the Rev. W. H. HUTCHINGS, M.A., Rector of Kirkby Misperton, Yorkshire. *Five Vols.* 32mo, *cloth limp, 6d. each; or cloth extra, 1s. each. Sold separately.*
Also an Edition *with red borders, 2s. each.*

OF THE IMITATION OF CHRIST. By THOMAS À KEMPIS. In Four Books.

THE CHRISTIAN YEAR: Thoughts in Verse for the Sundays and Holy Days throughout the Year.

THE DEVOUT LIFE. By ST. FRANCIS DE SALES.

THE HIDDEN LIFE OF THE SOUL. From the French of JEAN NICOLAS GROU.

THE SPIRITUAL COMBAT. Together with the Supplement and the Path of Paradise. By LAURENCE SCUPOLI.

Andrewes.—A MANUAL FOR THE SICK; with other Devotions. By LANCELOT ANDREWES, D.D., sometime Bishop of Winchester. With Preface by H. P. LIDDON, D.D. 24mo. *2s. 6d.*

Augustine.—THE CONFESSIONS OF ST. AUGUSTINE. In Ten Books. Translated and Edited by the Rev. W. H. HUTCHINGS, M.A. *Small 8vo.* 5*s.* *Cheap Edition.* 16*mo.* 2*s.* 6*d.*

Bathe.—Works by the Rev. ANTHONY BATHE, M.A.

A LENT WITH JESUS. A Plain Guide for Churchmen. Containing Readings for Lent and Easter Week, and on the Holy Eucharist. 32*mo*, 1*s.*; *or in paper cover*, 6*d.*

WHAT I SHOULD BELIEVE. A Simple Manual of Self-Instruction for Church People. *Crown 8vo.* 3*s.* 6*d.*

Bickersteth.—Works by EDWARD HENRY BICKERSTETH, D.D., Bishop of Exeter.

THE LORD'S TABLE ; or, Meditations on the Holy Communion Office in the Book of Common Prayer. 16*mo.* 1*s.* ; *or cloth extra*, 2*s.*

YESTERDAY, TO-DAY, AND FOR EVER : a Poem in Twelve Books. *One Shilling Edition*, 18*mo.* *With red borders*, 16*mo*, 2*s.* 6*d.* *The Crown 8vo Edition* (5*s.*) *may still be had.*

Blunt.—Works by the late Rev. JOHN HENRY BLUNT, D.D.

DICTIONARY OF DOCTRINAL AND HISTORICAL THEOLOGY. By various Writers. Edited by the Rev. JOHN HENRY BLUNT, D.D. *Imperial 8vo.* 21*s.*

DICTIONARY OF SECTS, HERESIES, ECCLESIASTICAL PAR-TIES AND SCHOOLS OF RELIGIOUS THOUGHT. By various Writers. Edited by the Rev. JOHN HENRY BLUNT, D.D. *Imperial 8vo.* 21*s.*

THE BOOK OF CHURCH LAW. Being an Exposition of the Legal Rights and Duties of the Parochial Clergy and the Laity of the Church of England. Revised by Sir WALTER G. F. PHILLIMORE, Bart., D.C.L. *Crown 8vo.* 7*s.* 6*d.*

A COMPANION TO THE BIBLE : Being a Plain Commentary on Scripture History, to the end of the Apostolic Age. *Two vols. small 8vo.* *Sold separately.*

   THE OLD TESTAMENT. 3*s.* 6*d.*   THE NEW TESTAMENT. 3*s.* 6*d.*

HOUSEHOLD THEOLOGY : a Handbook of Religious Information respecting the Holy Bible, the Prayer Book, the Church, the Ministry, Divine Worship, the Creeds, etc. etc. *Paper cover*, 16*mo.* 1*s.* Also the Larger Edition, 3*s.* 6*d.*

Body.—Works by the Rev. GEORGE BODY, D.D., Canon of Durham.

THE SCHOOL OF CALVARY ; or, Laws of Christian Life revealed from the Cross. A Course of Lectures delivered in substance at All Saints', Margaret Street. *Crown 8vo.*

THE LIFE OF JUSTIFICATION : a Series of Lectures delivered in substance at All Saints', Margaret Street. 16*mo.* 2*s.* 6*d.*

THE LIFE OF TEMPTATION : a Course of Lectures delivered in substance at St. Peter's, Eaton Square ; also at All Saints', Margaret Street. 16*mo.* 2*s.* 6*d.*

Boultbee.—A COMMENTARY ON THE THIRTY-NINE ARTICLES OF THE CHURCH OF ENGLAND. By the Rev. T. P. BOULTBEE, formerly Principal of the London College of Divinity, St. John's Hall, Highbury. *Crown 8vo. 6s.*

Bright.—Works by WILLIAM BRIGHT, D.D., Canon of Christ Church.

LESSONS FROM THE LIVES OF THREE GREAT FATHERS : St. Athanasius, St. Chrysostom, and St. Augustine. *Crown 8vo. 6s.*
THE INCARNATION AS A MOTIVE POWER. *Crown 8vo. 6s.*
IONA AND OTHER VERSES. *Small 8vo. 4s. 6d.*
HYMNS AND OTHER VERSES. *Small 8vo. 5s.*
FAITH AND LIFE : Readings for the greater Holy Days, and the Sundays from Advent to Trinity. Compiled from Ancient Writers. *Small 8vo. 5s.*

Bright and Medd.—LIBER PRECUM PUBLICARUM EC-CLESIÆ ANGLICANÆ. A GULIELMO BRIGHT, S.T.P., et PETRO GOLDSMITH MEDD, A.M., Latine redditus. [In hac Editione continentur Versiones Latinæ—1. Libri Precum Publicarum Ecclesiæ Anglicanæ ; 2. Liturgiæ Primæ Reformatæ ; 3. Liturgiæ Scoticanæ ; 4. Liturgiæ Americanæ.] *Small 8vo. 7s. 6d.*

Browne.—AN EXPOSITION OF THE THIRTY-NINE ARTICLES, Historical and Doctrinal. By E. H. BROWNE, D.D., formerly Bishop of Winchester. *8vo. 16s.*

Campion and Beamont.—THE PRAYER BOOK INTER-LEAVED. With Historical Illustrations and Explanatory Notes arranged parallel to the Text. By W. M. CAMPION, D.D., and W. J. BEAMONT, M.A. *Small 8vo. 7s. 6d.*

Carter.—Works edited by the Rev. T. T. CARTER, M.A., Hon. Canon of Christ Church, Oxford.

THE TREASURY OF DEVOTION : a Manual of Prayer for General and Daily Use. Compiled by a Priest. *18mo. 2s. 6d. ; cloth limp, 2s. ; or bound with the Book of Common Prayer, 3s. 6d. Large-Type Edition. Crown 8vo. 5s.*

THE WAY OF LIFE : A Book of Prayers and Instruction for the Young at School, with a Preparation for Confirmation. Compiled by a Priest. *18mo. 1s. 6d.*

THE PATH OF HOLINESS : a First Book of Prayers, with the Service of the Holy Communion, for the Young. Compiled by a Priest. With Illustrations. *16mo. 1s. 6d. ; cloth limp, 1s.*

THE GUIDE TO HEAVEN : a Book of Prayers for every Want. (For the Working Classes.) Compiled by a Priest. *18mo. 1s. 6d. ; cloth limp, 1s. Large-Type Edition. Crown 8vo. 1s. 6d. ; cloth limp, 1s.*

[*continued.*

Carter.—Works edited by the Rev. T. T. CARTER, M.A., Hon. Canon of Christ Church, Oxford—*continued.*

SELF-RENUNCIATION. From the French. 16mo. 2s. 6d. *Also the Larger Edition. Small 8vo.* 3s. 6d.

THE STAR OF CHILDHOOD ; a First Book of Prayers and Instruction for Children. Compiled by a Priest. With Illustrations. 16mo. 2s. 6d.

Carter.—MAXIMS AND GLEANINGS FROM THE WRITINGS OF T. T. CARTER, M.A. Selected and arranged for Daily Use. *Crown 16mo.* 2s.

Compton.—THE ARMOURY OF PRAYER. A Book of Devotion. Compiled by the Rev. BERDMORE COMPTON, M.A. 18mo. 3s. 6d.

Conybeare and Howson.—THE LIFE AND EPISTLES OF ST. PAUL. By the Rev. W. J. CONYBEARE, M.A., and the Very Rev. J. S. HOWSON, D.D. With numerous Maps and Illustrations.
LIBRARY EDITION. *Two Vols. 8vo.* 21s.
STUDENT'S EDITION. *One Vol. Crown 8vo.* 6s.

Crake.—HISTORY OF THE CHURCH UNDER THE ROMAN EMPIRE, A.D. 30-476. By the Rev. A. D. CRAKE, B.A. *Crown 8vo.* 7s. 6d.

Creighton.—HISTORY OF THE PAPACY DURING THE REFORMATION. By the Rev. CANON CREIGHTON, M.A., LL.D. *8vo. Vols. I. and II.,* 1378-1464, 32s. *Vols. III. and IV.,* 1464-1518, 24s.

Devotional Series, 16mo, Red Borders. *Each* 2s. 6d.

BICKERSTETH'S YESTERDAY, TO-DAY, AND FOR EVER.
CHILCOT'S EVIL THOUGHTS.
CHRISTIAN YEAR.
DEVOTIONAL BIRTHDAY BOOK.
HERBERT'S POEMS AND PROVERBS.
KEMPIS' (À) OF THE IMITATION OF CHRIST.
ST. FRANCIS DE SALES' THE DEVOUT LIFE.
WILSON'S THE LORD'S SUPPER. *Large type.*
*TAYLOR'S (JEREMY) HOLY LIVING.
*———   ———   HOLY DYING.
These two in one Volume. 5s.

Devotional Series, 18mo, without Red Borders. *Each* 1s.

BICKERSTETH'S YESTERDAY, TO-DAY, AND FOR EVER.
CHRISTIAN YEAR.
KEMPIS' (À) OF THE IMITATION OF CHRIST.
WILSON'S THE LORD'S SUPPER. *Large type.*
*TAYLOR'S (JEREMY) HOLY LIVING.
*———   ———   HOLY DYING.
These two in one Volume. 2s, 6d.

Edersheim.—Works by ALFRED EDERSHEIM, M.A., D.D., Ph.D., sometime Grinfield Lecturer on the Septuagint, Oxford.

THE LIFE AND TIMES OF JESUS THE MESSIAH. *Two Vols.* 8*vo.* 24*s.*

JESUS THE MESSIAH : being an Abridged Edition of 'The Life and Times of Jesus the Messiah.' *Crown 8vo.* 7*s.* 6*d.*

PROPHECY AND HISTORY IN RELATION TO THE MESSIAH : The Warburton Lectures, 1880-1884. 8*vo.* 12*s.*

TOHU-VA-VOHU ('Without Form and Void') : being a collection of Fragmentary Thoughts and Criticism. *Crown 8vo.* 6*s.*

Ellicott.—Works by C. J. ELLICOTT, D.D., Bishop of Gloucester and Bristol.

A CRITICAL AND GRAMMATICAL COMMENTARY ON ST. PAUL'S EPISTLES. Greek Text, with a Critical and Grammatical Commentary, and a Revised English Translation. 8*vo.*

1 CORINTHIANS. 16*s.*

GALATIANS. 8*s.* 6*d.*

EPHESIANS. 8*s.* 6*d.*

PASTORAL EPISTLES. 10*s.* 6*d.*

PHILIPPIANS, COLOSSIANS, AND PHILEMON. 10*s.* 6*d.*

THESSALONIANS. 7*s.* 6*d.*

HISTORICAL LECTURES ON THE LIFE OF OUR LORD JESUS CHRIST. 8*vo.* 12*s.*

Epochs of Church History. Edited by the Rev. CANON CREIGHTON, M.A., LL.D. *Fcap. 8vo.* 2*s.* 6*d.* each.

THE ENGLISH CHURCH IN OTHER LANDS. By the Rev. H. W. TUCKER, M.A.

THE HISTORY OF THE RE-FORMATION IN ENGLAND. By the Rev. GEO. G. PERRY, M.A.

THE CHURCH OF THE EARLY FATHERS. By the Rev. ALFRED PLUMMER, D.D.

THE EVANGELICAL REVIVAL IN THE EIGHTEENTH CENTURY. By the Rev. J. H. OVERTON, M.A.

THE UNIVERSITY OF OXFORD. By the Hon. G. C. BRODRICK, D.C.L.

THE UNIVERSITY OF CAM-BRIDGE. By J. BASS MULLINGER, M.A.

THE ENGLISH CHURCH IN THE MIDDLE AGES. By the Rev. W. HUNT, M.A.

THE CHURCH AND THE EASTERN EMPIRE. By the Rev. H. F. TOZER, M.A.

THE CHURCH AND THE ROMAN EMPIRE. By the Rev. A. CARR.

THE CHURCH AND THE PURI-TANS, 1570-1660. By HENRY OFFLEY WAKEMAN, M.A.

HILDEBRAND AND HIS TIMES. By the Rev. W. R. W. STEPHENS, M.A.

THE POPES AND THE HOHEN-STAUFEN. By UGO BALZANI.

THE COUNTER-REFORMATION. By ADOLPHUS WILLIAM WARD, Litt. D

WYCLIFFE AND MOVEMENTS FOR REFORM. By REGINALD L. POOLE, M.A.

THE ARIAN CONTROVERSY. By H. M. GWATKIN, M.A.

Fosbery.—Works edited by the Rev. THOMAS VINCENT FOSBERY, M.A., sometime Vicar of St. Giles's, Reading.

VOICES OF COMFORT. *Cheap Edition. Small 8vo.* 3s. 6d.
 The Larger Edition (7s. 6d.) may still be had.

HYMNS AND POEMS FOR THE SICK AND SUFFERING. In connection with the Service for the Visitation of the Sick. Selected from Various Authors. *Small 8vo.* 3s. 6d.

Garland.—THE PRACTICAL TEACHING OF THE APO-CALYPSE. By the Rev. G. V. GARLAND, M.A. *8vo.* 16s.

Gore.—Works by the Rev. CHARLES GORE, M.A., Principal of the Pusey House ; Fellow of Trinity College, Oxford.

THE MINISTRY OF THE CHRISTIAN CHURCH. *8vo.* 10s. 6d.
ROMAN CATHOLIC CLAIMS. *Crown 8vo.* 3s. 6d.

Goulburn.—Works by EDWARD MEYRICK GOULBURN, D.D., D.C.L., sometime Dean of Norwich.

THOUGHTS ON PERSONAL RELIGION. *Small 8vo,* 6s. 6d. ; *Cheap Edition,* 3s. 6d.; *Presentation Edition, 2 vols. small 8vo,* 10s. 6d.

THE PURSUIT OF HOLINESS : a Sequel to 'Thoughts on Personal Religion.' *Small 8vo.* 5s. *Cheap Edition,* 3s. 6d.

THE CHILD SAMUEL : a Practical and Devotional Commentary on the Birth and Childhood of the Prophet Samuel, as recorded in 1 Sam. i., ii. 1-27, iii. *Small 8vo.* 2s. 6d.

THE GOSPEL OF THE CHILDHOOD : a Practical and Devotional Commentary on the Single Incident of our Blessed Lord's Childhood (St. Luke ii. 41 to the end). *Crown 8vo.* 2s. 6d.

THE COLLECTS OF THE DAY : an Exposition, Critical and Devotional, of the Collects appointed at the Communion. With Preliminary Essays on their Structure, Sources, etc. *2 vols. Crown 8vo.* 8s. *each.*

THOUGHTS UPON THE LITURGICAL GOSPELS for the Sundays, one for each day in the year. With an Introduction on their Origin, History, the Modifications made in them by the Reformers and by the Revisers of the Prayer Book. *2 vols. Crown 8vo.* 16s.

MEDITATIONS UPON THE LITURGICAL GOSPELS for the Minor Festivals of Christ, the two first Week-days of the Easter and Whitsun Festivals, and the Red-letter Saints' Days. *Crown 8vo.* 8s. 6d.

FAMILY PRAYERS compiled from various sources (chiefly from Bishop Hamilton's Manual), and arranged on the Liturgical Principle. *Crown 8vo.* 3s. 6d. *Cheap Edition.* 16mo. 1s.

Haddan.—APOSTOLICAL SUCCESSION IN THE CHURCH OF ENGLAND. By the Rev. ARTHUR W. HADDAN, B.D., late Rector of Barton-on-the-Heath. *8vo.* 12s.

Hatch.—THE ORGANIZATION OF THE EARLY CHRISTIAN CHURCHES. Being the Bampton Lectures for 1880. By EDWIN HATCH, M.A., D.D. *8vo.* 5*s.*

Hernaman.—LYRA CONSOLATIONIS. From the Poets of the Seventeenth, Eighteenth, and Nineteenth Centuries. Selected and arranged by CLAUDIA FRANCES HERNAMAN. *Small 8vo.* 6*s.*

Holland.—Works by the Rev. HENRY SCOTT HOLLAND, M.A., Canon and Precentor of St. Paul's.

CREED AND CHARACTER : Sermons. *Crown 8vo.* 7*s. 6d.*

ON BEHALF OF BELIEF. Sermons preached in St. Paul's Cathedral. *Crown 8vo.* 6*s.*

CHRIST OR ECCLESIASTES. Sermons preached in St. Paul's Cathedral. *Crown 8vo.* 3*s. 6d.*

GOOD FRIDAY. Being Addresses on the Seven Last Words, delivered at St. Paul's Cathedral on Good Friday. *Small 8vo.* 2*s.*

LOGIC AND LIFE, with other Sermons. *Crown 8vo.* 7*s. 6d.*

Hopkins.—CHRIST THE CONSOLER. A Book of Comfort for the Sick. By ELLICE HOPKINS. *Small 8vo.* 2*s. 6d.*

James.—COMMENT UPON THE COLLECTS appointed to be used in the Church of England on Sundays and Holy Days throughout the Year. By JOHN JAMES, D.D., sometime Canon of Peterborough. *Small 8vo.* 3*s. 6d.*

Jameson.—Works by Mrs. JAMESON.

SACRED AND LEGENDARY ART, containing Legends of the Angels and Archangels, the Evangelists, the Apostles, the Doctors of the Church, St. Mary Magdalene, the Patron Saints, the Martyrs, the Early Bishops, the Hermits, and the Warrior-Saints of Christendom, as represented in the Fine Arts. With 19 etchings on Copper and Steel, and 187 Woodcuts. *Two Vols. Cloth, gilt top,* 20*s. net.*

LEGENDS OF THE MONASTIC ORDERS, as represented in the Fine Arts, comprising the Benedictines and Augustines, and Orders derived from their Rules, the Mendicant Orders, the Jesuits, and the Order of the Visitation of S. Mary. With 11 etchings by the Author, and 88 Woodcuts. *One Vol. Cloth, gilt top,* 10*s. net.*

LEGENDS OF THE MADONNA, OR BLESSED VIRGIN MARY. Devotional with and without the Infant Jesus, Historical from the Annunciation to the Assumption, as represented in Sacred and Legendary Christian Art. With 27 Etchings and 165 Woodcuts. *One Vol. Cloth, gilt top,* 10*s. net.*

THE HISTORY OF OUR LORD, as exemplified in Works of Art, with that of His Types, St. John the Baptist, and other Persons of the Old and New Testaments. Commenced by the late Mrs. JAMESON ; continued and completed by LADY EASTLAKE. With 31 etchings and 281 Woodcuts. *Two Vols.* 8*vo.* 20*s. net.*

Jennings.—ECCLESIA ANGLICANA. A History of the Church of Christ in England from the Earliest to the Present Times. By the Rev. ARTHUR CHARLES JENNINGS, M.A. *Crown 8vo. 7s. 6d.*

Jukes.—Works by ANDREW JUKES.

THE NEW MAN AND THE ETERNAL LIFE. Notes on the Reiterated Amens of the Son of God. *Crown 8vo. 6s.*

THE NAMES OF GOD IN HOLY SCRIPTURE: a Revelation of His Nature and Relationships. *Crown 8vo. 4s. 6d.*

THE TYPES OF GENESIS. *Crown 8vo. 7s. 6d.*

THE SECOND DEATH AND THE RESTITUTION OF ALL THINGS. *Crown 8vo. 3s. 6d.*

THE MYSTERY OF THE KINGDOM. *Crown 8vo. 2s. 6d.*

Keble.—MAXIMS AND GLEANINGS FROM THE WRIT-INGS OF JOHN KEBLE, M.A. Selected and Arranged for Daily Use. By C. M. S. *Crown 16mo. 2s.*

SELECTIONS FROM THE WRITINGS OF JOHN KEBLE, M.A. *Crown 8vo. 3s. 6d.*

Kennaway.—CONSOLATIO; OR, COMFORT FOR THE AFFLICTED. Edited by the late Rev. C. E. KENNAWAY. *16mo. 2s. 6d.*

Knox Little.—Works by W. J. KNOX LITTLE, M.A., Canon Residentiary of Worcester, and Vicar of Hoar Cross.

THE CHRISTIAN HOME. *Crown 8vo.*

THE HOPES AND DECISIONS OF THE PASSION OF OUR MOST HOLY REDEEMER. *Crown 8vo. 3s. 6d.*

THE THREE HOURS' AGONY OF OUR BLESSED REDEEMER. Being Addresses in the form of Meditations delivered in St. Alban's Church, Manchester, on Good Friday, 1877. *Small 8vo. 2s. ; or in Paper Cover, 1s.*

CHARACTERISTICS AND MOTIVES OF THE CHRISTIAN LIFE. Ten Sermons preached in Manchester Cathedral, in Lent and Advent 1877. *Crown 8vo. 3s. 6d.*

SERMONS PREACHED FOR THE MOST PART IN MANCHES-TER. *Crown 8vo. 7s. 6d.*

THE MYSTERY OF THE PASSION OF OUR MOST HOLY REDEEMER. *Crown 8vo. 3s. 6d.*

THE WITNESS OF THE PASSION OF OUR MOST HOLY REDEEMER. *Crown 8vo. 3s. 6d.*

THE LIGHT OF LIFE. Sermons preached on Various Occasions. *Crown 8vo. 7s. 6d.*

SUNLIGHT AND SHADOW IN THE CHRISTIAN LIFE. Sermons preached for the most part in America. *Crown 8vo. 7s. 6d.*

Lear.—Works by, and Edited by, H. L. SIDNEY LEAR.

CHRISTIAN BIOGRAPHIES. *Crown 8vo. 3s. 6d. each.*

> MADAME LOUISE DE FRANCE, Daughter of Louis XV., known also as the Mother Térèse de St. Augustin.

FOR DAYS AND YEARS. A Book containing a Text, Short Reading, and Hymn for Every Day in the Church's Year. *16mo. 2s. 6d. Also a Cheap Edition, 32mo. 1s.; or cloth gilt, 1s. 6d.*

FIVE MINUTES. Daily Readings of Poetry. *16mo. 3s. 6d. Also a Cheap Edition. 32mo. 1s.; or cloth gilt, 1s. 6d.*

WEARINESS. A Book for the Languid and Lonely. *Large Type. Small 8vo. 5s.*

THE LIGHT OF THE CONSCIENCE. *16mo. 2s. 6d. Also the Larger Edition. Crown 8vo. 5s.*

A DOMINICAN ARTIST: a Sketch of the Life of the Rev. Père Besson, of the Order of St. Dominic.

HENRI PERREYVE. By A. GRATRY.

ST. FRANCIS DE SALES, Bishop and Prince of Geneva.

THE REVIVAL OF PRIESTLY LIFE IN THE SEVENTEENTH CENTURY IN FRANCE.

A CHRISTIAN PAINTER OF THE NINETEENTH CENTURY.

BOSSUET AND HIS CONTEMPORARIES.

FÉNELON, ARCHBISHOP OF CAMBRAI.

HENRI DOMINIQUE LACORDAIRE.

DEVOTIONAL WORKS. Edited by H. L. SIDNEY LEAR. *New and Uniform Editions. Nine Vols, 16mo. 2s. 6d. each.*

FÉNELON'S SPIRITUAL LETTERS TO MEN.

FÉNELON'S SPIRITUAL LETTERS TO WOMEN.

A SELECTION FROM THE SPIRITUAL LETTERS OF ST. FRANCIS DE SALES.

THE SPIRIT OF ST. FRANCIS DE SALES.

THE HIDDEN LIFE OF THE SOUL.

THE LIGHT OF THE CONSCIENCE.

SELF-RENUNCIATION. From the French.

ST. FRANCIS DE SALES' OF THE LOVE OF GOD.

SELECTIONS FROM PASCAL'S THOUGHTS.

Library of Spiritual Works for English Catholics. *Original Edition. With Red Borders. Small 8vo. 5s. each. New and Cheaper Editions. 16mo. 2s. 6d. each.*

OF THE IMITATION OF CHRIST.

THE SPIRITUAL COMBAT. By LAURENCE SCUPOLI.

THE DEVOUT LIFE. By ST. FRANCIS DE SALES.

OF THE LOVE OF GOD. By ST. FRANCIS DE SALES.

THE CONFESSIONS OF ST. AUGUSTINE. *In Ten Books.*

THE CHRISTIAN YEAR. *5s. Edition only.*

Liddon.—Works by HENRY PARRY LIDDON, D.D., D.C.L., LL.D., late Canon Residentiary and Chancellor of St. Paul's.

THE DIVINITY OF OUR LORD AND SAVIOUR JESUS CHRIST. Being the Bampton Lectures for 1866. *Crown 8vo. 5s.*

ADVENT IN ST. PAUL'S. Sermons bearing chiefly on the Two Comings of our Lord. *Two Vols. Crown 8vo. 5s. each. Cheap edition in one Volume. Crown 8vo. 5s.*

CHRISTMASTIDE IN ST. PAUL'S. Sermons bearing chiefly on the Birth of our Lord and the End of the Year. *Crown 8vo. 5s.*

PASSIONTIDE IN ST. PAUL'S. Sermons bearing chiefly on the Passion of our Lord. *Crown 8vo. 5s.*

EASTER IN ST. PAUL'S. Sermons bearing chiefly on the Resurrection of our Lord. *Two Vols. Crown 8vo. 5s. each. Cheap Edition in one Volume. Crown 8vo. 5s.*

SERMONS PREACHED BEFORE THE UNIVERSITY OF OXFORD. *Two Vols. Crown 8vo. 5s. each. Cheap Edition in one Volume. Crown 8vo. 5s.*

THE MAGNIFICAT. Sermons in St. Paul's. *Crown 8vo. 2s. 6d.*

SOME ELEMENTS OF RELIGION. Lent Lectures. *Small 8vo. 2s. 6d. ; or in Paper Cover, 1s. 6d.*
The Crown 8vo Edition (5s.) may still be had.

SELECTIONS FROM THE WRITINGS OF H. P. LIDDON, D.D. *Crown 8vo. 3s. 6d.*

MAXIMS AND GLEANINGS FROM THE WRITINGS OF H. P. LIDDON, D.D. Selected and arranged by C. M. S. *Crown 16mo. 2s.*

Littlehales.—Works Edited by HENRY LITTLEHALES.
A FOURTEENTH CENTURY PRAYER BOOK : being Pages in Facsimile from a Layman's Prayer Book in English about 1400 A.D. *4to. 3s. 6d.*

THE PRYMER OR PRAYER-BOOK OF THE LAY PEOPLE IN THE MIDDLE AGES. In English, dating about 1400 A.D. Part I. Text. *Royal 8vo. 5s.*

Luckock.—Works by HERBERT MORTIMER LUCKOCK, D.D., Canon of Ely.

AFTER DEATH. An Examination of the Testimony of Primitive Times respecting the State of the Faithful Dead, and their Relationship to the Living. *Crown 8vo. 6s.*

THE INTERMEDIATE STATE BETWEEN DEATH AND JUDGMENT. Being a Sequel to *After Death. Crown 8vo. 6s.*

FOOTPRINTS OF THE SON OF MAN, as traced by St. Mark. Being Eighty Portions for Private Study, Family Reading, and Instructions in Church. *Two Vols. Crown 8vo. 12s. Cheap Edition in one Vol. Crown 8vo. 5s.*

[continued.

Luckock.—Works by HERBERT MORTIMER LUCKOCK, D.D., Canon of Ely—*continued.*

THE DIVINE LITURGY. Being the Order for Holy Communion, Historically, Doctrinally, and Devotionally set forth, in Fifty Portions. *Crown 8vo.* 6s.

STUDIES IN THE HISTORY OF THE BOOK OF COMMON PRAYER. The Anglican Reform—The Puritan Innovations—The Elizabethan Reaction—The Caroline Settlement. With Appendices. *Crown 8vo.* 6s.

THE BISHOPS IN THE TOWER. A Record of Stirring Events affecting the Church and Nonconformists from the Restoration to the Revolution. *Crown 8vo.* 6s.

LYRA APOSTOLICA. Poems by J. W. BOWDEN, R. H. FROUDE, J. KEBLE, J. H. NEWMAN, R. I. WILBERFORCE, and I. WILLIAMS; and New Preface by CARDINAL NEWMAN. 16mo. 2s. 6d.

LYRA GERMANICA. Hymns translated from the German by CATHERINE WINKWORTH. *Small 8vo.* 5s.

MacColl.—CHRISTIANITY IN RELATION TO SCIENCE AND MORALS. By the Rev. MALCOLM MACCOLL, M.A., Canon Residentiary of Ripon. *Crown 8vo.* 6s.

Mason.—Works by A. J. MASON, D.D., formerly Fellow of Trinity College, Cambridge.

THE FAITH OF THE GOSPEL. A Manual of Christian Doctrine. *Crown 8vo.* 7s. 6d. *Large-Paper Edition for Marginal Notes.* 4to. 12s. 6d.

THE RELATION OF CONFIRMATION TO BAPTISM. As taught by the Western Fathers. A Study in the History of Doctrine. *Crown 8vo.*

Mercier.—Works by Mrs. JEROME MERCIER.

OUR MOTHER CHURCH: being Simple Talk on High Topics. *Small 8vo.* 3s. 6d.

THE STORY OF SALVATION: or, Thoughts on the Historic Study of the Bible. *Small 8vo.* 3s. 6d.

Moberly.—Works by GEORGE MOBERLY, D.C.L., late Bishop of Salisbury.

PLAIN SERMONS. Preached at Brighstone. *Crown 8vo.* 5s.

THE SAYINGS OF THE GREAT FORTY DAYS, between the Resurrection and Ascension, regarded as the Outlines of the Kingdom of God. In Five Discourses. *Crown 8vo.* 5s.

PAROCHIAL SERMONS. Mostly preached at Brighstone. *Crown 8vo.* 7s. 6d.

SERMONS PREACHED AT WINCHESTER COLLEGE. *Two Vols. Small 8vo.* 6s. 6d. *each.*

Mozley.—Works by J. B. MOZLEY, D.D., late Canon of Christ Church, and Regius Professor of Divinity at Oxford.

ESSAYS, HISTORICAL AND THEOLOGICAL. *Two Vols. 8vo.* 24s.

EIGHT LECTURES ON MIRACLES. Being the Bampton Lectures for 1865. *Crown 8vo.* 7s. 6d.

RULING IDEAS IN EARLY AGES AND THEIR RELATION TO OLD TESTAMENT FAITH. Lectures delivered to Graduates of the University of Oxford. *8vo.* 10s. 6d.

SERMONS PREACHED BEFORE THE UNIVERSITY OF OXFORD, and on Various Occasions. *Crown 8vo.* 7s. 6d.

SERMONS, PAROCHIAL AND OCCASIONAL. *Crown 8vo.* 7s. 6d.

Mozley.—Works by the Rev. T. MOZLEY, M.A., Author of 'Reminiscences of Oriel College and the Oxford Movement.'

THE WORD. *Crown 8vo.* 7s. 6d.

LETTERS FROM ROME ON THE OCCASION OF THE ŒCUMENICAL COUNCIL 1869-1870. *Two Vols. Cr. 8vo.* 18s.

Newbolt.—Works by the Rev. W. C. E. NEWBOLT, Canon Residentiary of St. Paul's.

THE FRUIT OF THE SPIRIT. Being Ten Addresses bearing on the Spiritual Life. *Crown 8vo.* 2s. 6d.

THE MAN OF GOD. Being Six Addresses delivered during Lent 1886, at the Primary Ordination of the Right Rev. the Lord Alwyne Compton, Bishop of Ely. *Small 8vo.* 1s. 6d.

COUNSELS OF FAITH AND PRACTICE. Being Sermons preached on Various Occasions. *8vo.* 7s. 6d.

THE VOICE OF THE PRAYER BOOK. Being Spiritual Addresses bearing on the Book of Common Prayer. *Crown 8vo.* 2s. 6d.

Newnham.—THE ALL-FATHER : Sermons preached in a Village Church. By the Rev. H. P. NEWNHAM. With Preface by EDNA LYALL. *Crown 8vo.* 4s. 6d.

Newman.—Works by JOHN HENRY NEWMAN, B.D. (Cardinal Newman), formerly Vicar of St. Mary's, Oxford.

PAROCHIAL AND PLAIN SERMONS. *Eight Vols. Cabinet Edition. Crown 8vo.* 5s. *each. Popular Edition. Eight Vols. Crown 8vo.* 3s. 6d. *each.*

[*continued.*

Newman.—Works by JOHN HENRY NEWMAN, B.D. (Cardinal Newman), formerly Vicar of St. Mary's, Oxford—*continued.*

SELECTION, ADAPTED TO THE SEASONS OF THE ECCLE-SIASTICAL YEAR, from the 'Parochial and Plain Sermons.' *Crown 8vo.* 5*s.*

FIFTEEN SERMONS PREACHED BEFORE THE UNIVERSITY OF OXFORD, between A.D. 1826 and 1843. *Crown 8vo.* 5*s.*

SERMONS BEARING UPON SUBJECTS OF THE DAY. *Crown 8vo.* 5*s.*

LECTURES ON THE DOCTRINE OF JUSTIFICATION. *Crown 8vo.* 5*s.*

*** *For the Catholic Works of Cardinal Newman, see Messrs. Longmans & Co.'s Catalogue of Works in General Literature.*

THE LETTERS AND CORRESPONDENCE OF JOHN HENRY NEWMAN DURING HIS LIFE IN THE ENGLISH CHURCH. With a Brief Autobiographical Memoir. Arranged and Edited by ANNE MOZLEY. *Two Vols. 8vo.* 30*s. net.*

Osborne.—Works by EDWARD OSBORNE, Mission Priest of the Society of St. John the Evangelist, Cowley, Oxford.

THE CHILDREN'S SAVIOUR. Instructions to Children on the Life of our Lord and Saviour Jesus Christ. *Illustrated.* 16*mo.* 3*s.* 6*d.*

THE SAVIOUR-KING. Instructions to Children on Old Testament Types and Illustrations of the Life of Christ. *Illustrated.* 16*mo.* 3*s.* 6*d.*

THE CHILDREN'S FAITH. Instructions to Children on the Apostles' Creed. *With Illustrations.* 16*mo.* 3*s.* 6*d.*

Oxenden.—Works by the Right Rev. ASHTON OXENDEN, formerly Bishop of Montreal.

THE PATHWAY OF SAFETY ; or, Counsel to the Awakened. *Fcap. 8vo, large type.* 2*s.* 6*d. Cheap Edition. Small type, limp.* 1*s.*

THE EARNEST COMMUNICANT. *Common Edition.* 32*mo.* 1*s. New Red Rubric Edition.* 32*mo.* 2*s.*

OUR CHURCH AND HER SERVICES. *Fcap. 8vo.* 2*s.* 6*d.*

FAMILY PRAYERS FOR FOUR WEEKS. First Series. *Fcap. 8vo.* 2*s.* 6*d.* Second Series. *Fcap. 8vo.* 2*s.* 6*d.*

LARGE TYPE EDITION. Two Series in one Volume. *Crown 8vo.* 6*s.*

COTTAGE SERMONS; or, Plain Words to the Poor. *Fcap. 8vo.* 2*s.* 6*d.*

THOUGHTS FOR HOLY WEEK. 16*mo.* 1*s.* 6*d.*

DECISION. 18*mo.* 1*s.* 6*d.*

Oxenden.—Works by the Right Rev. ASHTON OXENDEN, formerly Bishop of Montreal—*continued.*

THE HOME BEYOND ; or, A Happy Old Age. *Fcap. 8vo. 1s. 6d.*

THE LABOURING MAN'S BOOK. *18mo, large type, cloth. 1s. 6d.*

CONFIRMATION. *18mo, cloth. 9d. ;* sewed, *3d. ; or 2s. 6d. per dozen.*

COUNSELS TO THOSE WHO HAVE BEEN CONFIRMED ; or, Now is the Time to serve Christ. *18mo, cloth. 1s.*

THE LORD'S SUPPER SIMPLY EXPLAINED. *18mo, cloth. 1s. Cheap Edition. Paper. 6d.*

PRAYERS FOR PRIVATE USE. *32mo, cloth. 1s.*

WORDS OF PEACE ; or, The Blessings of Sickness. *16mo, cloth. 1s.*

Paget.—Works by the Rev. FRANCIS PAGET, D.D., Canon of Christ Church, and Regius Professor of Pastoral Theology.

THE SPIRIT OF DISCIPLINE : Sermons. *Crown 8vo.*

FACULTIES AND DIFFICULTIES FOR BELIEF AND DIS-BELIEF. *Crown 8vo. 6s. 6d.*

THE HALLOWING OF WORK. Addresses given at Eton, January 16-18, 1888. *Small 8vo. 2s.*

PRACTICAL REFLECTIONS. By a CLERGYMAN. With Prefaces by H. P. LIDDON, D.D., D.C.L. *Crown 8vo.*

> Vol. I.—THE HOLY GOSPELS. *4s. 6d.*
> Vol. II.—ACTS TO REVELATION. *6s.*
> THE PSALMS. *5s.*

PRIEST (THE) TO THE ALTAR ; Or, Aids to the Devout Celebration of Holy Communion, chiefly after the Ancient English Use of Sarum. *Royal 8vo. 12s.*

Pusey.—Works by the late Rev. E. B. PUSEY, D.D.

MAXIMS AND GLEANINGS FROM THE WRITINGS OF EDWARD BOUVERIE PUSEY, D.D. Selected and Arranged for Daily Use. By C. M. S. *Crown 16mo. 2s.*

PRIVATE PRAYERS. With Preface by H. P. LIDDON, D.D. *32mo. 2s. 6d.*

PRAYERS FOR A YOUNG SCHOOLBOY. Edited, with a Preface, by H. P. LIDDON, D.D. *24mo. 1s.*

SELECTIONS FROM THE WRITINGS OF EDWARD BOUVERIE PUSEY, D.D. *Crown 8vo. 3s. 6d.*

Richmond.—CHRISTIAN ECONOMICS. By the Rev. WILFRID RICHMOND, M.A., sometime Warden of Trinity College, Glenalmond. *Crown 8vo. 6s.*

Sanday.—THE ORACLES OF GOD: Nine Lectures on the Nature and Extent of Biblical Inspiration and the Special Significance of the Old Testament Scriptures at the Present Time. By W. SANDAY, M.A., D.D., LL.D. *Crown 8vo. 4s.*

Seebohm.—THE OXFORD REFORMERS—JOHN COLET, ERASMUS, AND THOMAS MORE: A History of their Fellow-Work. By FREDERICK SEEBOHM. *8vo. 14s.*

Stephen.—ESSAYS IN ECCLESIASTICAL BIOGRAPHY. By the Right Hon. Sir J. STEPHEN. *Crown 8vo. 7s. 6d.*

Swayne.—THE BLESSED DEAD IN PARADISE. Four All Saints' Day Sermons, preached in Salisbury Cathedral. By ROBERT G. SWAYNE, M.A. *Crown 8vo. 3s. 6d.*

Tweddell.—THE SOUL IN CONFLICT. A Practical Examination of some Difficulties and Duties of the Spiritual Life. By MARSHALL TWEDDELL, M.A., Vicar of St. Saviour, Paddington. *Crown 8vo. 6s.*

Twells.—COLLOQUIES ON PREACHING. By HENRY TWELLS, M.A., Honorary Canon of Peterborough *Crown 8vo. 5s.*

Wakeman.—THE HISTORY OF RELIGION IN ENGLAND. By HENRY OFFLEY WAKEMAN, M.A. *Small 8vo. 1s. 6d.*

Welldon. — THE FUTURE AND THE PAST. Sermons preached to Harrow Boys. (*First Series,* 1885 *and* 1886.) By the Rev. J. E. C. WELLDON, M.A., Head Master of Harrow School. *Crown 8vo. 7s. 6d.*

Williams.—Works by the Rev. ISAAC WILLIAMS, B.D., formerly Fellow of Trinity College, Oxford.

A DEVOTIONAL COMMENTARY ON THE GOSPEL NARRATIVE. *Eight Vols. Crown 8vo. 5s. each. Sold separately.*

THOUGHTS ON THE STUDY OF THE HOLY GOSPELS.

A HARMONY OF THE FOUR GOSPELS.

OUR LORD'S NATIVITY.

OUR LORD'S MINISTRY (Second Year).

OUR LORD'S MINISTRY (Third Year).

THE HOLY WEEK.

OUR LORD'S PASSION.

OUR LORD'S RESURRECTION.

[continued.

Williams.—Works by the Rev. ISAAC WILLIAMS, B.D., formerly Fellow of Trinity College, Oxford—*continued.*

FEMALE CHARACTERS OF HOLY SCRIPTURE. A Series of Sermons. *Crown 8vo. 5s.*

THE CHARACTERS OF THE OLD TESTAMENT. A Series of Sermons. *Crown 8vo. 5s.*

THE APOCALYPSE. With Notes and Reflections. *Crown 8vo. 5s.*

SERMONS ON THE EPISTLES AND GOSPELS FOR THE SUNDAYS AND HOLY DAYS THROUGHOUT THE YEAR. *Two Vols. Crown 8vo. 5s. each.*

PLAIN SERMONS ON THE CATECHISM. *Two Vols. Crown 8vo. 5s. each.*

SELECTIONS FROM THE WRITINGS OF ISAAC WILLIAMS, B.D. *Crown 8vo. 3s. 6d.*

Woodford.—Works by JAMES RUSSELL WOODFORD, D.D., sometime Lord Bishop of Ely.

THE GREAT COMMISSION. Twelve Addresses on the Ordinal. Edited, with an Introduction on the Ordinations of his Episcopate, by HERBERT MORTIMER LUCKOCK, D.D. *Crown 8vo. 5s.*

SERMONS ON OLD AND NEW TESTAMENT SUBJECTS. Edited by HERBERT MORTIMER LUCKOCK, D.D. *Two Vols. Crown 8vo. 5s. each.*

Wordsworth.—Works by ELIZABETH WORDSWORTH, Principal of Lady Margaret Hall, Oxford.

ILLUSTRATIONS OF THE CREED. *Crown 8vo. 5s.*

ELIZABETH AND OTHER POEMS. *Crown 8vo. 6s.*

Younghusband.—Works by FRANCES YOUNGHUSBAND.

THE STORY OF OUR LORD, told in Simple Language for Children. With 25 Illustrations on Wood from Pictures by the Old Masters, and numerous Ornamental Borders, Initial Letters, etc., from Longmans' New Testament. *Crown 8vo. 2s. 6d.*

THE STORY OF GENESIS, told in Simple Language for Children. *Crown 8vo. 2s. 6d.*

Printed by T. and A. CONSTABLE, Printers to Her Majesty, *at the Edinburgh University Press.*